The Girl with the Wrong Name

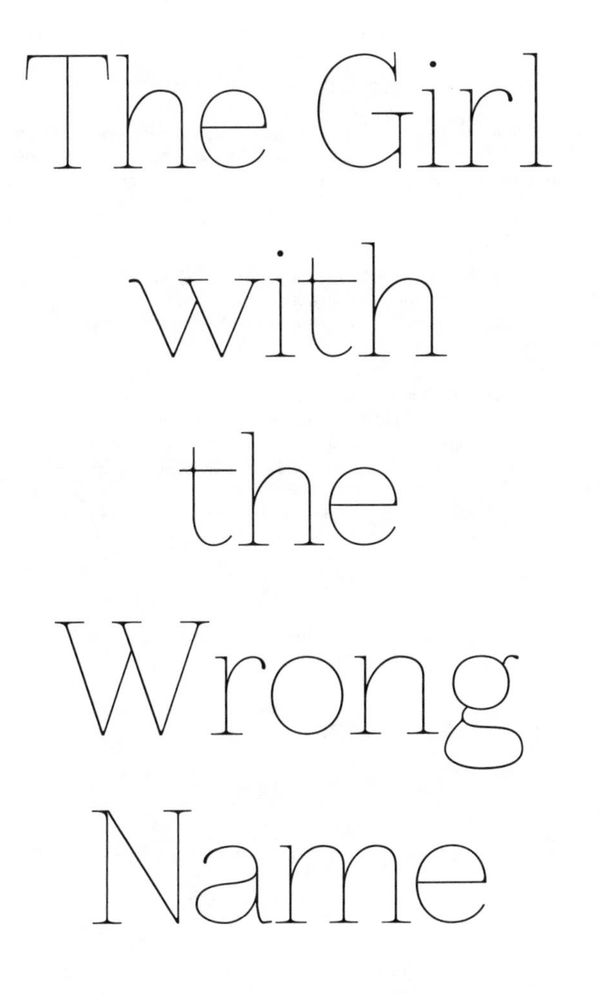

BARNABAS MILLER

Published in the United States by Soho Teen
an imprint of
Soho Press, Inc.
853 Broadway
New York, NY 10003

Library of Congress Cataloging-in-Publication Data

Miller, Barnabas.
The girl with the wrong name / Barnabas Miller.

ISBN 978-1-61695-194-8
eISBN 978-1-61695-195-5

1. Memory—Fiction. 2. Mental illness—Fiction. 3. Love—Fiction.
4. Documentary films—Production and direction—Fiction. I. Title.
PZ7.M61216Gi 2015
[Fic]—dc23 2015014947

Interior design by Janine Agro, Soho Press, Inc.

Printed in the United States of America

10 9 8 7 6 5 4 3 2 1

For H.H.M.

The Girl with the Wrong Name

Chapter One

Notes for My New Documentary Project, Tuesday, September 3rd
(Putting the Wedding Project on hold)

Possible working titles for new project:

THE LOST BOY
BEAUTIFUL STRANGER
STRANGER AT THE WINDOW
THE BOY AT THE WINDOW
~~*WINDOW BOY*~~

Window Boy?

Jesus, Theo, you are in serious need of sleep. Just stick with "The Lost Boy" for now—at least you've finally given him a name. And the title's not important; you know that. The only important thing is that you stay still and quiet and calm. You're an impartial documentarian—a neutral observer trying to make sense of your new subject. A decent cinematographer should at least be able to KEEP HER SUBJECT IN FRAME.

AND STOP YELLING AT YOURSELF IN ALL CAPS.

Stop writing now, because he's at the window again. You need to FOCUS, Theo. Brain and lens. Brain and lens . . .

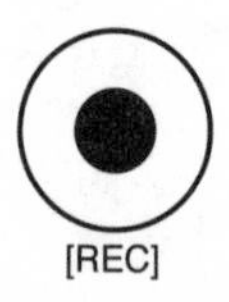

It's the third time I've seen the Lost Boy at the Harbor Café. My hidden button cam is sewn into my jacket collar, tracking his every move. I wonder if he knows that the freakish girl in the corner secretly films him, scrutinizing his image on her iPhone under the table, fighting to figure out what he has lost. Why does he come here every day at exactly 11:45? And how could anyone be so shamelessly beautiful but so palpably sad?

When I first saw him on Sunday, I was transfixed. Then he saw me. So I was embarrassed for the next twenty minutes—the kind of shame that makes your face glow bright red. I swear I could actually feel my scar burning. I had to turn down to the tabletop when I pictured that morning's *New York Times*'s "Weddings and Celebrations" section, page ST15:

> ***Emma J. Renaux, 30, daughter of James and Sally Renaux of Charleston, S.C., will marry Lester A. Wyatt, 30, son of George and Leona Wyatt of Dallas, Tex., on Sunday. The couple officially met as 15-year-old sophomores at New Hampshire's Phillips Exeter Academy, but unknown to Mr. Wyatt, they had in fact met a year earlier.***
>
> ***"We'd shared one dance to R. Kelly's 'I Believe I Can Fly' at the freshman Winter Formal," Ms. Renaux confessed sheepishly, "but my hair was so different that he didn't recognize me. It took me 10 years to admit that I'd watched him across a crowded room for hours before we ever spoke. I knew before I'd even asked him to dance. I knew I was going to marry him."***

Yes, I have a near-photographic memory when it comes to *New York Times* wedding announcements. And no, I have no explanation or defense for it. I only know that each and every blurb tends to prove some inevitable fact of life, and my inevitable fact is this: When a beautiful girl watches a beautiful boy across a crowded room, it's a delightful anecdote in the Sunday *Times.* It's an enchanting scene of timeless romance from an Italian foreign language Oscar nominee.

When an ugly girl watches a beautiful boy across a crowded room, it's a disturbing German indie on the Sundance channel about a budding young female serial killer.

To be clear, I am not a budding young female serial killer. I've just looked like one ever since June seventeenth, The Night in Question. Or, more specifically, since the early morning of June eighteenth, when I woke up feeling bruised and battered on every inch of my body. When I limped my way to the bathroom and found a four-inch gash running down the side of my jaw.

Now I can feel every woman in the café watching me watching him. I can hear them thinking: *Oh, that poor little teenage demi-troll, all dressed in black. She doesn't know that she's a hideous creature with toilet-paper skin and an involuntary perma-frown. She somehow doesn't see that he is a Glorious Golden God-Prince whose babies will grow up to be congressmen and Fox News anchorwomen and teenage country music divas.*

Well, to them I say, Lower Manhattan Yoga Elites, I know. I know I'm deformed. I know my attempts to hide it are futile—that a ton of concealer and Olay Regénerise under a pile of peekaboo black hair only draws more attention to what I'm hiding. What I *don't* know, you gawking little scone-eaters, is what happened to me on the night of the seventeenth. A horrific accident? A violent assault? Or maybe the boogeyman in my closet just finally lost his cool after years of menacing me silently from behind the laundry hamper?

All I can remember is going to sleep that night in the safety of my own bed. Apparently, the "trauma was so acute" that I've "repressed the entire blah blah blah . . ."

Dr. Silver keeps encouraging me to talk about it.

Too bad for him; the damage is already done. It was done long before The Night in Question. It was done on the day I was born, the day my parents made the inexplicable decision to name their one and only daughter Theodore.

I've imagined the post-birth conversation so many times:

"*Congratulations, Mrs. Lane, it's a girl! What are you going to name her?*"

"Well, we'd like her to grow up as socially maladjusted as possible. We'd like little boys to look at her disdainfully and say, 'You've got a boy's name' from the nursery all the way through sixth grade. That way she can get a solid jump-start on her existential alienation."

But Mom and Dad and Dr. Silver and everyone else have made a crucial mistake. They've all failed to understand: I am not Theodore. I am another lighter, airier, prettier girl. I have another lighter, airier, prettier name like Rachel or Hope or Samantha. They are just too blind to see it. "*Theodore will be your name,*" I can hear my cold-blooded mother cooing at the baby version of me. *"And if all goes according to plan, you'll be spending your entire seventeenth summer huddled in the corner of your bedroom, shutting out the world with a pair of scuffed-up Beats headphones, blasting the Beatles' 'Revolution 9' on repeat until your ears begin to chafe and not-so-metaphorically bleed. 'Number nine . . . number nine . . . number nine . . . number—'"*

I shake my head. *Focus, Theo. FOCUS.*

My thoughts tend to attack without warning now. They riddle my head like machine-gun fire and zoom off in a trail of smoke before I can make sense of them. That's why I try to capture as much as I can on video, so I can actually experience my life at some later date when my mind has stopped racing and snacks are more readily available.

I can't lose sight of the Lost Boy—can't, won't—because he is a compelling subject, whether he knows it or not. To be clear, I'm not here to save him. I'm not here to save anyone. I'm a cool, collected observer. I'm a cinematic scientist. I'm blending invisibly into his natural café habitat so I can observe his natural café habits and behaviors, untainted by—

Shit, he's on the move!

I crane my neck so my button cam can keep him in frame. (My documentarian trick: I run the cable through an incision in my jacket pocket so I can monitor all the shots on my phone.) He drifts past my table. I glance up and catch a glimpse of the blond flecks in his brown stubble and the light sprinkle of freckles on his ski-slope nose. Speed Stick deodorant is slipping out from the mesh side pocket of his overstuffed backpack. There are tiny rips and tears at the bottom of his worn-out white V-neck T-shirt.

I know those jagged little holes are telling me a story, but the only one I can think of is the story of what his chest looks like underneath that shirt.

This has nothing to do with sex! I want to yell at the tittering scone-eaters. *Vulgar Walmart romance is not my motivation, and if you people knew anything about me, you would know that.*

But for the split second that he and I are in the same orbit, I'm a lit cigarette, and I don't even smoke. The feeling is so intense, I can't even tell if it's a good sensation or a bad one. I've heard about the fine line between pleasure and pain, but this is the first time I have the slightest clue what it means.

Then he's past me, and it fades.

I take a few deep breaths and swipe my clammy palms across my jeans, swiveling in my seat to get him back on camera. I need to stay perfectly still. He grabs the last wrinkled copy of the *Times* and settles into his seat at the marble table closest to the door. Of course he chooses the *Times*—it's just one of the twenty-three things we have in common.

Thing Number Nine: he has to be an obsessive like me, because he has repeated this noontime routine with near-clinical precision every single day since Sunday.

It always starts on the café's front lawn. He shows up at the window and plants his black Chuck Taylors firmly in the manicured grass. There he stands, the Hudson River stretching out behind him. He looks out across the water at the Statue of Liberty. Then he turns to Ellis Island. It's like he's triangulating himself with those two monuments, orienting himself in a specific geographical position on the earth's grid, but I have no idea why. This is *killing* me.

Once he comes inside, he never orders anything. He just grabs the *Times*, drops down at his table, and begins what I call his "forlorn gazing." Every time the door swings open, his head darts up. He scans each new patron like an abandoned puppy tied to a hydrant, hopelessly spot-checking every pair of shoes and eyes for signs of his master.

Who are you looking for, Lost Boy?

I need to know. Did you miss your rendezvous with the mother ship? Are you part of some nomadic species of J.Crew model, wandering helplessly through Battery Park City in search of your Nantucket beach house? Or maybe you spent your last dime on a bus ticket to New York with dreams of becoming a hip-hop dancer, only to find yourself in an underground dance-crew battle where you got viciously and irreparably "served"?

I wish it could be that. I wish it could be something laughable and absurd, but I know it's not. I know something terrible has happened to him.

I turn away for just a moment and scrawl these notes in my production book: *What really happened to him? What kind of tragedy? What can I do to ~~save~~*

I give myself a swift bop to the head, hoping no one has noticed.

IMPARTIAL, I scrawl, breaking my all-caps rule again. *You are here to document the truth. You're not a part of his story; you're not even going to tell his story. You're going to let him tell his own story. That's the movie.*

Chapter Two

I would have shot the Lost Boy for another hour if it hadn't been for Max's fifth text:

MAXCELL: WTF? Please tell me you didn't decide to drop out of school on the first day of senior year. We discussed this in last night's session. It's 12:30 in the afternoon. Where ARE you? Lou and I are at the Trout talking about you. If you want to know what we're saying, you'll have to come back to school like the rest of the senior class.

It was a brilliant play on Max's part. I mean, relatively brilliant for a basketball stool. (That would be Max-Lou-Theo shorthand for stupid fool.) Even after all this time apart, he knows I seek the truth above all else. He knows it's not that I want to know what they're saying about me; it's that I *need* to know what they're saying about me—at the exact moment they're saying it.

Mostly it's a brilliant play because no one at Sherman Prep has seen me since The Night in Question—not even Max and Lou.

If you truly want to know whether you've changed over the summer, you need to see yourself reflected in their eyes. You can try to see the pretty version in the mirror, but their eyes will tell you the whole truth—their eyes are the only mirrors that count. Yes, I hate mirrors more than anything in the world now, but I'm no different than any other girl: I still need to look.

That being said, the second I walked into the Trout, I knew it was a huge mistake.

THE DINER TWO BLOCKS from school is actually called Le Burger Place. But when you open the door, you're bitch-slapped by a foul odor. Think of a trout that ate a whole roasted garlic clove for breakfast, played four hours of racquetball, and then skipped his shower to meet up with his trout coworkers for a Coors Light. So Max, Lou, and I renamed Le Burger Place "the Sweaty Trout," which we shortened to just "the Trout."

I only made it halfway through the door when the first wave of nausea attacked. It wasn't the stink; five years at the Trout had left me immune. It was this:

Lou was sitting in Mike DeMonaco's lap.

Once or twice, I've heard Lou accuse Max of "smelling like sex," and I've thought to myself: *That's disgusting. Not to mention impossible.* "What could sex possibly smell like?" I'd ask. "Cigarettes and cheap vodka? Latex and Axe body spray? Prom corsages and shame?" But now I swore I could actually smell it. Like sarin gas permeating the entire room. Toxic and sticky. Acrid and humid. Warm, pubescent bodies in a can.

So let me just repeat the image: Louise Cho—my best female friend in the world, fellow A/V aficionado at the Sherman News Studio (was that an *orchid* in her hair?), violin virtuoso, early acceptance to the Oberlin Conservatory—was superglued (was that a *minidress*?) via her ass to the crotch of Mike "Me Like" DeMonaco, linebacker for the Sherman Sharks, future secretary of the Date Rapists of America, President and CEO of all things stool.

What in God's name is happening here? I should have howled.

Thank God I'd doubled up on my Lexapro. The earth was clearly spinning in the wrong direction. I'd somehow traveled through a wormhole to an alternate universe. Had I ever seen a more ludicrous pairing? Yes, maybe I had, in the *New York Times* "Weddings and Celebrations" section from Sunday, October 10, 2010, page ST12:

> ***Sylvie Rifka Birnbaum, daughter of Saul and Ruthie Birnbaum, was married Saturday to Aidan O'Flaherty, son of Seamus and Molly O'Flaherty. Miss Birnbaum, 56, is a professional matchmaker for widowed Jewish seniors. Mr. O'Flaherty, 23, is a ghost hunter and Irish step dancer at Walt Disney World's Epcot Center. The ceremony was held at Disney's Enchanted Tiki Room amidst the tropical serenades of mechanical parrots and seabirds. Ordained Universal Life Minister and Def Poet "Da' T.R.U.T.H." officiated, with Rabbi Gunter Hirschberg taking part.***

Lou would have razzed me for remembering the wedding announcement verbatim, but Lou was nowhere to be found. She'd been replaced by that sparkle-faced doppelgänger sitting in Mike's lap.

"Theo!" Max yelled.

I relaxed when I heard his voice. But then I remembered. My fingertips instinctively jumped to my cheek, making sure my gel-hardened hair curtain was pasted to my chin. I wobbled to his booth in the corner and ducked in across from him.

"Okay, what the hell is going on with Lou?" I whispered.

"I'm fine, thanks," Max said flatly.

I dug into the last of his soggy fries, trying to ignore the amount of time that had passed between us, deflecting it. Max had grown. The kid had at least three days of stubble going. Shrouded in his gray hoodie, dark curls sneaking out on all sides, his eyes popping like neon-blue saucers . . . I think he was going for *Game of Thrones* chic, but it was coming across more Jewish android.

He leaned in closer, playing the mortifying Get Theo to Look Me in the Eye game. "Um, where the hell have you been since eight this morning?"

The strange thing was, I knew that was going to be his first question. But when he actually asked it, I found myself fighting back tears. It was a few more seconds before I even understood. They were tears of relief.

This was Max's first opportunity to make an official statement about my face. I'd kept my relationship with him and Lou "phone only" since June. But God bless Max Fenton, he didn't even flinch for that (almost) imperceptible second like the men who'd come before him: namely my doorman Emilio, and Todd, my complete simp of a stepstool. No, Max just said what he would have said if there had been no scar, if I had not hidden myself away for two months.

PLOTWISE, MY AND MAX'S friendship had gone down almost exactly like the standard teen flick. Step 1) Cool Jock needs to pass Algebra II to stay on the team. Step 2) Teacher forces Geek Girl to tutor Cool Jock even though they're from vastly different social circles. Step 3) Cool Jock and Geek Girl discover all their hidden commonalities and become unexpectedly close, etc.

But there were a few key differences between our story and the cliché. For one thing, Cool Jock actually got tutored by *two* Geek Girls (me and Louise). Secondly, and most importantly, nobody fell in love in any way, shape, or form—so that thirdly, there were no shocking last-minute betrayals at "the big dance" or "the big game," requiring any grand gestures like running through the rain or having surprise gospel choruses sing "our" song. Instead, we all just stayed friends, reasonably drama free.

Point being: I don't know where I'd be without Max and our late-night phone sessions. A girl can only play *Dark Side of the Moon* so many times without wanting to kill herself or go on a funnel cake bender. I am more grateful for Maximus than I could have possibly expressed—so, of course, I didn't.

"You answer my question, and I'll answer yours," I said as I chewed on his fries.

"What was your question?" he asked.

"What the hell is going on with Lou?"

"Oh, that." Max nodded with a knowing laugh. "Yeah, that is some classic A.B.O. right there."

"Classic what?"

"A.B.O. You know, all bets are off."

"What bets? Who's betting?"

"Oh, come on, Thee, this is a well-documented senior year phenomenon." He lowered his voice. "We've all been slaves to the same social structure since at least junior high, right? Mike could never hook up with a girl like Lou because the Sharks would have given him shit. Same for Lou. Imagine what the entire first violin section would have done to her—imagine what *you* would have done to her if she'd ever confessed her scorching pelvic desire for a dude who endorses butt chugging."

"Okay, ew."

Max laughed. "All I'm saying is, none of it matters now. We don't have to pay the price for our secret interspecific crushes anymore, because we're never coming back here again. We're in uncharted territory. Black is white, and white is black. All bets are off. A.B.O."

When he said it again, I was struck by a vivid sequence: *A bite-sized version of me is sledding down the Lost Boy's freckly ski-slope nose. I've somehow gotten caught in a snowstorm on his face. I shut my eyes and brace for death, but his gigantic thumb and forefinger snatch me from certain doom. I slowly morph into Snuggle the Bear. He cups me in his hands and scratches my furry brown head and under-chin like a treasured pet—like Lennie from* Of Mice and Men.

How sick is that? What did it even mean?

Max snapped his fingers in my face. "Theo? Come on. Please don't make me say, 'Earth to Theo'; we're better than that."

"What?"

"I said it's your turn."

"For what?"

"I answered your question; now you have to answer mine. Where the hell have you been since eight o'clock this morning?"

"Asleep," I said. "I just overslept. What's the big?"

Max smiled. "At least you haven't gotten any better at lying."

I smiled back. "That's why you trust me."

Chapter Three

Lost Boy Project Notes, Wednesday, September 4th

He's BACK. Fourth day in a row.
What am I doing? Why am I scribbling project notes when I should be . . .

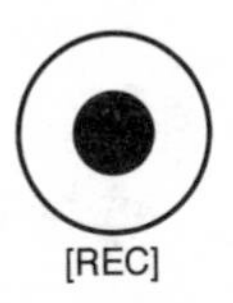

Nothing but pixels and jitters as my shaky button cam warms to life. I can't get myself still today. I'm a mess—everything's off.

The second the lunch bell rang, I raced down to my Trek 7500 hybrid and pedaled my ass off to make it here by 11:45, but some mall-haired Real Housewife of New Jersey tried to run me over on Water Street. "Hey, Dragon Tattoo! Get a frikkin' haircut!" Now I'm fifteen minutes late and covered in a sticky coat of bike sweat, and I've missed the Lost Boy's first act at the window.

He's already grabbed his *Times* and is well into the forlorn gazing stage.

Some yoga mom with a stroller the size of a space shuttle has taken my spot. She leaves me no choice but to grab a seat much closer to him than I want to be. I don't even know how to position my collar for a shot from this table. I keep shifting around in my seat, leaning my head left and right, looking like a ten-year-old with ADHD on her first day of Chicken McNugget detox. I'm drawing too much attention.

When I finally get him in frame, all I can see is a blurry mess of a man. Boy? Man? It's one of the most compelling things about him: he looks like a man from one angle and a boy from another—it really depends on how you shoot him. I don't think he could be much older than nineteen, but I can't say for sure. His face is a blur on my screen, like it's been rendered by a French Impressionist or a toddler with a tray of runny watercolors. The door swings open, and his head darts up.

A girl's voice shouts from somewhere off camera. "Oh my God, it's you!"

The paper falls from his hands. He lifts his head. It's the first time I've seen his veil of sadness drop away. Now I can see what his face really looks like—what it's supposed to look like. Now he's the boy and not the man.

He peers at the mystery girl. I tilt my chair back on its heels to get her into frame, feeling my heart rate spike.

Steady, Theo, steady.

I finally get her in the shot. She's skinny and blonde with huge boobs. Of course she is. She's the perfect vessel for his golden angel babies, and so chipper that I have to squint to look at her. Okay, *cringe* is the better word.

"I'm at the Harbor Café," she squeaks. "Where the hell have *you* been, girl?"

Why is she calling him "girl"? Is the Lost Boy transitioning?

I think he and I realize it at the exact same moment. She's not talking to him. She has dragged us into a little game that Max dubbed "Bluetooth or Psycho?" (It's a fun game, because it's so hard to tell the difference in New York, given the uncommon number of both raving lunatics and assholes on hands-free calls—and that they both tend to wear huge, flowy scarves.) I lift my head from the screen and watch him turn back to his paper.

Wait.

Did I see a tear on his cheek?

I tell myself that I can't be sure. I even consider rewinding and looking back through the footage to confirm, but I've learned the hard way that I can never look back through the raw footage until it is time to edit. I just end up all-capsing the crap out of myself for the shots I've missed and the scenes I've lost forever.

I don't need to see the footage. Not really. I know what I saw; I just don't want to face it. The problem is this: I suffer from a disease I call Self-Mutilating Empathy.

That is to say, when I see a man crying, I literally want to marry him. At least for the next fifteen to twenty minutes. Usually I can overcome it, but the Lost Boy is different. Watching him hurt in turn hurts *me*, and it has since the moment I laid eyes on him. He ducks his head down. He's trying to pass off the tear as an itch. He doesn't want anyone to see his face. I know that feeling so well that it turns my throat bone dry—I can't make myself swallow. I flip open my notebook and start scrawling rapidly.

IMPARTIAL IMPARTIAL IMPARTIAL IMPARTIAL

But it's useless. It's a fight I can't win. Despite everything I know and everything I am, the pen falls from my hand, and I stand up out of my chair, stashing the phone in my jacket pocket. My fingers rise to my face, checking to be sure my hair is a curtain over my scarred cheek, and I begin what feels like the longest walk anyone has ever taken in an eight-hundred-square-foot café.

Just go to the left and out the door, I keep telling myself. *You have to leave. Left, and out the door. Left, and out the door.*

"ARE YOU OKAY?"

I've startled him half to death. That was not the plan—I didn't even have a plan. The plan was to leave, but I didn't.

Now he looks confounded and maybe embarrassed, I'm not sure. Either way, he is staring at me, not answering, and I've run out of things to say. Mostly because, God help me, he's even more remarkable up close. The camera is still recording in my pocket, but a camera can't do what my eyes can do.

How can I explain it? He has no idea that he's the star of my movie, yet this is the first time I've truly seen the star up close. It's like that thing where you see a famous person on the street and you realize why they call them "stars." They actually do shine a little brighter than normal people. It's the shift from two-dimensional to three. Everything is crisper—his golds are golder; his angles are more angular; his skin is that much more, I don't know, succulent? Ew, no, that is *not* what I mean.

And then there's that tear. I can still see its faint trace on his cheek.

Self-Mutilating Empathy kicks in, and my scar suddenly feels like it's roasting. I'm dying to scratch it. It's as if I'm sitting too close to a campfire. I panic about my concealer—it's going to melt away, and he'll see me in all my repulsive glory. What have I done? This is New York. People don't just walk up to you and ask if you're okay. Even if you've just been shot, they tend to stand on the curb, craning their necks curiously, waiting to see if someone *else* will ask if you're okay.

"I'm sorry." I take a deep breath. "I didn't mean to . . ." I whirl around.

"Wait," he says.

I freeze, then turn back. There's a slight quaver in his voice. His accent is southern or western—maybe both. Texan? I think of the *New York Times* "Weddings and Celebrations" section, Sunday, June 3, 2012, page ST14:

> ***Elana T. Silverman, a daughter of John and Miriam Silverman of New Brunswick, N.J., was married Saturday to Brick Colton, the son of Ford and Louanne Colton of Temple, Tex. The Rev. Rudy B. Pickins (known fondly to***

parishioners as "Rev. Rudy") officiated. Mrs. Colton, 22, was a graduate student in Political Science at New York University, but has opted to forego her academic career and join Mr. Colton, 27, on his sustainable sheep farm in Texas.

"Ever since I met Brick, all I really care about is sheep," Mrs. Colton said.

"Yeah, I call her my little sheep," Mr. Colton added.

"To be honest," Mrs. Colton said, "I was so in love with him, I would have raised Tibetan yaks with him."

"You just saw a grown man crying, didn't you?" the Lost Boy asks.

I stiffen, and my hair becomes a blockade between my eyes and his. "What? No, I didn't see any—"

"It's okay. You saw what you saw," he says. "And I'm not. I'm not okay."

Well then, I'll marry you, I barely manage not to say. *I'll marry you, and we can fly back to Texas and raise a host of farm animals—pigs, cows, sheep, whatever—and slowly but surely, I'll help you recover from whatever has happened to you. I already have the dress, which is vintage and kind of funky.*

I say none of that. All I actually say is (again): "I'm sorry." The two emptiest, most meaningless words in history.

"Don't be," he replies, his voice quiet. "I don't even know how long I've been sitting here. You're the first person that's talked to me."

"New Yorkers," I say with a pathetic excuse for a laugh. "I mean, I assume you're not from New—"

"Oh, *hell,* no." He laughs. His laugh is warm and real. Not like my uncomfortable mouth farts. "I'm from Austin."

Texas. I knew *it.*

"Austin, Texas," he clarifies, perhaps reacting to my slack jaw.

"No, I know; I'm just—"

"I'm Andrew," he says, putting out his hand. "Andrew Reese."

I look at his outstretched hand and go numb. The last thing I want to do is hurt Andrew any more than he's hurting, but I can't bring myself to shake.

IT'S NOT THAT I'M afraid to touch Andrew Reese. Not exactly. It's because of my father.

I have only two memories of the man who brought me into this world. One is of him wrapping a blanket around my shoulders by a fire in some gray, snowy campsite, whispering, "Don't be afraid, darlin'. Don't you ever, ever be afraid." The other is of him gripping the lapels of my navy peacoat, shaking me too roughly, saying, "Don't talk to strangers, darlin'. Don't you ever, *ever* talk to strangers."

Yeah, thanks for the super-consistent advice, Pops. Not like you'll turn me into a walking manic-depressive contradiction for the rest of my life or anything.

The point is, while Andrew Reese waits five seconds too long for a simple handshake, I'm forced to face the harsh reality: he is a complete and total stranger. My inner five-year-old squeals at me to shut my mouth and run. But I slide down cautiously into the seat across from him, keeping my arms tightly crossed.

"Theo," I finally respond. "Theo Lane."

WHY DID YOU JUST give him your real name?

I jump at any opportunity to give myself a fake name. Doling out fake normal names is one of my few remaining pleasures in life, and Starbucks is usually my only outlet. Now I've given him the only Google tool he needs to find my address and plan my murder. Then again, sixty seconds ago, I was prepared to offer him my hand in marriage.

He pulls his hand back under the table. "Theo," he says, trying to move on from the awkwardness. "That's a cool name."

"No, it's not. It's not even a name, it's an address."

"What?" More than ever, he looks capital-L Lost.

"As in, 'Driver, take me to Number Nine Theo Lane.'"

"Oh, right." He nods with a forced smile. "Right." His eyes drift back toward the window, and my heart sinks. This isn't the first conversation I wanted with him. Not even close.

"Andrew, I'm sorry. I really just wanted to make sure you were—"

"Andy," he says. "All my friends call me Andy."

"Oh. Well, Andy—not that I saw you crying, but . . . why were you crying?"

His smile disappears. The silence lasts long enough to make me regret having asked. "I'm waiting for someone," he finally says.

"Who?"

"A girl."

Of course it's a girl. Deep down, didn't I know that already? Hadn't I put it all together? Besides, what's to put together? He's a boy, and he's sad. Why is he sad? Because of a girl.

"Her name's Sarah," he says.

Of course her name is Sarah.

"Well, where is she?" I ask. I wish I hadn't. The look on his face . . .

"I don't know. She was supposed to meet me here at eleven forty-five."

"Well, come on, she's not even an hour late. I'm assuming she's a 'Pretty Girl'?"

"She *is* pretty." He frowns at my air quotes.

"An hour late is nothing in Pretty Girl time. That's, like, ten minutes."

He almost smiles again. "Well, it's been longer than an hour," he says. "She was supposed to meet me at eleven forty-five on Sunday."

This is the part where I feign surprise. "You've been waiting here for four days?"

"Oh, man, has it been four days?"

I bite my lip, feeling a little bewildered. "I don't understand. Is Sarah your girlfriend or—?"

He lets out a single, joyless laugh. "I guess not. I don't know. What do you think, Theo? Can someone be your girlfriend if you've only known her for a day?"

I'm not qualified to answer that question, so I don't.

"I was just bumming around New York before school. I was supposed to head back to Austin on Saturday morning to start at UT. I met her as I was walking out of here. She was sitting right at this table. She'd just come from helping her friend plan a wedding at some place near here where they do weddings. Battery Green or Battery—"

"Battery Gardens," I say. "Yeah, I know it." This didn't seem like the best time to tell him about a) my wedding announcement obsession or b) how I'd been coming here all summer to shoot footage of the newlyweds walking in and out of Battery Gardens' forbidding ivy gates. Besides, that project is a thing of the past. He's been my new project for exactly four days. My star. Not that he needs to know that, either.

"Yeah, that's it!" He smiles, truly and fully, for the first time. *Star,* I think again; the smile is that bright. "Battery Gardens. Anyway, we just hit it off, you know—it was just one of those things. We talked, and we talked some more, and then we walked, and we walked some more till we were up in, like, Harlem or something, and we just ended up spending the whole day together. And Theo, believe me, I know how corny this sounds, I do, but we just . . ." He turns away and shakes his head.

"You just *what?*" I press.

"We fell in love; we just did. Love at first sight. It's real, you know? And she asked me to stay in town another week and be her date to her friend's wedding next Sunday, and I was like, *hell, yeah.* Then we went out that night till whenever, and she told me to meet her back here for brunch the next day at eleven forty-five. I got here at exactly eleven forty-five, and she just . . . didn't. She never showed. And being the total fool I am, I never got her number—I never even got her *last name.*" He shoots me a glance, probably regretting sharing so much with a stranger.

"So I just keep coming back. Hoping she'll be here this time. All I know is, this is her favorite café."

"It's a good place," I say, not even sure what I mean.

"She said she liked to watch all the newlyweds coming out of Battery Gardens—you know, just starting the rest of their lives together, just beginning like we were. Like I thought we were. And I know what you're thinking. You're thinking, 'Hey, Dumbass, she's just not that into you.' But you want to know what I think?"

I nod. "I do."

"I think something happened to her. Something really bad. Something, you know, terrible. I got nothing to prove it—I got nothing to tell it's so; I just know it. If she could have been here by eleven forty-five, then she would have been here no matter what."

I nod again.

He suddenly locks eyes with mine. "Do you believe me?"

I'm not ready for the question. What do I believe? Did I just sit down next to a creepy stalker who can't get the hint? My head and my heart start beating the crap out of each other as he stares at me, waiting for my answer. What do I believe? I don't know what I believe, but I know what I feel: Jealous. Jealous that a guy could fall so deeply in love with a girl in just one day. So much so that he'd be willing to look for her each and every day after.

"Your silence speaks volumes," he cracks, his drawl coming through.

"I believe you," I hear myself say.

"You do?"

"I do."

"So?"

"So what?"

"So will you help?"

I shake my head in confusion.

His eyes drop. "I'm sorry. Forget that. Forget I said that. It was just, when you walked over here, I thought—"

"No, it's not—I mean, I don't even know what I could do to . . ." *Don't talk to strangers, darlin'.* I glance at the clock. "God, is it . . . ? I'm supposed to be back at school. I didn't even realize what time it was."

He nods and looks down at his hands. "I didn't mean to keep you."

"No, you didn't keep me. It's not—"

Don't you ever, ever talk to strangers.

"You should go," he says. He flips to the next page of his paper.

I don't know what else to say. I only know that I'll be back tomorrow morning.

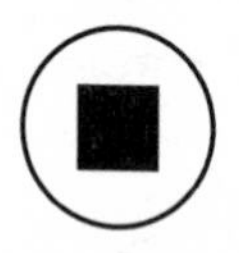

Chapter Four

"Can you please pass the peas, Theo?"

There was no point in answering my simpering stepstool. Best to just ignore him.

How could I have left Andy Reese there? How could I have just abandoned him at the Harbor after Sarah had done the very same thing? After I'd seen his tears up close? No, it wasn't even about Andy; it was about the raw footage. How could I have walked out in the middle of such a pivotal scene? I'd just started getting all the good stuff—

"Theo, the peas?" Todd was still gazing at me expectantly.

Oh, Todd. You may look like a middle-aged man, but you're one evolutionary step away from sock puppets. And the Mozart hair doesn't make you look cool; it makes you look like the love child of Betty White and Dr. Zaius from Planet of the Apes.

"Theodore!" Mom's fist came crashing down on the table like a gavel.

My fork fell from my hand. "What?" I asked, sounding more like a little girl than I'd planned.

Even Todd looked surprised.

My mother does not emote. At least, not toward me. Our dinner ritual usually consists of silence, followed by three disinterested questions about my day, followed by the Complaints: when Mom and Todd discuss their students' inability to "grasp the postmodern underpinnings of Thomas Pynchon." Yes, Mom and Todd are both NYU lit professors, and no, I have not read any Thomas Pynchon.

"Todd asked you for the peas," Mom said. "Will you please pass your father the peas?"

I'd retired the "he's not my father" retort by age twelve. It was too Lifetime movie. By fifteen, I'd moved past "Why did you even have a kid if you were just going to name her Theodore and treat her with the cordial but distant reserve of a weekend guest at your bed-and-breakfast?" Still, for some reason, on this particular night, it stung.

"Did my father like peas?" I asked politely, passing Todd the bowl of peas.

"Excuse me?" Mom said.

"My biological father," I said. "Was he a pea lover like Todd? Or was he more of a big zucchini man?"

Mom shot eye daggers at me. "Don't go there, Theodore. Not tonight."

"Let's go easy on your mother tonight," Todd whispered. "You know it's September, Theo. Beginning of the semester. Let's try to keep it light."

Oh, right, Mom's "fall semester stress." It was the one time a year when you could actually see glimpses of anxiety behind her stoic façade. I guess the prospect of teaching *Gravity's Rainbow* to another batch of untrained minds was enough to give any lit professor night terrors—even the otherwise unflappable Margaret Lane.

"Sorry, Mom," I said. "I didn't mean to probe so deep on the vegetable thing."

"It's all right," she said, starting work on a new slice of turkey meatloaf.

"So just tell me again why you despise my actual father?"

Mom threw her knife down on the plate.

"Okay!" Todd barked a nervous laugh and clapped, rubbing his hands together like he was trying to make a fire. "What's for dessert tonight, Meg?"

My mom still didn't answer me. She didn't have to. I hadn't seen my father since I was five years old, but her stare told me the same thing I'd heard since I was old enough to start asking questions. *"Stop treating a divorce like some crippling mystery. The answers do not change with time. Your father and I could not see eye to eye. We were from two different worlds. He was much too young for me, and he was completely unprepared for any kind of real relationship. He just wasn't a good man."*

Todd started to open his mouth, but the shrill ring of the doorbell cut him off.

Mom began to rise, grabbing hold of the edge of the dining table, her knuckles white. The only thing that bothers my mother more than a new class of ignorant freshmen is an unannounced visitor at the door. She once spent twenty minutes chewing out our doorman Emilio for letting a Chinese food delivery guy upstairs without calling first.

Of course, she'd assumed I was the culprit.

"Who is it?" she mouthed, like I was Anne Frank and the Nazis had just discovered our secret annex.

"I don't know," I mouthed back.

"Did you invite someone over?"

"I did not. Mom, can you chill, please?"

The thought of finding Andy Reese behind that door didn't even occur to me till I was reaching for the doorknob. It sailed across my mind like a gust of wind, somewhere between the shave-and-a-haircut knock and the drawn-out, steady thump-thumping that seemed to imitate a heartbeat.

HERE'S A QUICK TIP: when your junior year is winding down and your mother asks a question like, "Have you started your college applications yet?," don't give her a vaguely existential answer like, "I can't even picture my life past the age of eighteen."

This will set off an ultrasonic suicide alert that only parents and school counselors can hear. The next thing you know, you'll be sitting across from Dr. Harold Silver in an office full of Gustav Klimt posters and African folk art, trying to clarify your answer as he writes you a prescription for Lexapro. You'll try to explain that you're not the least bit suicidal; you've just always pictured a big empty frame after your eighteenth birthday, but he'll already be listing off potential side effects.

Later you'll come to realize that those potential side effects are "everything."

In my case, the worst was world-class insomnia.

So then you'll tell Dr. Silver that you're struggling with insomnia, and he'll prescribe Ambien. While on Ambien, you will bake and eat an entire pan of Pillsbury crescent rolls in your sleep and have a terrible nightmare about the Pillsbury Doughboy, staring at you with this really judgy look in his eyes. After enough of those bad dreams, you'll stop the Ambien, but you won't tell your mother or Dr. Silver because you don't want to try the next thing he has to offer.

At least, I didn't.

So now it's just me and my dear frenemy Lexapro. Sometime I just call him "Lex." He halfheartedly wards off my depression and anxiety all day, but then keeps me awake all night so I can dream up more depressing and anxious scenarios for him to ward off come dawn. It's the neurotic circle of life! Or not. He's like a pet or a little brother you don't even want.

Dr. Silver told me that as long as I never missed a pill and continued to stick with the program, the side effects would wear off after the first few weeks. But that never happened, which is fine with me. Honestly? I need Lex's side effects more than ever now. Lex saves me every night.

After all, I can't possibly have another Night in Question if I'm only asleep two to three hours at a time.

I DID NOT OPEN our front door to find Andy Reese. I opened it to find Louise Cho, my putative best friend, holding a bunch of white daisies.

"What's wrong?" Lou asked, disappointed. "They're daisies. Your wedding flower? Your all-time favorite?" She shook them a little to make them more enticing. "They match the Dream Ring. No?"

"Yeah, thanks," I said. I tried to smile; I really did. I accepted the flowers from her and took a long whiff of their earthy sweetness.

"Um. So, hi?" Lou said.

"What up," I mumbled. Awkward silence.

"I really like your hair," she said cautiously. She reached out to touch it, but I couldn't help jerking my head back. I turned to the floor and smoothed my hair against my cheek. I knew what she was trying to say; I just wish she hadn't said it. Max had known better.

"Thanks," I said. Without noticing, I'd begun to tap my foot.

"Okay, what?" Lou threw up her hands. One of them landed on her bony hip.

"Whut-whut?" I replied reflexively, imitating some long-dead MC.

"Why so gangsta?" She laughed, uncomfortable. "What is your thing today? You didn't answer any of my texts this morning, you avoided me at the Trout, and you didn't find me after school. We were totally fine on the phone last night. What changed?"

"*You did,*" I didn't say. "*You drank the girly-girl Kool-Aid in Florence, and now you're hunting meat-brained linebackers as sexual prey.*"

"Who is it, dear?" Mom asked.

Lou peeked over my shoulder and announced herself with a smile. "It's Louise, Mrs. Lane."

"Sort of," I muttered. I scanned her tight red dress and strappy sandals.

Lou laughed. "Is that what this is about? My dress? Come on, Thee. My mom made me get this dress for the final concert in Florence. I thought it would be a funny outfit for the first day back."

"It's not the dress."

"Well then what?"

"Aren't you coming in, Louise?" Mom asked pointedly.

"I'm trying, Mrs. Lane." Lou dug her hand into her new suede saddlebag. "Okay, look, I can prove it's me. Look." She put her glasses on and slipped them up the bridge of her nose. Then she pulled her hair back into its familiar ponytail. "Mr. Schaffler, this editing bay was built in the late *'90s*!" she exclaimed earnestly. "We need to upgrade *all* the A/V equipment in this room. I *cannot* produce the Sherman News in these conditions!"

I lowered my head so she couldn't see me smile. Louise Cho was doing Louise Cho, and it was a damn good impression.

"Admit it, Ms. Rinaldi," she went on. "The Tchaikovsky concerto was invented to mangle the slender fingers of Asian teens—"

"Okay." I glared at my mom over my shoulder. *See?* I asked silently, eyebrows raised. *Not an intruder.*

Lou grabbed my shoulder and steered me toward my room. "Thee, I need your brilliance. I need a Cyrano letter."

THE CYRANO LETTERS HAD started in seventh grade. Lou would fall in love with some sensitive young geek in the viola section, or a fellow techie in the middle school production of *Godspell*, and she wouldn't have the guts to approach him. Instead she'd beg me to help her compose a "Declaration of Romantic Intent." (Not to be confused with a "Love Letter." Lou felt that, much like the word *genius*, the word *love* was tossed around far too prematurely and far too often.)

I'd developed an early obsession with Cyrano de Bergerac, based on Steve Martin's modern adaptation *Roxanne*. I guess the idea of pining for an unattainable love hit home with a dour seventh-grader who was always planning her wedding day when she should have been planning her bat mitzvah.

Now, as we sped down the hall to avoid one of Mom's generic Lou interviews ("How was your summer?" etc.), a dark irony was dawning. Lou probably hadn't even realized it yet, but substitute an impossibly huge schnoz with a hideous scar, and I *was* Cyrano de Bergerac.

"I have some ideas for the first paragraph," Lou said breathlessly. She knew exactly where to find the blank composition notebooks on my desk, even buried under a heap of Mountain Dew cans, half-eaten desserts, and memory cards. "But this has to be all you, Thee. You're the wordsmith here."

"Yeah, and I have two words for you already," I said, tossing the daisies onto my bed. *"Hell, no."* I shut my bedroom door and flopped onto the mattress. I quickly realized my hair was hanging off my face—exposing said scar—so I slid back against the wall, holding a pillow between my knees and chin. "But thanks for the flowers. This room could use them."

Lou scowled. She grabbed a notebook from my desk and cleared one of the piles of dusty Sunday *New York Times* from my formerly white couch, carving out a seat for herself. "I might have to repo them. You don't get it. I need this one bad, Thee. Like *really* bad."

"Who's it for?" I asked. I knew, but I wanted to hear it from her.

Her lips twisted in a secret smile. "I can't tell you. It's too embarrassing."

"See, that's a red flag right there. You can't write a love letter to someone you're too embarrassed to love."

She groaned. "It's not a love letter, it's a Declaration of—"

"Romantic Intent," I finished. "I know, Lou. Would now be a good time to remind you you've never actually given one of these Declarations to any of the boys we've written them for?"

"Well, this time I will. I have to. It's my last chance."

"Oh, right, because 'all bets are off.'"

Lou's eyes narrowed. "What bets? Who's betting?"

"I am just stating for the record that I absolutely refuse to play any part in this disgusting A.B.O. senior year crossbreeding. It's unnatural."

"A.B. *what*? Can you just slow down? I feel like we're not communicating."

"I *know* who it is," I declared.

"You do?"

"Jesus, I was at the Trout this afternoon, remember? I saw the whole thing."

Her face flushed. She giggled. "Oh, God, was I that obvious?"

"'Obvious' doesn't really do it justice. I'd call it 'stripper-pole obvious.'"

I could see the flush of pink climbing up her cheeks. "So you hate me now."

"Oh, please. It's more a mix of shock and dismay, and maybe the first few seeds of disrespect." I nodded toward the desk. "Funnel cake?" I offered, pointing toward the last stale piece from last night's bender.

"No, thanks," she said, crinkling her nose.

"Sorry, I don't have any low-fat scones or dried kale chips."

She tossed the notebook to the floor. "Thee, why are you being like this?"

"Like what? I thought you loved my dry wit. I thought I gave the Sherman News its bite."

She was looking at me seriously now. "You have a bite, but you're not mean. Who are you today?"

"Who am *I*? Are you kidding me right now? Who are *you*? It's like you showed up at school a completely different person."

"No, I have a different outfit, and I let my hair down. I'm being serious. Where were you this morning? Whatever happened to you this morning, you're different."

"Oh, you think it was this morning? You don't think something might have happened to me, say, two and a half months ago that might have changed me a little bit? Maybe just a *little bit*?"

Lou blinked. Her lips trembled. I couldn't believe those words had come from my mouth. I never brought up The Night in Question anymore. At least, not consciously or out loud.

My outburst left a cloud of black silence between us. The kind of silence that has physical mass and weight. Lou stood as if someone else had taken over, as if an invisible hand had yanked on her marionette strings.

"I am so sorry," she whispered. "I don't know what I was thinking. I mean, I wasn't thinking. I wasn't. I think I should just go. I'll go."

"No." I jumped out of bed and grabbed her hand before she got to the door. "That was totally my fault," I said. "I don't know why I said that, I really don't. Stay. I'll help you with the letter. I'll totally help you. I mean, duh, of course I'll help you, girl."

"You don't have to."

"I want to," I lied. "I really want to."

THREE MINUTES LATER, I tore a page from my notebook and handed it to Lou. She'd stayed glued to her phone as I'd scrawled out the first paragraph—reading the latest post from *The A.V. Club*, I prayed, and not some depraved sext from Mike.

A Declaration of Romantic Intent

Dear M,

I really, really, really, really want to have vigorous sexual intercourse with you, preferably in the back of a smelly taxi, or perhaps in one of those pee-stained bathroom stalls in the boys' locker room (or the girls' locker room, if you think that is hotter. I'm cool either way).

"Theo, come on," Lou grumbled, trying not to laugh, and failing. "I thought you were going to help."

"What? I'm helping. Good writing is all about conservation of words. Actually, you're right; we don't need that many *reallys*."

She shoved her phone into her pocket. "Okay, if you're going to be mean—"

"No, okay." I sat up straight and held my pen over a fresh page. From under my hair, I tried to stop smiling. "What do you want it to say?"

"Well, I'd prefer if it didn't say anything about vigorous sexual intercourse. Or urine. Or taxicabs. Let's start there."

"Oh, so you want it to be romantic," I said.

She laughed again. "I want to find a way to tell him."

"Tell him what?"

"To really *tell* him this time. You know, to tell him that I'm . . ." I looked up and watched her struggle for the words. How any girl—especially one as smart as Lou—could search her heart so valiantly and sincerely for Mike DeMonaco was *beyond* beyond me. "To tell him that I'm the one who sees it."

"Sees what?"

"That he's not just, you know, that *dude* that everybody else sees—that . . ."

I believe "stool" is the term you're looking for?

"That '*guy*,'" she said in the silence. "He's not just 'that guy' in a jock jersey, cracking jokes."

"I'm pretty sure he *is* that guy."

Lou's face soured. "Well, you're wrong. Because I've watched him for years. I mean, I watch him when he doesn't even know I'm watching him."

"Yeah, maybe we leave out the stalker part."

"And I can see," she went on, ignoring my snarky comments, "that there's this whole other side to him. A romantic side. A heroic side that he's too embarrassed to show anyone. You can't see it, Thee, but I can. And I think that's when you know that you're meant to be with someone. When you can see the part of him that no one else sees. Does that make any sense?"

I fully intended to joke about the part of Mike DeMonaco no one else should see, but I found myself tongue-tied.

"And once you've seen it," Lou continued, "once you know how you feel, you have to let him know in, like, no uncertain terms—you have to just tell him flat-out. Because you think it's the most obvious thing in the world. You think, 'How could he not know how I feel? Every single person in this room is staring at me, and they all know exactly how I feel.' I mean, you said I was stripper-pole obvious at the Trout, right?"

"Yeah," I said, my voice barely audible. "Like hooker obvious." I wanted to hug Lou right then, despite her new tragic taste in men.

Lou rolled her eyes. "Right. Hooker obvious. Well, you know what? I don't think he noticed at all. I don't think he has a single solitary clue how I feel. That's why I need you to put it all in the letter. So there is no way he could possibly miss it."

I nodded. The epiphany had come slowly at first, as Lou was finishing her monologue. It snaked its way through the shoddy plumbing in my head, and my eyes drifted up to my bedroom ceiling—up to a grimy, pencil-thin, half-woman/half-fish-shaped outline that had once been a sticker of Ariel from *The Little Mermaid.* I began projecting blurry images onto the blank white space where Ariel's face used to be: half-baked guesses at Sarah's facial features—dimpled chin, rounded chin; high cheekbones, rounded cheeks . . . every version with those oversized, lifeless eyes that stare back at you from a police composite sketch taped to a subway teller's plexiglass window.

"What's wrong?" Lou asked.

The words finally leaked from the corner of my mouth. "She doesn't know."

Lou looked confused. "Who doesn't know what?"

"Sarah. She doesn't know that he loves her."

"Sarah who? Sarah Bingham? Sarah Pratt? Crop Top Sarah? There's, like, a billion Sarahs."

"No, nothing," I said. "Nothing, never mind."

"Are you kidding? Now you have to tell me. Who's Sarah?"

"I'll tell you later, but I'm feeling inspired here. Don't worry; it has nothing to do with this."

"Oh, then go, go, go." She jumped next to me on the bed.

I dropped pen to paper and began to scribble furiously, reciting to Lou as I wrote.

"I really need to talk to you. Please don't be alarmed by the heading of this letter, but our time is running out here at Sherman, and I couldn't forgive myself if I didn't tell you how I truly feel . . ."

"Oh, that's good," Lou purred. "That's really good."

Chapter Five

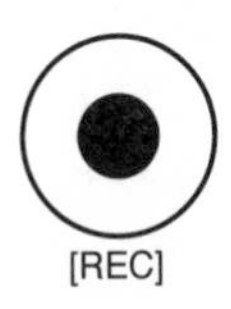

"I don't think she knows."

I say this first, instead of "hello" or "I'm sorry for abandoning you like a cowardly ass yesterday." I say it first, because it's the most important thing—the missing piece of the puzzle, if my hunch is right. I say it also because Andy's eyes lit up on me the second he stepped through the Harbor door. For *me* this time. Not for the walking pair of boobs in the corner; not for Sarah, his lost golden goddess (I know she's blonde—she has to be blonde); not for anyone but the half-faced troll camped out at his favorite table with her button cam recording.

I expect him to say, "You came back," with enthusiastic emphasis on "back." That's supposed to be his line. That's what he said when I pictured this moment while biking down Water Street in the rain. After all, I'd risked serious injury to surprise him with my heroic return from Alienating New York Bitchhood.

But he doesn't say anything. He just stands across the table from me, soaking wet from the downpour—somehow smiling without smiling.

Or *is* he smiling? Is he smiling at me, or is he thinking about the awesome grilled cheese sandwich he had for breakfast? Where do beautiful boys learn that unreadable gaze? Is it inherited? Is it taught by elder Jedi beautiful boys, by secret Handsome-Man Yodas across the country?

So I'm the one who ends up saying it, or adding it, really: "I came back."

He drops his backpack to the floor and lands in his seat with a puzzled grin. His hair has turned darker brown from the rain. He slicks it back with both hands, droplets trickling down his forehead, and leans across the table. "She doesn't know what?" he asks. "Are we talking about Sarah? Are you going to help me?"

"Yes, we're talking about Sarah. She doesn't know you're in love with her. I mean, that you fell in love with her that day. I don't think she knows."

"Nah, that's impossible," he says.

"Listen to me. I've done a lot of research on relationships." (More than two hundred weeks of wedding announcements, though he doesn't need to know that.) "This is one of the only categories where Pretty Girls are like everyone else. When they fall in love, they are just as insecure about being loved back as Normal Girls."

"I don't know." Andy shakes his head, leaning back.

"But I do, so here's my version of Sarah's Sunday morning. Nothing terrible happens to her. Nothing unthinkable. I can see it. She wakes up, groggy, her mouth still tasting of beer. She pulls the sheet up over her head to block out the sun, and that's when that first physical memory of you bubbles to the surface. And then *boom,* she's drowning so deep in embarrassment, she can barely breathe. Not because she feels like a slut, but because she's one hundred percent certain that *you* think she's a slut."

"She is?" he asks doubtfully.

"Yes, because she's made every rookie mistake in the book. She confessed secrets about herself way too early. She asked you to stay with her for an entire week on your first date. I mean, Jesus, she gave herself to you on the first night. That's, like, an instant disqualification for true love."

He smirks. "'Gave herself?' How do you know that?'"

"Andy, please." I gesture toward his rain-soaked torso without looking at it directly. "Look, you can use whatever terminology you want. The point is, she thought she'd ruined it already. She didn't want to show up at eleven forty-five and sit here for three hours like a pathetic fool, knowing you'd lost all respect for her, knowing you'd probably forgotten her name already."

"Oh, man." Andy sighs. "If three hours makes her a pathetic fool, then what do you call the guy who waits for five days?"

"No! I mean . . . I didn't mean *you* were a pathetic fool for waiting—"

"But that's what you were thinking."

"No, listen to what I'm telling you." I finally drum up the courage to lean a little closer. "Sarah does love you. She just doesn't know that you love her back. The only thing worse than loving someone who doesn't love you back is sleeping with someone who doesn't love you back. If she'd known you loved her, she would have been here at eleven-freaking-fifteen with an orchid in her hair and the prettiest dress she owned. All we need—I mean, all you need to do is find her and tell her that."

He furrows his brow. "I think you might be missing the point here. I can't find her. I don't even have her last name or her number. So when you say 'we,' you're right."

"Well, what else have you tried?"

"Tried?"

"Yeah, what other ways have you tried to find her besides coming here?"

I'd fallen so deep into the conversation, I'd almost forgotten who he was for a minute. Then I see that familiar look sail across his eyes again. The Lost Boy look. Not exactly forlorn, not exactly confused, just clearly at home in a place that isn't here.

"But this is where we're supposed to meet," he says, mostly to himself.

"I know, but haven't you tried anything else? Like retracing your steps, or asking around the café to see if anyone else knows her?"

He rubs his eyes like a toddler waking from a nap. I study his face, trying to understand the sudden glitch in the conversation. I know he's not stupid. He's not naïve, either. But there's something going on with him. It reminds me of that awkward three-second delay in a satellite news interview. Like half his brain is an over-taxed processor, trying to load, and the other half is frustrated at the slow pace.

"Andy?" I tilt my head to see him from a different angle. "Are you okay?"

His hands drop. "We did go to her house."

"Her *house*? Jesus, you know where she *lives*?"

"I didn't say that." There was a glimmer of hope, but it's gone. He glances out the window at the rain. "She wanted to stop by her place to change into something fancy for our date. I went with her, but I don't have a clue where we went. We took one subway, we took another subway. I wasn't looking at subway stops, I was looking at her. I was looking at her eyes and her mouth. I was thinking, *How does this girl get that big ballsy laugh through that fragile little neck of hers?* I didn't know if we were on a subway to Greenwich Village or New Jersey, and I didn't care."

"New Jersey. Did you take the PATH train?"

He laughs hopelessly. "The *what* train? See, I'm totally screwed."

"I don't think so. If you really want my help . . . I can help. We can do this. You just need to focus. Did you notice the names of any of the subway stops?"

Andy's staring out at the river now, at the swells and whitecaps lapping against the pier. Again, his brain seems to be working much too hard to answer an easy question. "Maybe," he says. "Maybe Clark Street? Is that a stop?"

"Yes, it is! Clark Street is on the Number Two line. Were the numbers red when you walked into the station?"

"Maybe," he says, sounding more focused now. He turns back to me.

"Well, what did it look like when you came out of the train? What kinds of buildings?"

"The blocks were real calm and peaceful. Not like the city. We walked past a lot of those little row houses."

"Brownstones."

"Right, brownstones. Just one after the other down the whole block—all of them kind of fancy. You could see big chandeliers through some of the windows, and all those books. Almost every one of those places had wall-to-wall shelves of books."

"Brooklyn," I say. "Probably near Clark Street, too."

"You think?"

"I know it." I can't sit still. Blood starts rushing to my head, liquid determination. "Okay, here's what we're going to do. After school, I'm going to come back here, and we're going to get on the Two train and get off at every stop after Clark Street until something looks familiar. And if we don't find anything on the Two, then we'll try the Three and the Four and the Five and the L and the F and—"

"How come you're being so nice to me?" he interrupts. "I thought you were a bona fide New Yorker and all that."

"Well, it's one of our best-kept secrets," I say. "We're actually really nice people, we just don't tell the tourists about it. Then we'd have to talk to them."

It's the first time I've offered a real smile to a stranger in two and a half months. But then again, he's not really a stranger anymore. As a filmmaker, I work my over-wide ass off to steer clear of corny clichés, but I have to admit Andy never really felt like a stranger to begin with.

THAT SAME AFTERNOON, WE board the 2 train at Chambers Street and get off at each stop in Brooklyn, beginning with Clark Street. I suspect Andy doesn't have much money after five extra days in New York. He wears the same outfit every morning and never orders so much as a coffee at the Harbor. I offer to pay his train fare, but he refuses. Every time we approach a new station, he races out ten eager steps ahead of me and then runs down the stairs, burrowing his way into the crowd.

Then he finds me again on the other side.

I wonder if he's jumping turnstiles, but I think better of it. He isn't some Brooklyn skate rat looking for a free ride; he's a genuine Texan, born and bred. He proves it by letting me have the seat on the train every time.

On again, off again five straight times: we walk a block or two from each station and backtrack if nothing looks familiar, checking around corners and down avenues, hoping he'll recognize a store or a landmark.

As we pull into the ninth station, he speaks the words so softly I almost miss it.

"Bergen Street."

I bounce up from my seat. "You recognize it?"

"Yeah," he says with the beginnings of a smile. "Because I thought it was Burger Street, and she thought it was hilarious that Andy Reese was strutting down Burger Street."

"Yeah, that's hilarious if you're five."

He frowns at me. "Theo, when you're in love, everything someone says is hilarious. Come on." He weaves his way through the onslaught of hipsters pouring onto our train and races up the stairs. None of those hipsters would ever dare utter a line like the one he just pulled off—with total sincerity, no less. They would all be seething with envy.

"Andy, slow down!" I do my best to cut through the rush-hour crowd, thinking of all the useless, shaky footage my button cam is recording as I climb to the surface. Nothing but shoulders, chins, messenger bags, and shuffling feet.

I'll have to find a few minutes to upload the footage to my cloud drive, so I can keep recording.

INSTINCT SEEMS TO CARRY him the next five rainy blocks. Pizza places, wine shops, and trendy little ten-seat restaurants give way to those well-appointed brownstones he'd remembered—thick slabs of Old New York limestone and brick, squeezed together along peaceful, tree-lined streets.

His smile grows wider. His trot turns into a jog and then a sprint, until he stops at a redbrick townhouse between Nevins and Bond.

I'd considered that it might take three or four tedious days of meeting him after school to find the house. I'd also considered that there was a very decent chance we'd never find it at all.

Three hours. That's all it took. I guess Andy had been paying a little more attention to his surroundings than he thought.

"Holy crap!" He drops his backpack to the ground and breaks into a celebratory dance, with that unbridled "king-of-the-world" howl that Leo DiCaprio somehow manages to slip into every movie he's ever made. "You did it, Theo! You found her! Come here, girl." He reaches for me, grinning.

"Whoa!" I lurch away from those outstretched arms.

"Whoa," he echoes. He raises his hands as if I'd pulled a gun.

I laugh, blood rushing to my face. My scar twitches. "No, it's just—"

"Sorry, sorry." He takes a very deliberate step back, keeping his hands up. "Got a little too excited there. I will never attempt to hug you again, I swear."

I try to keep laughing, try to get to the next moment quickly. "No, you just need to *warn* me first . . . Anyway, this is big. This is huge. You know what? We've got to record this."

I hadn't planned on this exact moment, but I know a rain-spattered button cam in the gray twilight will yield me next to no usable footage. He can only be the unknowing star of his own documentary for so long.

I disconnect the cord in my pocket, pull out my iPhone, and start recording him head-on.

"Oh, hell no!" he shouts. In a flash, he blocks the camera with his palm, the same sort of reflexive reaction I had to his attempted hug. "What do you think you're doing?"

"It'll be tasteful, I promise—"

"No way," he says. "I already look stalkery enough showing

up like this. I don't need the Publishers Clearing House camera crew standing behind me when she opens the door."

"Are you kidding me?" I'm ducking and jumping. "You and your lovely wife Sarah will thank me some day. How often does a moment this intimate get caught on film? The beginning of your life together, preserved for all your Golden Angel Children and Grandchildren to enjoy!"

"Shut up." He laughs, turning his back to the camera. "I don't even think she's home. Look up at the windows. It's darker than dead in there."

"Nice try."

"No, I'm serious. Point the damn camera over there!" Suddenly, he's not laughing anymore.

"Dude. It's just a camera."

"All right," he says, barely turning to me. "You want the truth?"

"Always."

"I mean, what the hell, you've already seen me cry like a baby. The truth is . . . I'm camera shy," he declares.

"That's ridiculous. There is no possible way you're camera shy."

"Why not?"

"Have you looked in the mirror lately? People who look like you and claim they're camera shy are liars. Are you a liar?"

"I am not. But let me tell you something about people like me. People like me couldn't drop their first deuce in the toilet without their folks turning it into a feature-length film. It's called *Andy's First Deuce on the Toilet.* I can send it to you if you don't believe me. It has its moments, but it's nothing compared to *Andy's Second Deuce on the Toilet* or *Deuce Three: Caribbean Vacation.* Shit literally did not happen in my house unless someone took a pic or a video of it happening. *Literally.*"

At least he's smiling again.

"You *are* a liar," I say.

"Theo, I'm begging you. I'd rather this moment not feel like I was dropping a deuce for my mama's video scrapbook, okay?"

I shove the phone back in my pocket and curse myself for

taking it out in the first place. But inside my pocket, my fingertips find the tip of the button cam cord and guide it carefully back into the phone connector.

Yes. Still recording.

"Okay, it's off." Now I'm a liar, too.

"So what do you think?" he says. "To ring or not to ring?"

I climb the stairs and jab the button before he can argue. There are muffled chimes inside.

"Theo!" he whispers.

My heart thumps as I take my first good look at the building. Sarah isn't just a Pretty Girl; she's a Pretty Rich Girl. The double doors are carved antiques. But as I look closer, I notice the signs of age. A crack running down one of the second-story windows that any self-respecting Brooklynite would have repaired. Dead leaves and twigs piled up in the window boxes. Every other window box on the block is bursting with colorful flowers or at least a few splashes of green.

I feel a hole growing in the pit of my stomach. It's not a specific thought or emotion, just a rush of vague anxiety: loss and time and neglect. I might not have even felt it on a sunny day, but here in the darkness, with the rain trickling down the red bricks, it looks like the building is in tears.

"Wait," Andy says. He does a wet golden retriever shake of his head. "She didn't want me to come in through the front. She wanted me to give her a few minutes and then meet her at the second-floor window around back."

"Oh, isn't that so Romeo and Juliet," I mumble.

"Shut up."

"Okay. So Rapunzel?"

"Just stay here." He jumps down the stoop, snatches up his backpack, and steps up to the wrought-iron gate that guards the maintenance alley next to Sarah's house. He peers through the bars. The next thing I know, he's tossing his bag over the spikes and scaling the gate. Maybe he did jump all those turnstiles?

Then he's gone. "Andy?" I whisper into the alley.

No response, just the sound of rainwater pouring down from the gutters on the roof. The hole in my stomach expands. It's dark outside. The trees on Bergen Street are huge and leafy. They block the streetlamps. This isn't the East Village, where the streets are lit up like a film set. Night actually looks like night in Brooklyn, and the moon is nowhere to be found. I unplug the button cam and pull my phone back out of my pocket to keep me company. If camera-shy Andy wants to disappear, at least I can shoot some quality HD footage of the house. I pan along the red bricks, up to that long crack on the second-story window, then back down to the arched window over the front doors, where I zoom in on the address. Two-Twenty-Four spelled in wrought iron—

"Excuse me. What do you think you're doing?"

I nearly fall down the steps.

A thirty-something mother and her child are standing at the bottom of the stoop. The mother has slim, pinched features and pointy cheekbones. A black headband keeps her hair firmly slicked back, and she wears a full-length tailored black coat—*The Matrix* by way of Boerum Hill. Her little girl wears a red rain hat, purple raincoat, and aqua galoshes. Her mother holds a Disney's Little Mermaid umbrella over her head.

"Hello," I croak, trying to smile. "Is this your house?"

"Can I help you?" the mother asks sternly.

I sense it in her voice immediately. Fear. There's a soaking-wet stranger with a weird-ass haircut skulking around her doorway. Probably a homeless meth-head casing her apartment for a box of Sudafed or a few Adderall from her medicine cabinet. I need to ease her mind.

"Oh my God, where are my manners?" I giggle. "Might Sarah be home, by any chance?"

Her eyes zero in on my phone. "Why were you filming my house?"

"Oh, no, I was only—"

"Are you filming me now?"

"No, no, I was just . . ." I shove the phone back in my pocket and feel around to plug the button cam back in.

Still recording. Still a liar.

The girl gawks at my ghostly pale face. All I can think of is myself at that age—maybe five or six—before I'd read any Nietzsche or Dostoevsky, before I'd wanted anything more in life than the rare gift of Ho Hos from my mother as an after-school snack.

I try to smile. Her ruby lips part in what looks like horror. She dives back behind her mother's coat.

Now I feel the same horror, a moment of realization: *all that time in the rain.* It had washed away the concealer and foundation—even the extra-firm gel in my hair. I'd spread the curtain wide open, and she'd seen the monster. The Phantom of the Opera unmasked. The only thing missing was the booming thunderclap when you cut to my gruesome close-up.

"Sorry, I'm Emma," I manage, turning back to the mom. I shuffle quickly down the steps and distance myself from them on the sidewalk. "Emma Renaux," I add as they bound up the steps. "I'm a friend of Sarah's from school—"

"There's no one here by that name," the woman says, rifling through her purse for her keys. "You have the wrong house."

"No, I'm pretty sure this is the place."

"There are plenty of other houses like this one." She shoves her daughter through the doorway. "My husband is right upstairs. *Dale,* can you come down here, please?"

I wonder if Dale is actually home or if there even is a Dale. I also wonder if Dale has just found Andy Reese toppling through his bedroom window from the fire escape.

"No, ma'am, that's all right!" I assure her. "I really didn't mean to bother you. It's my mistake. I must have the wrong address. I am so sorry to disturb—"

She slams the door, turning all three locks so I'm sure to hear them.

I wonder if she is still watching me through the shutters. I wonder if I'm about to hear her little girl screech when she finds the imposing Texan boy in her living room.

"Psst, Theo," Andy whispers from the alley, "are they gone? You think she's still watching through the window?"

I storm over to the gate. "Where the hell were you?"

He finally emerges under two pale slivers of streetlight, gripping the wet bars, his face jutting out like a prisoner's. "I was searching the courtyard, trying to find a way in," he whispers. "Then I heard y'all talking outside."

"So why didn't you come out and help me?"

"I told you. Sarah doesn't want her folks to see me."

"This isn't even Sarah's place. That wasn't her mother. We have the wrong house."

"How do you know?"

"Andy, that woman would have to have given birth at *fourteen* to be Sarah's mother. We have the *wrong house.* There are plenty of other—can we not have this conversation here, please? If she sees me standing here, she's going to call the cops."

"Okay, chill, woman." He scales back over the gate and lands on the sidewalk, quickly dusting himself off.

I hurry us down the block, trying to get as far from the house as possible before he says another word.

THE RAIN FINALLY STOPS, but we've strayed from the more populated half of Bergen Street into "the other half" of Brooklyn—the sketchier half, where abandoned buildings and empty lots pop up on every other block. Some part of me knows to turn around and walk back toward Not-Sarah's-House, toward a subway that will take us home. But the other part wants to keep moving in the direction we're going.

"I mean, that was her place," Andy says, as if I've been arguing. "I mean, I get that it's not her place, but it *was.* Shit, I don't know what I'm talking about. What's the matter with me?"

I sneak a glimpse at his face. Confused and weary, that familiar hopeless set of his brow. I have to admit it was a little strange that he'd picked the wrong house after seeming so sure about 224 Bergen Street. But I'm beginning to develop a theory.

"Andy . . ."

"Yeah?"

"Don't get mad when I ask you this question, all right?"

"At you? I can't even believe you're still hanging out with me right now."

"Okay. How drunk were you on Saturday night?"

He actually laughs. "A couple of beers, no more," he says. "Believe me, nobody knows blotto better than I do, but I wasn't even close. I didn't want to make a fool of myself."

"Yeah, scratch that." I rack my brain for another explanation. "I suppose there's one other possibility."

"What's that?"

"Well . . . what if it wasn't her house?"

"What do you mean? We know it's not her house."

"No, I mean, what if it was the house she took you to, but it wasn't actually *her* house?"

Andy stops abruptly. I case the street; we're in front of a decrepit old warehouse. There's a collage of bright-yellow rat poison warnings pasted on the garage door behind him—big fat rat silhouettes with dark-red NO symbols slicing through their stomachs.

"You mean, like she lied to me?" he says.

Seconds of ugly silence begin to stack up between us. This is the longest I've been away from my room in weeks, and I'm beginning to feel the side effects of cocoon-less living.

"You know what? I have no idea what I'm saying—"

"No. You're saying she lied to me."

"No, no." I wave my hands. "I didn't mean it like that. Andy, I don't even sleep at night. There's nothing but scrambled eggs in my brain after six or seven. But I'm doubling up on my meds, so—"

"Why would she take me to a house that wasn't her house?"

he demands. "Why would she send me off to the alley, break in, steal a sexy dress, and meet me at the back window for a quick getaway? Why?"

"She so clearly did *none* of those things. Andy, I do the news at school. I'm always trying to find 'the big story' when there's no story at all. I make documentaries." I'm jabbering now, but I can't stop. "After a while, you just start taking all your random footage and forcing it together into a story. It's like my disease—"

"No, but what if you're right?" he says with a crack in his voice. "Oh, man . . . she took me to a fake house." He backs up against the garage door and slides down its steel ridges until he's crouched on the sidewalk, shoulders slumped. "She could have been lying about everything. What if everything she told me was a lie?"

I crouch next to him, not wanting to get my butt wet on the rain-slicked sidewalk. "Just forget the house, okay? It could have been the next street over or a completely different neighborhood; it doesn't matter. Let's just move on—let's keep retracing your steps. Where did you go after you picked her up?"

He rubs his eye and takes a long breath. "We went out to a place," he says.

"Could you be a little more specific?"

"It had flowers everywhere." He stares vacantly at the empty lot across the street. "Daisies," he says, snapping his fingers with a burst of new energy. "Daisies are her favorite flower."

I try not to smile. I know that loving daisies is far from unique, but the thought of having anything in common with Andy's Golden Goddess feels like a shot of whiskey warming my chilled bones. "So you went to a park? Central Park?"

"No, not a park," he says. "There were flowers everywhere, but they were inside."

"Like the Botanical Gardens?"

"No, not the Botanical Gardens, but . . . the *Magic* Garden!" He claps, giving me a start. "That's what it was called, the Magic Garden."

"Like a club?"

"A club."

I whip my phone out and Google "the Magic Garden club NYC." I scroll through a bunch of hits for some children's television show from the '70s.

On the third page, I strike pay dirt.

"Here! This is it. The Magic Garden." I read aloud from the club's homepage: *"Some of us spend our whole lives looking for paradise, never knowing that Eden was right beneath our feet. And only two blocks from the F Train! Get out of the Urban Jungle, people. Come and play with us."* Then, at the bottom, a rhyming couplet: *"So come on in without a fuss, 'cause the Magical Garden is waiting for us!* Well, that's just adorable," I deadpan.

"I didn't say it was a cool place."

"Do you have a decent shirt in that backpack?" I ask.

"I guess. Why?"

"Why do you think? The Magical Garden is waiting for us."

"No way." He shakes his head. "You've done too much already. I can find her on my own."

I realize in that moment that Andy knows even less about me than I know about him. He has no idea how far I'll go to feed an obsession. He has no idea that *he's* been my obsession for the last five days, or that a brand-new obsession has just taken his place.

I have to find Sarah. I have to find her for Andy, no matter what. Even if it means facing one of my darkest fears: putting on a dress.

Chapter Six

At the time, I owned exactly two dresses. One was the vintage wedding dress I kept wrapped in tissue paper, creaseless and pristine, inside the cedar Glory Box at the foot of my bed. (I preferred the Australian term *glory box* to the more traditional *hope chest.* It just sounded ballsier.) The other was a little black cocktail dress—a sleeveless pleated funeral smock that my mom had forced me to purchase at Ann Taylor last year because she wouldn't let me wear a black hoodie and matching jeans to Todd's Distinguished Teaching Award ceremony at NYU.

I'd argued that nothing said "New York University" like a black hoodie and black jeans. I'd even thrown the words of her favorite American transcendentalist back in her face. "Didn't Henry David Thoreau tell us to beware all enterprises that require new clothes?" But Mom said that no amount of transcendentalism could justify a black hoodie at an awards ceremony. Then she threatened to put me in therapy if I didn't get over my issues with my "perfectly normal-size derriere." I told her my fluctuating ass had nothing to do with my no-dress policy, but she had already won the war. Ann Taylor funeral smock, black tights, and clunky sensible pumps all the way.

I stood at the bathroom sink in my black bra, tights, and Beats headphones and stared into the drain. The Darkness's "I Believe in a Thing Called Love" was blasting through my ears at max volume. It was loud, and it was funny, and I needed the distraction if I was going to make it through this.

It had taken me almost a month to perfect this, but I could now look in the mirror without actually looking in the mirror. The trick was to focus your eyes on an extreme close-up at all times and never zoom out to full frame. I could focus in and pluck an eyebrow, or trace my lips with lipstick, or smooth down a hair that had curled out of place. But one false move and I might catch a glimpse of my entire self—bony elbows, pale stomach, disproportionate ass, goose neck, and, of course, the red gash.

It could all be avoided in the daytime. Sweatshirts, T-shirts, and jeans could be applied mirror-less. The scar cover-up was more of an art project than a makeup job. But "pretty makeup" and evening wear were a completely different story. You can't apply "pretty makeup" strictly in close-up; you have to see it in context. You think you've got the blush and mascara right, then you zoom out, and you're staring at a Goth circus clown with Egyptian mummy eyes—or worst-case scenario: you're that ninety-year-old lady at the diner.

The same with a dress. You can't judge it all by feel. You have to look and see if it zigs where it's supposed to zag, or if the tag is showing, or if the hanger straps are creeping out under the arms, and you have to look at the ass. You *have* to. No woman—not even one as allergic to mirrors as I—can leave the house without checking the ass.

A notification alert buzzed through my headphones: Max's tenth consecutive text. He'd been texting me at fifteen-minute intervals since 7 P.M., and I'd been forcing myself to ignore them. He clearly needed me, but I knew if I answered even one, I'd get sucked into a long conversation, at which point I'd lose my nerve to go clubbing with Andy.

MAXCELL: Where u at? Need a session NOW.

MAXCELL: Dude, please don't do the Invisible Theo routine right now. NEED emergency session.

MAXCELL: When I say NEED, I mean NEED. A session. Now.

MAXCELL: Hello? Fine, I'll say it. EARTH TO THEO! MAYDAY, MAYDAY.

MAXCELL: Okay, u are beginning to suck now.

MAXCELL: Now u are fully sucking.

MAXCELL: Unprecedented suckage. Your suckage mocks me . . .

MAXCELL: Hello, Theo, it's your friend Max. Might you have a brief moment to speak? Would be so greatly appreciated. ☺

MAXCELL: Oh, the humanity

I yanked off the headphones and shoved the phone into the old-lady purse that Mom had made me buy with the dress. Then I checked my ass in the mirror, gasped with horror, grabbed my pumps, and tiptoed to the back door in the kitchen while Mom and Todd discussed Ayn Rand in the living room.

I KNEW THERE WAS no way I could get past my doorman Emilio without a conversation, but I tried. I moved swiftly through the lobby—as swiftly as I could in my barely used, clunky pumps—and ducked my head like a movie star leaving a Hollywood hot spot.

"Hot date tonight?" Emilio grabbed the doorknob but wouldn't open the door.

"Oh, please." I laughed. "Emilio, have you ever seen me go on a date?"

"First time for everything, right?" He smiled. "I'm gleaming with pride." He was from Guadalajara and still carried an accent. *Everything* sounded like *every-sing*.

We don't live in a fancy building. Emilio doesn't hail people cabs or wear one of those vaguely military outfits with tassels on the shoulders. He doubles as the building's superintendent and maintenance man, and opts for loose-fitting khakis and a shirt that was always opened one button too many, revealing a dense forest of graying man-fuzz.

"I think you mean 'beaming' with pride," I said.

"Oh, I'm gleaming and beaming."

"Well, you shouldn't do either, because it's not a date."

"Jew look pretty fancy."

We'd worked through the accent-related "Jew" confusion a long time ago. When I was about twelve—and I had just seen *Annie Hall* for the first of my nine times—I told Emilio to watch the scene where Woody Allen describes an NBC executive's unfortunate lunch inquiry: *Jew eat? No, not 'Did you eat?' but JEW eat? JEW?* Emilio thought it was so hilarious that we agreed to make it an essential part of any conversation.

"No, Jew doesn't look fancy," I said. "You've just never seen Jew in a dress."

"No, it's not the dress," he said. "It's a vibe."

"A vibe?"

"Yeah, Jew have the vibe."

"There's no vibe, Emilio."

"*Vibe,*" he insisted with an all-knowing nod. "My daughter had this same vibe the night she met my son-in-law Estefan. Now I have two beautiful grandkids and counting. Trust me, I know the vibe."

I started compulsively flattening my hair against my cheek. "There is no *vibe*," I groaned. "It's not a date, it's, it's a—I'm going to an awards ceremony, okay?"

"Oh. Well, I hope it's the Vibe Awards, because Jew would win tonight."

"Jew doesn't win, Emilio. Jew never wins." I swatted his hand from the doorknob and swung the door open, sliding by him as he laughed gleefully.

"Jew have a beautiful night, Teodoro!"

Outside, I searched the block for Andy.

When I heard him call my name, I followed his voice and found him rising from a stoop across the street. He had his backpack hoisted over one shoulder, and he was still in his jeans, but he'd swapped out the frayed white V-neck for a crisp white Oxford shirt, untucked and open at the collar.

I'd seen a thousand "dudes" crisscrossing the East Village on a Friday night in that exact same outfit. They traveled in teams of three, and they always reeked of desperation. That devil-may-care untucked shirt seemed so laughable to me, since they had obviously primped and gelled for hours, grasping at trends like thirteen-year-old girls. But as I clip-clopped across the street, wobbling my way toward him, I realized the man they were all trying to look like—the man they were all trying to be . . . was Andy.

If we had been on a date, this would have been the moment when we shared a quick hug or a casual peck on the cheek. But there was no hug and no peck. Instead we just stood in awkward silence, which only brought more attention to the absence of the hug or the peck, which in turn only magnified the date-like nature of the non-date.

"You put on a dress for me," he said finally.

"For Sarah," I corrected him too quickly.

"God. Do you really think we'll find her at that club?"

"I know we will."

He took a small step closer, erasing the last bit of distance between us. "Theo, I'm running out of ways to thank you."

I lifted my head to meet his, noticing for the first time that the pale beige freckles on his nose almost matched the color of his eyes. "You don't have to thank me."

I glanced back across the street and caught a glimpse of Emilio watching us through the front door. His easy smile had been replaced by a distrustful squint.

My cheeks suddenly flushed, but it wasn't because of Andy; it was simply this: I'd never had a father around to give my date the once-over—that withering "touch her, and I'll break your face" look. Having my overprotective doorman eye my non-date with fatherly suspicion was the closest I would ever come.

I COULDN'T GET THIS comparison out of my obsessive head: If Emilio was my doorman father, then the bouncer at the Magic Garden was most definitely my doorman mother. Ice-cold. A master in the art of silence. Impervious to even the most heartfelt of pleas. I thought Andy's Texan charm could work on any creature with a beating heart, no matter the gender, height, or pectoral size, but this bouncer was a six-foot granite statue in an Armani suit.

"Aw, come *awn*, man." It was the first time I'd heard Andy exaggerate his drawl for effect (I suspected it was a secret skill all Southerners possessed). "Forty-five minutes? We been standing on this line for forty-five minutes. Now that just ain't right, don't you think?"

Zero response from Granite Bouncer.

Maybe he saw the same tragedy I did: a massive herd of drunk girls in heels and crotch-length skirts, lining up in the cold as if it were their lifelong dream to be funneled into a vast, thumping abyss. Their toxic fusion of designer fragrances was making me woozy. I wasn't sure how much longer I could last.

Andy tried a new tack. "All right, look. I think you need to know the whole story here, man. The girl I love—I'm talking the love of my life, brother—I've been trying to find her for days, and I think she just might be inside that club right now. Only she doesn't know I'm out here. So we just need you to let us in so I can tell her that. Do you feel me, brother?"

We got nothing.

"Really?" Andy laughed, but the laugh was strained. I wasn't sure how much longer he could last, either. "I don't even get it.

I was just here on Saturday night, and they let us through in two minutes. What the hell changed?"

I slammed my eyes shut. I knew exactly what had changed. It was the hotness level of his companion. Sarah had walked him straight through that door because she looked like Sarah. But a bottom-heavy troll in funeral attire? That was a much harder sell.

"Excuse me, sir?"

Miracle of miracles, Granite Bouncer actually turned to me. Apparently, he responded much better to *sir* than he did to *dude, man,* or *brother.* Maybe I had cracked his code.

"What up, girl?" he asked.

"Hi, yes—if I could just point out . . . your website states that we should 'come on in without a fuss, because the Magical Garden is waiting for us.' But we have actually been waiting for *it* for about forty-five minutes. Doesn't that strike you as false advertising?"

When the bouncer smiled, he looked like a totally different person. Which is to say, he looked like a *person.*

"You're funny," he said. He said it as if his opinion had very deep and lasting significance. "I like funny girls." With that, he leaned over and unhooked the rope. I was so shocked, I didn't even move at first. "You coming in or not?"

"Yes, thank you, sir, yes," I said.

"Theo, let's go!" Andy called back to me, already through the door.

"Oh, and girl . . ." The bouncer grabbed my arm. "If I could also just point something out. This whole funeral brunch vibe you've got going—totally working." He waved his hand over me from head to toe. "I like a girl with a look."

I couldn't decide if I was flattered or insulted. It didn't matter. Andy and I were in.

I CUPPED MY EARS like an elderly librarian. It wasn't the bone-shaking bass drum or the screaming synthesizers—I liked my music set to "deafening." It was that I'd spent weeks alone in a small bedroom, living with a mother and stepstool whose preferred entertainment was quietly debating the postfeminist merits of Susan Sontag. I'd blasted plenty of music in my room, watched more than two hundred movies, played more than forty Xbox games, so I wouldn't have called it "sensory deprivation." But nothing on earth could simulate the crush of human bodies. And that was the Magic Garden: a cavernous garden of arms, legs, elbows, naked shoulders, and perfectly toned asses. I think they'd set the thermostat to "Deathly Oppressive Humidity" for the sake of all the flowers.

And there were so many flowers. Mounds of fresh flowers and green leaves sprouting up from tall Lucite pedestals that anchored plush, circular banquettes. The pedestals were lit up from within like trees in the Na'vi forest, casting an ethereal, blue glow on all the Crest-whitened smiles and tan summer flesh. It was so ugly and so beautiful at the same time.

It was Blue Hell with flowers, and I wanted out as much as I'd wanted in, but I wasn't leaving until I found Sarah and asked her at least one question:

Why on earth would you bring Andy here? Why not a kick-back barbecue joint in the West Village? Or a romantic restaurant where you could actually hear each other speak? Did we meet the same Andy Reese? Sensitive country boy? Ridding the world of irony one boyish smile at a time? You'd just spent a whole day with him, soulfully walking and talking *Before Sunrise*–style. Why would you close it out with this soulless urban dungeon? Are you one of the Beautiful People? I mean, I know you're beautiful, but are you one of them?

Okay, fine, that was nine questions.

"Andy," I shouted, straining my voice to overcome the din of the crowd and the pulsating beat even though he was less than a yard away, "if I'm going to spot her in this hellscape, it might be good if I actually knew what she looked like. How about some specifics?"

I felt a set of bony fingers crawl down my back. When I turned around, there was a pencil-thin party boy in a sleeveless Sex Pistols T-shirt and skinny jeans pushing me forward, his hands on my hips.

"Dude." I slapped his probing hands from my body. "What is your *problem?*"

I don't even think he heard me as he slid past. But when I turned back around, Andy was gone.

"Andy?" I called out, spinning in place. "Andy?" The bodies were cutting deeper into my personal space. There was nowhere to put my hands without touching some guy's sweaty back. Nowhere to breathe without inhaling some girl's Chanel-drenched neck. I crossed my arms over my chest and buried my fingers between my underarms, feeling sweat start to trickle down my elbows. *"Andy . . . ?"*

"Theo! Theo, look up!"

He was tall enough that I could see his backpack. He pointed above us and mouthed, "Bar. Meet me at the bar."

BY THE TIME I got upstairs, I felt like a used punching bag. I'd lost track of Andy again, but I was sure he'd find me. I pushed through two more layers of thirsty club kids and miraculously found an available stool. I set my elbows down on the glowing blue Lucite bar and buried my head under my hands. I knew it made me look like one of those psycho drunk chicks who'd had one too many lemon drops and a screaming fight with her boyfriend. But maybe that was a good thing. Maybe it made me invisible—

"Rough night?" a boy's voice asked, close to my ear.

I jerked away and became the Terminator, scanning the boy and assessing the threat level: *Casual gray sport coat over a spanking new white T-shirt. Even whiter teeth in a perma-smile. Close-cropped, wavy red hair with no product. Bud Light Lime on the napkin in front of him. A flat pug nose that probably left him begging for his frat brothers' sexual table scraps in college. Yes, undoubtedly a frat boy, but one of those kinder, all-inclusive frats that real frats made fun of.*

Conclusion: Douchey but harmless.

"Do you need a drink?" he asked.

"No, thank you," I said. "I didn't come here to drink."

"Oh, right on." He smirked. "Booze isn't your thing, then?"

"Right," I said.

"How about a water?"

I glanced over my shoulder for signs of Andy. He should have made it to the bar already. Now he had me talking to strangers again. "Okay, a water," I said flatly.

Douchey-but-Harmless raised his hand to the bartender. "Ray-Ray! A bottle of water for the lady!"

"Coming up!" Ray-Ray shouted back.

Clearly Douchey and the bartender were friends, and clearly Douchey wanted me to know this. The hordes were clamoring for Ray-Ray's attention, hollering drink orders, thrusting fifty-dollar bills between the beer taps, but Ray-Ray ignored them like the bouncer had ignored Andy.

Aha. Andy was a genius. He wanted us at the bar because that's where all the regulars hung out. The regulars were more likely to know Sarah if she partied here, and I was pretty sure I'd just found the Magic Garden's resident junior barfly. Time to unleash Theo Lane, P.I.

I turned to Douchey. "So do you come here a lot?" I demanded.

Douchey frowned. I shut my eyes, mortified. I'd just asked him a variation of the world's most clichéd pickup line by complete accident.

"Yeah," Douchey said cautiously. "I live just around the corner."

I mustered the courage to open my eyes.

"One water for the lady!" Ray-Ray slid up to our spot and poured half a bottle of Voss water into a floral-print glass. He had a square actor's face, annoyingly perfect jet-black hair, and overly manicured black stubble. "Who's this, Tim? Your little sister?"

I was relieved that Tim's real name was even more harmless than Douchey.

"No, this is my friend . . ." Tim looked to me to finish his sentence.

"Emma," I said.

"Well it's very nice to meet you, Emma." Ray-Ray reached over the bar, I assumed to shake hands. But when I reached for his hairy bear paw, he snatched my wrist. In a flash, he expertly fastened a thin strip of orange paper around it. "Welcome to the Magic Garden, Emma. You can have all the water and soda you want. It's on me."

Once free, I scowled and massaged my wrist. UNDERAGE was printed on my orange bracelet.

I needed to find Andy, and I needed to get out of here as soon as possible. "Listen, Tim, I was supposed to meet my friend Sarah here, but I haven't been able to spot her yet. Maybe you know her? Sarah? She comes here all the time. She's blonde and . . . she's ridiculously pretty."

"I know at least twenty ridiculously pretty blonde Sarahs who hang here," Tim said.

"Right. She's, uh . . . God, I don't know how to describe her. She was just here on Saturday with our friend Andy."

"Andy . . . ?" He was waiting for a last name.

"Andy Reese," I said. "But you probably don't know him—"

"Andy Reese?" Tim interrupted, dropping his voice to a whisper. He glanced over his shoulder and leaned close, hammering me with his cinnamon skunk breath. "Of course I know Andy. He's here almost every night. In the men's room."

"The men's room?"

"Yeah, I bet he's there now. Should we pay him a visit?"

I blinked, feeling vaguely sick. "Andy Reese? Is here every night? In the men's room?"

"Pretty much," Tim said, sliding off his stool and smoothing down his jacket.

"Like, since when? Since Saturday?"

"My boy Andy?" Tim laughed. "Nah, the kid's a year-round staple. He's what makes the Garden magic." He offered his hand, and I flashed back to the Harbor Café—to Andy reaching across our table for a supposedly innocent handshake. I wanted to tell Tim he was full of shit, that he had the wrong Andy Reese, that he had no idea what he was talking about. But one thing kept getting in the way: Andy had disappeared. Did he head straight to the men's room? Was he conducting "business" in there? What was he carrying in that overstuffed backpack that never left his side? Was the bouncer just pretending to ignore him? Just giving his pal Andy shit for hanging out with an underage girl?

No, this is ridiculous. Douchey is messing with your head because you're the ugly newbie at the bar. You know Andy. He couldn't even remember the name of this place until you helped him remember it.

But I'd known Andy Reese for less than twenty-four hours.

I knew him about as well as he knew Sarah No-Last-Name.

"Show me the men's room," I said to Tim.

"OH, ANDYYYYYY?" NO ONE seemed to care that Tim was cutting the long line to the men's room and ushering a clearly branded underage girl through the door. "Paging Andy Reese. I have a friend of yours who wants to say hello-ohhhh."

All the things that should have made my skin crawl didn't matter right now. Not Tim's increasingly annoying, singsong-y children's theater voice. Not the fact that I was entering a men's room, something I'd never done before, not even in an emergency. It was lined wall-to-wall with backs hunched drunkenly over shiny white urinals. I willed the symphony of zippers and pee and who-knows-what-else into the background because I needed to see him. I needed to see the real Andy Reese.

"Andyyyyy?" Tim called again. He smiled, showing those white teeth. "He's usually at the back." He led me down to the handicapped stall at the end of the room and tapped on the metal door. It was unlocked. "Mr. Reese?"

I barged in, ready to confront Andy, but praying I'd find what I found: the stall was empty. But then Tim stepped in behind me and locked the door.

I spun around in my clunky heels. "What are you doing?"

Tim giggled. "Just wait for it." He reached down the front of his pants and pulled out an old-model Samsung flip phone, then snapped open the battery compartment and pulled out a small plastic baggie filled with white powder. "Ta-daaa!"

My stomach dropped. "Okay, let me out."

Tim was blocking the door. He was stockier than I'd realized. "Oh, come on, Em. I'm not going to charge you."

"*'Em'?* We're not on a nickname basis, Tim. You said Andy was back here."

"And that wasn't code? Come on, you told me booze wasn't your thing."

"Just let me out!" My heart was thumping. "Open the goddamn *door.*" I tried to shove him aside, and the plastic baggie fell from his fingers, sprinkling a cloud of white dust all over the black tiles like confectioners' sugar.

"What the fuck?" he growled. He dropped down on his knee and tried to sweep the mess of powder back into the tiny bag. I lurched forward and got my hands on the lock, but he snatched my wrist and tugged me backward. "No, don't open that door."

That's when I screamed. I screamed from some well in my gut that I didn't even know existed. *"Get off of me!"* I broke out of his grip and slammed my fists against the stall's metal door. "Help me, Andy! Somebody help!"

Men started gathering around the stall, shouting. Maybe Tim shouted something back at them. Maybe he just sat there frozen on the floor, gawking at the spectacle of a screaming girl trapped in a tiny cage.

"Out!" a deep voice bellowed, silencing everything. "Everybody out!"

And then the stall door was swinging open, and a massive man with a corded earpiece and a shaved head was grabbing my arms, crossing them over my chest like a human straitjacket, lifting me off the floor, and carrying me out of the bathroom into the roaring music.

"Stay calm," the man breathed as the crowd cleared a path for us. I kept trying to wriggle free, but my feet weren't touching the ground. "Calm down. It hurts less if you stay still."

"Where are you taking me?" I moaned. "My boyfriend is still in there. I need my boyfriend."

"He'll find you outside. They always do." He used his shoulder to slam open an emergency exit and then placed me down on the sidewalk. "Thank you. Come again."

He slammed the door behind him.

I was alone.

The roaring beat was suddenly a muffled thump behind the door of the Magic Garden.

I stumbled two steps in my heels and nearly fell over. I could hear people chattering and laughing. I smelled cigarette smoke all around me, but the street was a dim and soggy blur, the stinging combo of pretty makeup and tears that I didn't even know were there.

I swiped at my eyes as they stared—all the other club rejects who'd stuck around this dingy back lot because they had no place better to go. All I wanted was Andy. The *real* Andy, not the Magic Garden's fictional drug dealer.

That's when I saw him. He rounded the corner and jogged toward me.

"Where *were* you?" I cried. My hands balled up into fists again, and I swung at his chest. "Where the hell did you go? Why did you leave me alone in there?"

The club rejects burst into laughter. I couldn't blame them.

But Andy was too quick for my punches. "Whoa, whoa, whoa!" He laughed nervously, eyes wide, dodging every swing like a pro. "Calm down, Theo, calm down!" he whispered. "I'm sorry. I didn't know which way was north in there. It was nothing like that on Saturday. I mean, it was crowded, but not . . . I should have stuck next to you. I thought I made it up to the bar pretty fast, but you were already gone."

"Yeah, that's my bad," I admitted, trying to catch my breath. I sat down on the curb. "This whole thing was my bad."

I felt sick again, at myself. I did know Andy; why did I let the world's douchiest cokehead convince me otherwise? If I'd just given him three more minutes to make it up to the bar, then everything would have been fine. We could have kept looking for Sarah.

"You should go back in," I said. "I'm the one who should be sorry. Go back in. You can still find her."

"No, I am not leaving you out here," he said. "No way."

"Don't worry about me. She's the only reason we're here. Go back in and find her."

"Theo. Hey." He crouched down beside me. "Let's be real. We were never going to find her in there." I saw an ocean of disappointment well up behind his eyes, but he tried to hide it with that familiar resolute half-smile. "Maybe it just wasn't meant to be."

I hid under my hair curtain. I wasn't ready to accept that. "Andy? Will you please take me home?"

"I'm way ahead of you," he said, standing to flag a cab. But we didn't have any luck until I finally found us one on Essex Street.

Chapter Seven

The Fates had been utter bitches to us tonight, but they at least did us one small favor: Andy was able to enter my building without being seen. Emilio's shift ended at eleven, sparing Andy ten excruciating minutes of faux-fatherly cross-examination. More importantly, no one would be calling up to my mom to announce Andy's arrival.

Not that it had ever been much of a problem. I could count the number of boys who'd come to my room on one finger, and that finger's name was Max. But it still took Mom more than three months to adjust to our tutoring sessions. I'd tried to reason with her: *Max is just my student—we're barely even friends.* (Only true for the first month.) *He's like my goofy older brother.* (We were the same age.) *He's not the kind of guy that sleeps around with girls.* (Untrue.)

None of it worked. Like most phobias, it was the repeated exposure that finally got Mom used to Max, and gave him clearance to my bedroom without an entrance or exit interview. But Mom still tended toward hourly bed checks, however thinly veiled. *Knock, knock. Max, I've just made some bergamot tea. Would you like a cup? Knock, knock. Max, Todd is about to watch the World Bocce Ball Championship. Perhaps you'd like to join him? Knock, knock. Theo, we're in the kitchen discussing Hawthorne's excessive use of symbolism. Thought you and Max might want to get in on that. We've broken out the hummus.*

As I dug through my old-lady purse for the keys, I jabbered in a hushed whisper to Andy about Mom's archaic visitor policies. I then raced through a description of next steps. We would take the maintenance stairs to the third floor, enter my apartment through the back door in the kitchen, and tiptoe like professional burglars to my room.

And it worked. At least something had gone according to plan tonight.

I LOCKED MY BEDROOM door. Andy collapsed between two piles of newspapers on my couch. I flopped onto the bed, finally yanking the cruel shoes off my blistered feet. I wanted to change into a sweatshirt and jeans, but the thought of having him so close to the bathroom door while I changed felt too weird. I stayed bound in the funeral smock.

I did manage a quick check of my makeup in the bathroom mirror. The raccoon eyes were horrifying. I had to use the extreme close-up method to wipe them clean with some Swisspers. But I was still so shaky that my eyes drifted off target and I caught a glimpse of Andy's reflection. He thought my back was turned, so he gave his optimistic smile a rest. I could see it: his heroic five-day quest for Sarah was a total bust.

I popped an extra Lexapro, hoping it would help tamp down my racing thoughts and numb all the exposed nerves.

When I stepped back into my room, Andy flipped the smile back on. "You okay?"

I put my finger to my lips, reminding him to stay quiet. I almost sat next to him on the couch, but opted for the wooden armrest instead. "You know, it's not over," I said. "There's still, like, a thousand other things we can try. We can go online and search for—"

"Theo, stop. Just stop." We sat in silence for a moment, and I tried to use the time to quiet my mind. "You know what I think?" he asked.

"Uh-uh," I replied, focusing on the cracks in my dilapidated Japanese coffee table.

"I think I've just been putting her in the wrong category."

"What do you mean?"

"I mean, maybe she's not supposed to be the love of my life. Maybe she's just supposed to be the best day of my life. Maybe she doesn't belong in my future. You know, she'll be that person. The one you never really fall out of love with, but you have to kind of lock them away in a story box in the back of your mind. So you can dig up the memory twenty years later—like when you're fishing on the lake with your kid and you need to tell him the story of the one that got away. You know what I mean?"

I nodded. "Yeah, I think so." But I had no idea what he meant. I'd never met anyone who fit that description. I'd never met "the one that got away" because I'd never met "the one."

I did know this much. When I finally fell in love, I sure as hell wouldn't bury him in some "story box" in the back of my mind. He would be standing right next to me, my ever-present soul mate and lawfully wedded husband—

"Theodore?" The urgent knock gave us both a start. "Theodore, I can hear you in there." Mom twisted and tugged at the doorknob. Thank God I'd locked it—it gave us a few extra seconds for evasive maneuvers. "Can you open this door, please? Where on earth have you been?"

"Shit, shit, shit," I whispered. I had to hide Andy. The bathroom shower was too risky. Under the bed was too '80s movie. "Closet," I whispered.

"On it," he whispered back, springing up from the couch. "It's not the first time I've hid in a girl's closet."

"Theodore!" Mom shouted. "I can hear you whispering. Open the door!"

I guided Andy to the clearing between two tall stacks of *Times* wedding sections. "What's with all the papers?" he mouthed.

I slid the closet shut before he could ask any more questions and dove for my bedroom door, swinging it open. "Sorry, Mom. Didn't realize I'd locked it."

She took in my dress and the faded remains of my lipstick and rouge. Her eyes were simmering. "Who were you talking to?" she demanded. "I heard you talking." She was so angry, she hadn't even used the proper *whom*. It was that bad.

"I was talking to Lou," I said. I grabbed the purse from my dresser, whipped out my phone, and held it up as if that somehow backed up my story.

"Where on earth were you tonight? Why are you so dressed up?"

"Lou had a recital, remember? I told you about it last week."

"I don't remember that. I would have remembered."

"Maybe your September stress has you a little frazzled? Oh, wait." I slapped my head. "Maybe I told Todd. Todd might not have told you."

"But how did you come in? We didn't even hear you come in."

"Through the kitchen like always. I told you, it's a faster route to my bed, and I am super-*duper* tired. The recital was epic—Brahms, your favorite. I think I just need to call it a night."

"Well, you can't call it a night, because you have a visitor."

"What visitor?"

Max stepped out of the dark hallway and raised his hand. "What up?" he mumbled.

I GRIPPED THE DOOR tightly. My knees were in danger of giving out from under me.

"Max!" I cried with a stupid grin. He was my human lie detector, the last thing I needed with Andy balled up in the closet. "What's up?" I asked, just to maintain the illusion of normalcy for Mom.

But it was a cruel insult to Max. He'd been begging for an emergency session since seven o'clock. He shrugged by way of response. I tried to find his ice-blue eyes in the dark recesses of his practice hoodie.

"I'll tell you what's up," Mom interjected. "Max has been

sitting with us in the dining room for over an *hour* trying to reach you—"

"Max, don't hate me," I interrupted. "I'm so sorry. I couldn't have my phone on during the recital."

He pulled off his hood and turned to my mother. "Mrs. Lane, do you think I could speak with Theo alone for just a few minutes? I know it's late."

Mom's lips tightened. "Of course," she said with a labored smile. "But just a few minutes, yes?"

Max took the liberty of closing the door in her face. I wanted to hug him.

"Okay," he whispered, turning back to me. "A recital? Seriously? Like I wouldn't know if Lou had a recital tonight? She's texted me about fifty times."

"Okay, no, sorry," I whispered. "It was a leftover lie."

"So then why? Why do you look like a . . . ?" He scowled, gesturing at various parts of my body. "You know, a . . ."

"Like a girl, Max? Is that what you're trying to say? Why do I look like a girl?"

"Yes." He crossed his arms. "Yes, you look eerily similar to a girl."

"Eerily similar? Nice. It's just a dress, Max. I'm wearing a dress."

"Just a dress? Theo, you own exactly two dresses—the one you're wearing, which your mom made you buy for Todd's Distinguished Teaching Award ceremony, and the wedding dress buried in your Glory Box, waiting for that magical prince to come along and unlock your—"

"God, will you shut *up*?" I glanced at the closet. Andy Reese now knew about my Glory Box. I took hold of Max's shoulders and tried to spin him toward the door. "Can we please just have this conversation tomorrow? I'm super-*duper* tired."

Max planted his feet. He wouldn't budge. "What, like you're going to go to bed now? You don't even go to sleep till four A.M."

"Yeah, why do you think I'm so super-duper tired?"

"Okay," he said quietly. "I don't know what's freaking me out more—that you're still lying to me or that you're trying to get rid of me." He peeled my hands from his shoulders. "What is this?" He lifted my left wrist. I still had the orange bracelet Ray-Ray had forced on me like a handcuff. "Did you go to a *club* tonight?"

I couldn't answer. My mouth moved, but nothing came out.

I saw the lightbulb go on in his eyes. "Jesus, do you have a guy in here?" He began to survey my room.

"Oh, come on." My knees began to wobble again.

"You picked up a Random at a club and brought him back home, didn't you? That's why you didn't text me back all night. That's why you keep disappearing all week."

"No."

"Jesus, Thee, what ever happened to saving yourself for Mr. Right? I mean, I know everyone's going completely A.B.O. bat shit today, but I think you're overshooting. It's supposed to be someone in school—someone you had your eye on for years, not some bar stool with a silk shirt and a pocket full of Trojans."

"Max, I am seriously going to throw up if you keep talking like that."

"Where is he?" He stepped into my bathroom and reached for the shower curtain. "No, shower's too risky," he mumbled, stepping back.

"Max, come on, stop."

He crouched halfway down to the floor next to my bed. "No, too '80s movie."

"Max . . ."

"Closet." His eyes zeroed in on the sliding wooden doors. "You never close your closet door."

My heart leaped into my throat, and my mouth went into overdrive. "Max-you're-being-ridiculous-this-is-totally-ridiculous-I-don't-even-know-what-the-problem-is-right-now-I-said-I-was-sorry-I-didn't-text-you-back." The babble floated past him like vapor as he stepped to the closet and slid the door open with a rusty screech. I bit down on my tongue. This was it.

But the Fates did me one last favor.

He'd opened the wrong side of the closet. He'd opened the *left-hand* side. Nothing to see but the usual mass of dirty laundry, cellophane-wrapped dry cleaning that I hadn't touched in a year, and more towering stacks of *The New York Times,* all of which helped to keep Andy hidden away on the other side.

"Max," I said quietly. "I really think you need to chill."

"Yeah, I know," he said, turning to face me. "I told you how bad I needed a session. We haven't even talked about—"

"Tomorrow," I interrupted. I couldn't let him spew any more embarrassing details for Andy's entertainment. "A full two-hour session after school tomorrow, I promise. Right now, I think we could both use some sleep, don't you?" I grabbed his arm and ushered him to the front door of my apartment as he tossed off some quick goodbyes to Mom and Todd. I locked the door behind him and rushed back toward my room.

"Theodore?" Mom called to me as I passed. "Our talk is not finished."

"In a minute!" I called back. "I've got to get out of this dress."

I HAD NO IDEA if Andy would be laughing in my face about the Glory Box, or pissed at me for shoving him into the closet for so long, or twice as depressed after ending his miserable night cooped up in a high school senior's bedroom. But when I opened the right-hand door, I found him crouched over a stack of my newspapers, grinning from ear to ear.

"What's so funny?" I asked.

"Nothing's funny." He was staring at the "Weddings and Celebrations" section at the top of the pile, the most recent edition from this past Sunday. *"This,"* he said, jabbing excitedly at one of the announcement photos. "*This* is the wedding."

"What wedding?"

"Remember? I told you Sarah wanted me to go with her to a wedding this Sunday. Theo, this is her friend."

I looked down at the two-inch square photo: a solo pic of a young woman, one of the few solo pics in a long column of ecstatic newlywed couples. She looked pert and lively, with a blonde bob and kind eyes—not a sex goddess, but the less cute friend of the sex goddess. "Are you sure?"

"I told you. Right before Sarah and I met, I saw her with her friend outside that Battery Green place."

"Battery Gardens."

"Battery Gardens, right. She was coming from Battery Gardens when she walked into the café, and that's the woman she was with. I saw them hugging through the window. I'm telling you, Theo, that's her in the picture. That's Sarah's friend, Emma—"

"Renaux." I finished his sentence. A cold rash of goose bumps rose on my arms and neck. Emma Renaux. I'd been using her name as my alias all day. I didn't even need to read her blurb because I knew it by heart. I'd read it the very first morning I saw Andy. Sunday, September 1, page ST15 . . .

> ***Emma J. Renaux, 30, daughter of James and Sally Renaux of Charleston, S.C., will marry Lester A. Wyatt, 30, son of George and Leona Wyatt of Dallas, Tex., on Sunday. The couple officially met as 15-year-old sophomores at New Hampshire's Phillips Exeter Academy, but unknown to Mr. Wyatt, they had in fact met a year earlier.***
>
> ***"We'd shared one dance to R. Kelly's 'I Believe I Can Fly' at the freshman Winter Formal," Ms. Renaux confessed sheepishly, "but my hair was so different that he didn't recognize me. It took me 10 years to admit that I'd watched him across a crowded room for hours before we ever spoke. I knew before I'd even asked him to dance. I knew I was going to marry him."***

"Theo." Andy stood. "You were right. It's not over. This is way better than a clue. We know *exactly* where she's going to be and when. Sunday, at Battery Gardens for Emma Renaux's wedding. Hey, are you okay? You're shaking like a leaf."

He was right. I was shaking. Maybe the sleep deprivation and the trauma of the Magic Garden and the way I'd handled Max were catching up with me. But right now, something was wrong. I felt like I'd been dropped into a bathtub full of ice, a child with a raging fever. I was freezing and burning at the same time.

"Are you okay?" Andy was still smiling, but his eyes began to narrow with worry. "Is something wrong?"

"No," I said. "No, this . . . this is amazing. This is all we need." I took a deep breath and forced myself to return his smile. Even in my current state, I was sure of one thing. "We don't have to wait till Sunday to find her. I think I know a faster way."

MY EXTENSIVE KNOWLEDGE OF *New York Times* wedding announcements is the closest thing I had to a superpower. I'm not bragging; it's the truth. Where some might have only seen a two-inch photo of Emma Renaux, I saw an opportunity for some expert deductive reasoning.

1) The solo bride pics appear in less than ten percent of the *Times* wedding announcements. 2) When they do appear, they are almost always Southern brides because 3) bride-only pics are mostly an old Southern tradition. Therefore, it was more than likely that 4) the Renaux family were fans of all the classic Emily Post wedding traditions. Ergo, therefore, and thus, I was ninety percent confident that 5) Emma Renaux would be hosting a traditional bridal luncheon before the wedding.

If I was right, then Andy had found her just in time, because the luncheon would most likely be happening tomorrow. It was just a question of where and when.

Chapter Eight

That morning, I did the unthinkable. I dressed in the exact same outfit as I had last night. I wore my funeral smock and pretty makeup to school.

True, it helped that I knew Emilio wouldn't be on duty when I left. But even if he had, I couldn't be stopped. I had a plan.

When the lunch bell rang, I walked a safe distance from school, about a block and a half, and Googled both of Emma's parents: James and Sally Renaux of Charleston, South Carolina. I cross-referenced their separate listings to confirm a shared phone number. The entire extended family would probably be in New York by now. I felt reasonably confident that they were a wealthy bunch, based partly on Emma's fancy Exeter education and partly on their affluent location and regal-sounding French name (admittedly not an exact science).

If I was right about the wealthy part, then I was willing to bet they had a maid or a housekeeper watching their place while they were away. I crossed my fingers, dialed the number, and held my breath through four long rings.

"Hello? Renaux residence," a woman with a heavy Southern twang answered.

"Oh, yes, *hi,*" I said, trying to mimic her accent. "This is Jenny Robinson. Who's this?"

"This is Vonda," the woman said. "I'm the housekeeper."

Jackpot.

"Oh, hi, Vonda! I'm guessing Jim and Sally are already in New York, right?"

Why the Southern accent? You sound like a mash-up of Scarlett O'Hara and Larry the Cable Guy. Don't you think they might have invited a few guests north of the Mason-Dixon Line?

"Oh, yes, Miss Robinson," Vonda answered politely. She was one of those people you could hear smiling over the phone. "The family flew out a few days ago."

"Oh, Vonda, honey, I sure hope you can help me out," I said. "I am in *such* a pinch. I lost that little card with the invitation. Would you happen to have the details on Emma's bridesmaids' luncheon? I'm praying to sweet Jesus I'm not late already." I bit my lip.

"Well, don't you worry," Vonda said. "I've got all the info on the fridge right here. The luncheon, let me see . . . Oh, you're golden, honey—it's not a luncheon, it's a cocktail party. Seven o'clock tonight. The Rise Bar and Terrace at the Ritz-Carlton Battery Park Hotel. Fourteenth floor."

Double jackpot. Maybe you're not so bad at being an over-the-top Southerner after all. "Vonda, sweetheart, you are a life saver!"

"Well, I'm just glad I could help!" Vonda said. "I'll let Ms. Renaux know you called. Your first name is—"

"Ooh, Vonda, honey, my cell is breaking up. Hold on now; just let me—"

I killed the call. I couldn't help but smile. I'd completed my undercover op and ascertained the time and location of Andy's date with destiny. Seven o'clock at the Ritz-Carlton. Fancy-schmancy, I knew it. I wasn't one to pat myself on the back, but my smile grew wider as I turned around to head back to school.

That's when I nearly crashed into Lou.

"WHO WAS THAT?" SHE spat. I think she'd gotten about as much sleep as I had—somewhere between sixty and ninety minutes, tops. Her eyes were underlined with dark, puffy circles, but they didn't make her look tired; they made her look poised for battle.

"No one," I said, watching her nostrils flare. "It was a wrong number. How long were you standing there?"

"Where were you last night?"

I needed a second to process the second question. "I'm not—"

"Just tell me where you were," she snapped. Her voice was hoarse. "No, forget it. I know where you were. You were with him all night, weren't you? All night and all morning."

"With—with who?" I stammered. "No—what are you talking about?"

"Thee, *don't*, okay. Don't. I've been up all night."

"Lou, I swear I don't know what you're talking about."

She smiled bitterly. "Really? Then maybe you want to tell me why you're dressed like that."

"Like what?"

"Thee, you own exactly two dresses. Why are you suddenly dressed like a girl?"

I laughed suddenly—not because anything was funny, but because she and Max must have had some kind of mind meld. I'd have to work on lying to my friends; they knew me too well. "Because . . ." My mind raced for explanations. This was what came out: "Why shouldn't I dress like a girl?"

"Ugh, you're the worst liar. You can't even make something up. Why didn't you text me back last night? I wrote you both, like, a hundred times. Tell me what he said to you. Why wouldn't either of you text me? You obviously never went home—you didn't even get a chance to change your clothes."

I shook my head. "Lou, I'm sorry. I am so confused right now. Can we just start from the top?"

"Fine!" she yelled. "From the top: You both went to Shanika Butler's party last night, but you left before I got there. You probably went out for falafels at Mamoun's afterward and laughed about me for two hours, and then you went back to his place for one of your marathon 'sessions,' and you *finally* got it out of your systems."

"Sessions? Wait . . . Are we talking about *Max* right now?"

She threw up her hands. "*Yes*, we're talking about Max. Who else would we be talking about?"

"You think I went home with Max last night, and we had . . ."

"*Sex.* Yes, it's called 'sex,' Thee. I guess you found your Mr. Right after all!" She pumped her fists in fake celebration.

"Okay, stop, *stop*—"

"Please tell me you at least found a decent rabbi to marry you first, otherwise you've wasted a year of quality celibacy."

"Lou, stop it. He's *Max*. I wouldn't do it, period. Neither would he! With *me*? Not in any parallel dimension on any planet in any universe."

"Well, then *why* are you dressed like that?"

Maybe it was my impulse control problem, or my lack of sleep, or maybe I just wanted to tell the truth for a change. Mostly I wanted to disabuse her of any more ludicrous notions about Max and me. "Okay, look." I glanced around and lowered my voice. "You have to swear this stays between us. Swear?"

She nodded. Her eyes slowly lost their warrior aggression.

"I was with a boy last night. But it wasn't Max."

Her sleepless scowl began to melt away and reshape itself into a smile of amazement. "Oh my God." She stopped in the middle of the street and leaped on me, grabbing me in her skinny arms. "She went on a date! She's all grown up! She's all—"

"No, it's not like that," I groaned, breaking free from the hug. "I'm just helping this guy find someone. It's more like a missing persons case. Sort of."

"Oh, no." She grimaced. "Oh, Thee. Please tell me you're not trying to help one of your iDoc subjects. Theo. Are you trying to help one of your newlyweds find a long-lost brother for his wedding or something?"

"*No,*" I said, and even though it was sort of the truth, I knew

I sounded like a liar. "I'm working on a totally different project now. I have a new subject."

Lou placed her hands on her bony hips and narrowed her eyes. "Thee, you know better. You can't help your subject. You can't be part of the story; that's, like, Rule Number One. You know what Mr. Schaffler would say. You're tainting the narrative."

"I am not. I'm just helping this guy out."

"Come on, Schaffler does the Observer Effect speech every year at News orientation. It's hard enough to get an unbiased portrait of your subject when he knows you're filming him. People always change when they know they're being filmed."

"Yeah, that's why I don't *tell* my subjects I'm filming them. Usually."

"No, what you're doing is way worse. You're putting yourself in the story. It's worse than the Observer Effect, it's the Butterfly Effect. You're changing his future when you're just supposed to be documenting it."

"I am not!" I took a few deep breaths and forced myself to remain calm. "I'm just making sure he ends up with the girl he's supposed to be with."

"How do you know who he's supposed to be with?"

"I just do."

"How do you even know him? What's his name? Where did you meet him?"

"His name is Andy. I met him at the Harbor Café."

"So you just started shooting this Andy guy at the café, and now you're his personal private eye? How do you know he's not an ax murderer? How do you know he's not reeling you into the Long Con? Has he asked you if you're rich yet?"

"The *Long Con*? What is this, *House of Games*?"

I was hoping to make Lou laugh with the reference to one of our favorite David Mamet movies. I could tell from her angry smile that she was reliving the movie in her head: a slightly fat Joe Mantegna spends days conning a slightly mannish Lindsay

Crouse into giving him eighty thousand dollars. Lou seemed to get the point: I was absolutely sure I was not Lindsay Crouse to Andy Reese's Joe Mantegna.

"Lou, *enough.*" I grabbed her hands and squeezed. "You don't have to worry. This guy is totally harmless. Besides, none of this matters anymore because the project is over. The whole story ends tonight. I found her. I found the girl he's looking for. And once I get them together, he's not going to need me anymore." My throat caught. Without a hint of warning, I found myself fighting off another ambush of tears.

Lou leaned closer. "Sweetie, are you all right?"

"People really need to stop asking me that." I took a deep breath. "I am fine. Don't pay any attention to this." I pointed to my moist eyes. "This has no actual meaning; it's just a thing that happens to me now. Just ignore it."

"Oh, God, Theo. Are you in love with this guy?"

"*What?* God, no. If I were in love with him, would I be helping him find his girlfriend? Hel-*lo*?"

"I thought we outlawed 'hel-*lo*' last year?"

I laughed in spite of myself. "Well played. How about this? I'll come over to your place around nine tonight, and you can help me start logging all the footage."

"Okay, fine," she said, still sounding unsure. "But you promise you'll come? You can't bag on me—not now."

"I swear," I said. "All I need to do is shoot the final scene."

Chapter Nine

It's 6:52 P.M. The sun has already sunk below New Jersey, leaving a dark violet sky in its wake. Andy and I are standing in a pocket of shrubs outside Wagner Park, across the street from the Ritz-Carlton Battery Park Hotel. Yes, we are hiding in the bushes.

I'd realized something crucial in my run-in with Lou. I'd gotten so involved in this search for Sarah that I'd forgotten my real purpose here, and that is to make a fantastic documentary. I'd let my obsessive mind throw me off course. I'd told Lou about the great footage I'd be showing her at nine o'clock, but I hadn't shot a stitch of video since our creepy visit to Bergen Street. So I stopped home after school, grabbed my jacket with the button cam, and plugged myself back in for the grand finale, the dramatic reunion of Sarah and Andy Reese.

Maybe it will be beautiful. Maybe it will be a disaster. Either way, it will be high-octane cinema, and that's the only reason I'm here. Camera-shy Andy doesn't need to know I'm shooting.

"I feel sick," he says now. "I shouldn't feel sick, right? I should be excited. Or maybe I'm so excited, it's making me sick? What do you think?"

It's too damn dark out. The button cam doesn't do well in low light. I should have picked a spot under some direct streetlight. I want to peek into my jacket pocket and check the screen, but I can't risk Andy catching on.

"Theo," he says, "throw me a bone here. This isn't the time to go quiet on me."

"Sorry. I feel queasy, too. I think it's excited-queasy. I mean, I'm sure it's excited-queasy."

"Totally," Andy says, wiping his clammy palms on his Oxford shirt. He spots two women across the street. They could be twins with their shiny elegant blonde hair and designer coats, shuffling their way into the Ritz-Carlton lobby on their Christian Louboutin stilettos. (Okay, I can't be sure; I just assume they're Christian Louboutins.) "You think those two are going to the party?" he asks.

"I am ninety-nine percent sure. Ninety-nine point nine-nine percent."

The lame semi-humor doesn't go over well. "Oh, man." He runs his hands through his sweat-slicked hair and shambles over to a nearby bench. "They're so freaking fancy. She's rich, isn't she? She's *rich.* I never even thought about it."

I sit down next to him. I reach to pat his knee, to comfort him, but hesitate at the last second. "Andy, who cares if she's rich?"

"I care. What if I can't give her the life she's accustomed to?"

"She's not going to care about that; she has *you.* Besides, we don't even know if she's rich. Just because Emma's rich doesn't mean all her friends are, too. Anyone can look fancy for one night."

"That's true," he says. He turns to me. "You look fancy tonight. Are you all secretly rich?"

I snort. "My parents are English professors. Do the math. They sure can't. And I don't look fancy. I look like I'm going to a gym teacher's memorial service."

"Well, I think you look beautiful."

He says this with zero irony, and the world goes still. Downtown New York City is suddenly so quiet; I can hear my own voice echoing in the back of my head. *He said it to be nice.*

I know that.

You were fishing for a compliment, and he responded in kind. He said, "Well, I think you look beautiful.*" It was a response, not a statement. If he'd just said, "I think you look beautiful," it would be entirely different, but that's not what he said.*

Yes, I know. *I just want to stop and remember the moment he said it, that's all.*

No, you don't, Theo.

I need an industrial-size jug of TUMS.

"Okay, I'm ready," he announces, getting up from the bench. "I'm ready for this. She can love me or she can hate me, but I am going in."

"No, Andy, wait." I stand, blocking his path.

"What?" he asks. "What's wrong?"

"Maybe I should go in first."

"Why?"

"Because . . ." *Because why?* "Because this party is just for the bridesmaids. It's ladies only. If a guy walks in, there will be a huge spotlight on you. You could cause a huge commotion."

His shoulders drop. "You think she doesn't want to see me?"

"No, I *know* she wants to see you. Look, I wore this dress so I could blend in at the party and scope out the situation first. I can find her upstairs and tell her you're down here waiting for her. That way you don't have your romantic love scene in the middle of Emma Renaux's party." I smile at him. "You know that the second-worst crime after murder is stealing a bride's thunder."

Why are you doing this? You want *maximum drama, or at least maximum carnage. Why are you trying to keep him from going upstairs?*

"Shit, maybe you're right," he says. "Maybe you should go up there first."

"Good." It's so preposterous, I almost laugh when I tell him, "I still have no idea what she looks like. I can't find her if I don't know what she looks like. I know she's tall and blonde, but what else?"

He arches an eyebrow. "Sarah's not blonde. When did I ever say she was blonde?"

I tilt my head, at a loss. "Of course she's blonde."

"No. She's not blonde. She's got dark hair, kind of your color, but much longer. And she's not tall. I don't think she's much taller than you are."

Now I can't move. I'm in shock. Not as much shock as when I thought he was a coke dealer at the Magic Garden, but more shock than the moment he pointed to Emma Renaux's picture in the paper. Sarah is not a blonde. How is that humanly possible? Never could I have pictured her as anything but a stick-thin, towering blonde with alien-size blue eyes—like every other woman filing into the lobby right now from their taxis and town cars and limos.

"What else?" I ask.

"She has dark eyes," he mutters uncertainly. "Definitely dark eyes. But it's the lips. That's how you'll recognize her. From her lips."

"What about her lips?"

"She has those—what do you call it?" He lifts his finger to my mouth and traces along its curves—not touching my upper lip, but hovering close enough to wake the writhing Ridley Scott alien in my chest. "What do you call this part here? Where the top lip kind of rises and falls in little arches?"

His finger floats over the peaks and valleys. He is very close.

I duck my head and back away.

"You know," he goes on, "kind of like a—"

"Bow," I say with a fraction of a breath.

"Right." His eyes twinkle. "Cupid's-bow lips. That little dip in the middle."

"Okay, I got it. I'm ready."

"No, Theo, wait." He steps in front of me, forcing me back on my wobbly granny-pump heels.

"What's wrong now?"

"I don't know," he says. He nervously massages the back of his neck. "It's just . . . I think I'm lying to you. I mean, I know I am. I'm lying."

I clutch at the bench rail for support. "About what?" It comes out more a croak than a question.

"About this feeling. I don't think it's excited-queasy. This is the other kind of queasy. The kind you get before a final exam. The kind you get when you drive into a bad neighborhood after midnight." He looks up at the treetops swaying over the edge of the fourteenth floor's outdoor terrace. "Maybe neither one of us is supposed to go up there. I don't know anything about this Renaux lady or this Wyatt dude, but I've got a bad feeling about them. I don't know. I don't think you should go."

I let go of the railing, feeling better. He's just stalling. "Is it because they're rich?"

"No."

"Is it because they like R. Kelly?"

He doesn't even crack a smile. "No. It's just a voice in my head, and it's saying, 'Don't let her go up there.'"

Standing this close to him, I can almost hear the voice, too.

"Is that it?" I ask.

"The voice, you mean?"

"No, is that the only thing you're lying to me about?"

His eyes meet mine. "Yeah," he states. "That's it."

"Okay. Ominous feeling noted and totally respected. And if I am not back down here with Sarah in twenty minutes, then I give you full permission to bust in there and ruin all of Emma's precious wedding memories."

THE BELL STRIKES FOURTEEN, and the golden elevator doors slide open to the sound of women laughing. The laughter is tasteful. It's the exact opposite of the laughter I heard at the Magic Garden. This is definitely a Rich People Party. As if to drive the point home, I hear a string quartet playing Bach somewhere down the hall. (I think it's Bach. Lou would know for sure.) I check the iPhone screen in my pocket and straighten the button cam on my collar. Picture and sound are good to go.

Before I can take another step, a waiter with a skinny tie offers me a tray of pink champagne. "Welcome," he says with a practiced smile. "There's a coat check—"

"I'll keep it," I blurt out.

"All right, then." He smiles, taking a tiny step back. "The ladies are straight ahead."

"Thanks," I reply, wondering if I qualify as one of "the ladies." My nerves get the better of me, and I grab two glasses from his tray. I feel like I'm gliding through a long dolly shot—the Art Deco walls falling away on either side of me as mahogany tables and bouquets of white orchids float past. The champagne hits my tongue with a sweet, delectable fizz, and I down the first glass without thinking. I can barely feel the blue-and-gold runner beneath my feet. I ditch the empty by a vase full of calla lilies and start on my second as "the ladies" begin to take shape at the end of the tunnel.

It's a bigger crowd than I'd thought.

Emma didn't just invite the bridesmaids; she invited all of her female friends and family. Staying hidden in the crowd will be much easier than I thought, but finding Sarah will be harder. I search the sea of flawless faces for a girl with dark hair, dark eyes, and Cupid's-bow lips. They all share a sort of high-society sameness, but there is one pocket of girls that stands out.

Two of the five are African American, one Latina. That's the first thing that catches my eye, but it's not what keeps my attention. They're the only ones not laughing or smiling. They're fidgety and uncomfortable. They're the outcasts, so I feel an instant kinship with them, even from twenty feet away.

I bring my glass to my lips as I study their faces. I tip it all the way back. That's two full glasses of champagne in less than three minutes. I haven't had a sip of alcohol in three months. I need to stop; I'm not here to get shit-faced.

I grab another beautiful and perfectly coiffed waiter as he passes, placing my empty on his tray and taking a fresh bubbly.

"Enjoy," he says with a wink.

It's not for enjoyment; it's for self-control. Hopefully, it will keep the camera steady for my first interview.

After two sips, I stride forward and pause at the two-foot social moat surrounding the girls. I look for the friendliest face in the bunch. I decide on the mocha-skinned Latina girl with the frumpy floral dress and the dried-out platinum-blonde ponytail. Her friends are all wearing ill-fitting, conservative floral dresses, too. Something is wrong with this picture—aside from the fact that they don't occupy the same tax bracket as the other guests—I just can't place it yet.

"Hey, do you know if Sarah is here yet?" I ask the girl.

She flashes a quick glance at her friends, like she's checking to see if it's cool to talk to me. "I don't think I know any Sarah," she says, sizing me up. She has a strong accent, Brooklyn or the Bronx. "Why?" she asks. "Are you with cops?"

I almost spit my champagne back into the glass. "Cops? Why would I be with—?"

"No, not *cops*." She laughs. "That's a giveaway. So you aren't K.O.P. I thought you might be the sixth ambassador."

Are we speaking in CIA code now? The sixth ambassador? It sounds like a bad political thriller that couldn't get George Clooney and had to settle for one of the Affleck brothers instead. *They thought diplomacy was dead. They hadn't counted on . . . THE SIXTH AMBASSADOR. This Fourth of July, Casey Affleck IS . . . The Sixth Ambassador.*

Okay, I'm drunk.

"I'm sorry," I say, trying not to smile and failing. My cheeks feel hot; the room swirls with a warm glow. "You lost me."

"No, *I'm* sorry. Oh, shit, you look so freaked out right now." She clamps her palm over her mouth, and her friends laugh. Her hand falls away. "My bad," she says. "Let's start again. I'm Helena."

I'm so tipsy that my real name leaks out. "Theo."

"What's up, Theo?"

"So . . . what's K.O.P?"

"The place that Mr. Wyatt and Ms. Renaux run on Parker Street . . . ?"

All the outcast girls are staring at me now. I'm obviously supposed to know this. Everyone else at the party knows this.

"You know," Helena continues in the buzzy silence. "It's, like, a place for girls. Like, girls who are going through sh—stuff back home or whatever, and they need a place to stay."

"You mean a shelter?" The question sounds overly loud in my ears.

Helena's eyes darken. "Yeah, like that," she mumbles, "but we don't really like that word. It's more like a hostel. But just for girls."

My complete lack of tact has done it yet again. I've managed to offend someone at a party I've crashed in, what, ten minutes? I gulp down what's left of the champagne. My mind races with this bizarre new information. Emma and her fiancé run a young women's shelter in Lower Manhattan. On Parker Street. Which is not far from the hotel or Battery Gardens. Not far from the Harbor Café, either.

"It's K.O.P.'s anniversary," Helena adds. "So Ms. Renaux planned the wedding, like, around the big anniversary so they could celebrate them together. You know what I'm saying?"

The girls are all squinting at me now, clearly wondering why the hell I don't know any of this.

"Oh, yeah, cool."

"Yeah, cool." Her voice is flat. "I'm saying they invited some of us to the wedding as, like, 'ambassadors,' so their friends and family could meet us and see how good we're doing—you know, thanks to K.O.P. That's why I thought maybe you were the sixth girl, because nobody's met her yet."

I'm still nodding and smiling, but I feel squirmy and disoriented. On the other hand, at least now I understand Helena's outfit—all their outfits. Hints of previously inked skin peek out from beneath their ill-fitting collars and sleeves. There are seven empty piercings along Helena's right ear, a pin-sized hole where her nose stud should be. They've all been "scrubbed" and de-pierced—made over with dull, conservative frocks to showcase the transformative powers of K.O.P.

K.O.P. Making the world a better place, one dowdy floral dress at a time.

I try to picture Sarah in one of those dresses. Could she be one of these girls? Could she be staying at this K.O.P. shelter? Is she the "sixth ambassador"? Is she somewhere at this party wearing a dress even uglier than mine?

First, she's not blonde; now, she's not rich.

Is that even possible? I know I told Andy she might not be rich, but I never really believed it. Now I think of the insane suggestion I made that rainy night—that Sarah tried to pass off that Brooklyn townhouse as her own. Could I have possibly gotten that whole thing right? I feel a steady throbbing in my temples, synced with my heartbeat.

Three glasses of champagne, you idiot.

The pewter clock over the oyster bar tells me I have thirteen more minutes before Andy initiates Operation *Rescue*.

Helena's voice drifts toward me. "Are you okay?"

"I need people to stop asking me that," I mutter.

"Maybe you should sit down," she says. "Do you want some water or something?"

Helena guides me to the couch, pulling the champagne glass from my hand. One of her friends runs to one of the bartenders and returns with a glass of water, which I pound down in three grateful glugs.

Then I suck in a deep breath. Three letters fall from my mouth as I exhale. "K.O.P."

"Say again?" Helena says.

"K.O.P.," I repeat. "What does K.O.P. stand for?"

"Oh. Keeping Our Promise. That's the full name. Mr. Wyatt says it's about the 'unspoken promise' we all make to help the poor and the needy, but all the girls know what it really means." Helena rolls her eyes. "You know, the promise every girl makes to keep herself p—"

"Ms. Renaux at two o'clock," her friend whispers.

Everything about Helena's demeanor changes in an instant. Her posture straightens, her smile doubles in size, and her voice doubles in volume, bubbling with fake joy.

"Oh my *God,* I could go on about Ms. Renaux and Mr. Wyatt for*ever,*" she gushes. "They are, like, the kindest, most amazing people I've ever met. I can't even believe they invited us to *every*thing—this awesome bar and the rehearsal dinner. It's like a dream."

Emma Renaux draws near. No longer a two-inch photo in the paper, but a living, breathing human being, moving slowly in my direction. The closer she gets, the woozier I feel. Sweat forms on my eyelids, stinging my left eye. Thank God the cam can pick up what I'm losing.

"And Mr. Wyatt, he is just the *best,*" Helena goes on. "It's, like, totally true what everyone says about him. He really is an honest-to-God *hero,* you know?"

"Oh, that's the *truth,*" her friend agrees far too loudly.

The conversation is clearly for Emma's benefit, but she doesn't seem to hear it. She's not looking at us. She's not exactly looking at anything. She's smiling, but it's the emptiest smile I've ever seen. It's like a mask that only covers the bottom half of her face. The top half—the eyes—are telling the real story. Whatever that story is, it doesn't jibe with the festive mood here. Even with my cloudy eye, I can see it. I wonder if anyone else can see it, because it doesn't seem they can. Nobody looks concerned or worried for her. Nobody's asking her what's wrong. Why am I the only one who sees it?

"Oh, shoot," Helena says, standing up and smoothing out her dress. "I forgot my soda at the bar. I'll be back in a few."

I know she's lying to make a quick exit, but that's fine. She floats out of frame, and my tunnel vision narrows to just one person. Emma. Her sad green eyes and slender shape are all I see now. Everything else is a blur. My bleary eyes follow her across the room—pink minidress hugging her tiny, twenty-five-inch waist; her blonde bob expertly cut with thousand-dollar highlights that shine like gold, even in the dim light. How could anyone that rich and skinny look so forlorn at her own bridesmaids' party?

I realize I'm not just following her with my eyes. I've begun to tail her. I'm up and walking past the velvet couches, not ten feet behind her as she weaves her way through friends and family toward the glass doors at the end of the bar, where the vast New York skyline glows. The outdoor terrace is empty. Too windy for girls with salon hair. The hotel hasn't even bothered to turn on the terrace lights.

But that's exactly what she wants. She wants to be alone.

EMMA WALKS THE LENGTH of the terrace, hair battered by the wind, peering back through the windows to be sure no one is watching her. I wait until she's on the far end before I step outside to join her. The wind is so deafening, there's no way she can hear me approach even with my clunky shoes crunching on the gravel.

Once she's sure she is safely hidden, she digs into her Fendi clutch and pulls out a cigarette, waging an epic battle with the wind to get it lit with a cheap Bic lighter. I know next to nothing about Emma Renaux, but I'm surprised that she smokes. Judging from the way she keeps looking over her shoulder, I'm guessing her friends and family would be surprised, too.

Finally the cigarette catches, glowing orange. She takes a long drag and exhales, waving the smoke away from her face. I don't know why, but I take the sudden stillness in the air as my cue to speak.

"Excuse me, where's Sarah?" I ask her. "She's supposed to be here, right?"

Emma gasps and drops her cigarette. She turns and her eyes lock with mine. In that instant, she whirls away, fixing her gaze on the white gravel beneath our feet. She hugs herself tightly, clutching her taut shoulders, and begins to shiver. I think I've somehow terrified her. Is she that nervous about getting caught with a smoke? I can only see a sliver of her face. I take a few steps closer and realize she's whispering something.

A prayer. She is whispering "Our Father."

Over and over.

". . . Forgive us our trespasses as we forgive those who trespass against us. And lead us not into temptation, but deliver us from evil . . ."

What did I do? How could I have frightened her this badly? I take another step, but her desperate voice stops me cold.

"Don't come any closer," she says, edging toward the railing, her back still turned to me. Her voice is quavering and weak. "Please. I know why you're here."

I want her to see me smile; I make my voice as light and apologetic as I can. "No, I don't think—"

"You don't have to say anything. Please don't say anything."

"No, I'm not—I'm just here for Andy. I'm just looking for—"

"Oh, God, *please* stay away from Andy," she begs. "This isn't his fault. He's a good man. He's only ever tried to do good. Please don't punish him now. I'll fix it, I swear."

When she says his name, I feel something rise inside me, scorching the back of my throat. "What's not his fault? What did Andy do?"

"Nothing." She's on the verge of tears. "Andy's a saint. He still loves you more than anything in this world. Please. Please don't come back here again." She finally turns to me, her face streaked with tears. "Please, Sarah. Let me make it right. I'll make it right."

She bolts past me, slipping through the door at the other end of the terrace. I follow her with my eyes, watching her stumble recklessly through the crowd until I see my own reflection in the glass.

I can't move. I can't find any oxygen to breathe. I can't hear anything. I'm stranded in deep space. The white gravel has become the surface of the moon. I'm weightless, suffocating, in a vacuum. I'll expand like a grotesque balloon and rip apart at the seams if I don't find some air.

Racing back downstairs registers only in snapshots: knocking Helena aside as I run back through the bar, stumbling through the golden elevator doors, smacking the LOBBY button, pulling off my shoes to find what was left of my balance. Running barefoot across Battery Place, dodging fast-moving cars with their horns blaring, until I'm back in the bushes near Wagner Park, where I find Andy nervously waiting for me on our bench.

When he sees me, his eyes go wide. "Jesus, what the hell happened?" He jumps up and reaches for me, but I back away. I know I owe him explanations and descriptions, but I can't. I can't say anything except, "Take me home."

"Theo, what's going on?" he demands. The less I say, the more frightened he looks. "Did you find her? Was Sarah up there or not?"

I don't even know how to answer. I see his lips forming question after question, but there is only one immediate need powerful enough to cut through the haze.

"Just take me home, Andy. Please take me home."

IS THE CAMERA STILL running? It must be, because I never pressed STOP. I didn't even check the screen once during the cab ride. I couldn't break free from my catatonic state, other than to give the cab driver my address and pay him whatever was in my wallet. Andy was right behind me, matching me step for step as I climbed the back stairwell to my apartment. He kept trying to make me talk in the cab, but I couldn't or didn't hear him. Now, as I lock my bedroom door, praying my mother hasn't heard us, he tries again.

"Theo, please," he whispers. "Please tell me what happened up there. You are scaring the shit out of me."

The dizziness is ten times worse after the bumpy cab ride. I drop my purse and shoes on the floor and take a few aimless steps around my room, still trying to find my center, still trying to get the world to stand the fuck *still* for just one second. I step to my bed, but sway back toward the couch. I step to the closet, but sway sideways toward my bathroom. Andy steps in front of me, blocking my route to the toilet.

"Theo, stop, just *stop*. You have to talk to me. You have to tell me what happened up there. Did you find Sarah or not?"

"What are you not telling me?" I whisper.

"Hallelujah, she finally speaks!" He smiles, and I feel my stomach rise.

"Don't. Don't try to charm me. She called me *Sarah*. Emma called me Sarah. Why would she call me that?"

"Wait, Emma Renaux? She talked to you?"

"She *knows* you. She knows who you are." I'm slurring the words.

"Theo, what are you saying? Are you drunk?"

"She begged me to leave you alone. Or no, not me, *Sarah*—she begged Sarah to leave you alone."

"To leave *me* alone?" Veins bulge in his forehead; he's stressed or lying or both. "I don't know what you're saying. I've never met that Renaux lady in my life. I told you, I just saw her hugging Sarah goodbye that day."

"Andy, we have all these things in common. Don't you realize that?"

"Who does?"

"Me and *Sarah*." I press on my chest to try and slow my heart.

"Okay, we just need to breathe here," he says. "We need to sober you up and calm you down. We need coffee—"

"We both love the Harbor Café," I say. "We both love to sit and watch the newlyweds at Battery Gardens. We both love daisies, for God's sake. Who loves daisies anymore?"

"Theo, please."

"We both have dark hair and Cupid's-bow lips. You said so yourself. Why are all your memories of her so fuzzy? It was just a few days ago."

"They're not fuzz—"

"If you love her so much, then why can't you remember her?

You couldn't remember which subway, you couldn't remember where she lived. You could barely remember the color of her eyes. Do you actually remember her or *not*?" Lava scrapes the back of my throat, and I begin to choke. "Shit, move," I croak. "Get out of the way."

"No, I am not moving until you talk to—"

"No, I'm going to be sick. I'm going to be—"

But it happens. I can't stop it. I would have done anything on earth to prevent the moment, but I can't. It flows over my tongue and spills from my mouth, an acrid pink champagne waterfall. Every heave is like fire. I feel the retching at the base of my stomach as the hot pink mess douses us both, soaking the front of his white Oxford shirt and the front of my black dress from top to bottom.

And then it's over.

I'M NOT SURE HOW long I stand there shivering, mortified—frozen in place like a child who's just had an accident in front of her kindergarten class. I wait for Andy's face to turn hard and cruel like Douchey Tim in the Magic Garden men's room. I wait for him to bark at me with disgust.

But when he speaks, his voice is quiet and calm and kind. "It's okay," he says.

"Andy," I whimper.

"It's okay. Just don't move."

He carefully unbuttons his soiled shirt and peels it off his sturdy shoulders, dropping it to the floor.

"I'm so sorry," I say. "I don't know what's happening to me."

"Let's just start with the jacket," he says. "Can you get the jacket off? Do you want me to help?"

I nod. I'm a puke-stained child, and Andy is the paternal voice of reason. I do whatever he tells me to do. He helps me slowly pull the jacket off and drop it to the floor next to his shirt. I know the button cam is shooting our feet now, or the rumpled folds of my jacket, or nothing at all.

"Okay, now the dress," he says. "How do we get it off?"

"Zipper in the back."

"Do you need me to help?"

"I can do it." I reach behind me and find the zipper. It slips twice from my sweaty fingers before I finally manage to pull it down. I peel off the revolting bodice and step out of the skirt, letting the dress fall to my ankles.

The moment it hits the floor, I wake from my kindergarten trance. I'm not a five-year-old girl, and Andy is not my father. He's a half-naked man, and I'm a full-grown woman, standing before him in a black bra and panties—close enough to feel his breath on my shoulder.

The rest of the world goes dark, leaving a white-hot spotlight glaring down on our skin. I'm drowning in my nakedness and blinded by his. I'd shamefully pictured his naked chest more than once. I'd seen glimpses of it behind the tattered holes of his V-neck; I'd seen its outline under soggy white cotton. But here it was, unveiled, in the flesh, and every contour, every freckle, every wispy blond hair is exactly as I'd pictured.

I look at his chest and think of Michelangelo's *David.* Then I think of my fat, funnel cake–induced ass. I think of my fleshy stomach. I think of the gash on my cheek, and I shove Andy aside and run to the bathroom sink, snatching my white towel from the floor and wrapping it around myself like a giant Ace bandage. I lean over the faucet and blast the cold water, splashing my clammy face and neck.

I grab the spearmint mouthwash next to the sink and drink in a huge mouthful straight from the bottle, swishing it around, spitting it out and taking a second mouthful—so much that it dribbles down the sides of my mouth. Then I flip off the cold water and flip on the hot until it's scalding. I douse myself twice with boiling-hot water, trying to scrub away my face, but when I look up at the mirror, it's still there.

I forgot to use my mirror technique.

I forgot to focus on the tight close-ups and the individual

features. Now I've accidentally taken in the whole picture, the whole face, the whole me. The hot water has fogged the mirror, enough to blur the scar. I can see the hint of a face; I'm just not sure I recognize her. I've tried not to look at her for so long. Who is this person with trails of tears pouring down her scoured cheeks? Who is this?

Andy steps into the bathroom and turns me around. "Please don't cry," he says. But it's too late; I'm already crying. I wouldn't have known if I hadn't seen it in the mirror.

"I'm seriously begging you," he says. "You can't cry. I have this problem when I see a girl cry, I just want to—"

"Why can't you *remember* her?" I plead for the answer now. "What really happened that night? What do you really remember about her? Anything?"

Steam rises from the faucet behind me, billowing like smoke. Andy looks down at my towel and then up at my face. The look in his eyes compels me to hide my jaw with a swath of wet hair.

"I remember that you were wrong," he says. "You were wrong about her."

"About what?"

"You said she 'gave herself' to me that night, but she didn't. Because she had never . . . you know . . . Sarah was still a—"

"Everything's the same. Everything about us is the same."

His eyes roam across the features of my face, down to my shoulders and back again. "You do look like her," he says quietly.

"But you said she was a Pretty Girl."

"She is." He steps into me. His bare right hip presses up against my stomach through the towel.

"But then I can't look like her."

"But you do. You look more and more like her every day." He leans his face past my last inch of personal space, his bangs brushing across my forehead, his nose grazing mine, his mouth a breath away from mine. His fingers engulf my left arm and climb my bare shoulder toward my neck. I've never given over to anything in my life. I never even knew what it meant. But I feel my entire body giving over to his.

My hands clutch the sink behind me, and I push myself up to meet his lips as my towel falls to the floor. But his caress doesn't stop at my neck. Before my lips can find his, his fingers climb past my chin all the way to the left side of my jaw. His fingernails inch toward my scar, and I'm stricken. My body goes rigid. I want to punch and kick and ravage and destroy. I want to run as far and as fast as I can. It all boils down to fight or flight. And I choose flight.

I duck down under him and grab my towel, draping it over my chest and running from the bathroom, jumping over the heap of ruined clothes and the puddle in the doorway. I grab a pair of sneakers and sweatpants by the closet. I trip as I climb into both, then grab a gray hoodie from the foot of my bed and rush out my door. I zip it up as high as it will go, pull the hood over my head, and run to the kitchen, to the back stairs, to the overcrowded street, to the only safe place in the world I know.

Chapter Ten

I hardly remember how I got to Max's apartment building from my house. Subway? Cab? On foot? All three? I'd been counting on my camera to remember things for me, but I'd conveniently abandoned my iPhone in the puke-stained jacket on the bedroom floor. Now I could only record events with my *actual brain*, which was proving to be my least reliable organ.

Miraculously, I was able to remember the key code to get into Max's building, but once I reached his floor, I could only pound on his apartment door for as long as it took him to answer. No texts to warn him, no emails, just my fist.

"Okay, shut up already!" I finally heard him holler from inside. I kept on knocking. "Whoever it is, I already hate you so much," he grumbled as he flipped the lock and swung open the door. "I seriously do. I hate you with a deep—Theo?"

Max stood tall and lanky in the doorway, his hair making all kinds of bed-headed decisions of its own, his blue track pants riding too low on his hips. I'd woken him up. He flipped on the foyer light, and I realized he was shirtless. The dark hair on his chest narrowed into a slim trail over his low-slung waistband.

I spun away and tugged my hood down over my eyes. "Where are the freaking *shirts* tonight, people?" I croaked. "For the love of *God*, where are the shirts?"

Max laughed groggily. "Excuse me? You just woke me up with

the whack-ass knocking. I thought you were the cops from *Cops.* I *had* to answer shirtless. Good thing my parents are out."

"I just need you to put on a shirt," I told the hallway carpet. "I'm not coming into this house until everybody puts on a shirt."

He yawned loudly. "I think I crashed watching *Sports Center.*"

"That still leaves you without a shirt."

"I've got a variety of shirts in my room. Come in, and I'll pick a real winner."

"I'll wait," I said.

I felt him staring at me. "You're serious?"

"Yes, Max, I'm serious. Just go put on a shirt, and I'll wait out here."

"Okay, fine," he huffed. "But you need to dial down the crazy by, like, thirty percent before I get back."

"I can't do that right now," I called to him as he shut the door.

An eternal half-minute later, Max swung his door back open in a black Shins T-shirt. His hair was still a wild black forest, but he'd made an effort to tame it. "Okay, I've shielded you from my nakedness. Now are you going to tell me what's wrong?"

"I need your help. I know I completely screwed you yesterday, but I'm just . . . right now, I just need you to . . ."

"Wait. Are you crying?" He tugged my hood down.

"What? Hell, no, this is just allergies." I pulled the hood back over my face and pulled my hands inside the sleeves.

He grabbed my stump of a hand. "You suck at lying, Thee. Anyone ever tell you that?"

THANKFULLY MAX'S PARENTS DIDN'T have any puritanical rules about coed visits from friends. Before The Night in Question, our sessions had always taken place on his bed. It was queen-size, large enough for each of us to stake out a full side of the mattress, flat on our backs, and stare at the ceiling ("the Freudian position," we called it). We got to his room, and he shut the door, switching on the chrome floor lamp next to his desk.

"No, too bright," I said.

He looked a little puzzled, but switched it off and turned on his TV instead, letting the fish tank screensaver light the room in a wash of aqua. "Better?"

I nodded, then threw myself onto his bed and shimmied across the mattress till my back was against the wall. He crouched down to take his usual side, but something inside me screamed for him to back off.

"I need the whole bed," I whispered. "Could you just sit next to me?"

He rose, his forehead creased. "Okay," he agreed.

Even in the pale digital glow, I could see the concern in his eyes. Or was it pity? I felt like an injured pigeon he'd just found on the street. The room grew pin-drop quiet. His apartment was downtown, on the twentieth floor of a converted office building, shielded from everything below with soundproof windows. Normally I loved it here; it was the antidote to my dilapidated, secondhand disaster area, all blond wood and white paint and chrome. (His mom had decorated the whole place). But tonight, I felt like I was trapped inside a huge IKEA fishbowl. Like I was on display for the whole city to see.

"Thee, you have to tell me what's going on," Max urged. "Wherever you've been going, whoever you've been seeing, you have to tell me. You can't keep going like this."

I pushed myself onto my knees and peered at Max across the rumpled bed. I hesitated, trying to find the perfect words, but it all just spilled out like tweaker babble. "Max, you're the sanest person I know, and I need that right now. I need your sanity because I know what's happening to me can't actually be happening. It's just that people said some things to me tonight, and someone called me by the wrong name, and Lou has been saying all this stuff to me about how I'm a different person ever since, you know, ever since that night. I'm meaner and faster. And I haven't really looked at myself in the mirror since that morning. I couldn't really bear to look at myself for weeks, but tonight I looked, I *really* looked, and I just . . . I couldn't tell. The mirror was so foggy, I know that's all it was, it's not some kind of ghostly possession, there's not some freakish metamorphosis happening here. I just need you to confirm that it's not happening."

Max didn't answer right away. I couldn't blame him; he probably wanted to be certain I was completely finished with my deranged rant. Eventually he took a deep breath.

"Okay," he began. "Can you just clarify what's not happening? I'm not totally clear on what's not happening."

"I just need you to look at me and tell me what you see."

"I see a hood."

I ripped back the hood and turned to the left, showing him the side of my face that wasn't ruined. "What do you see?"

"I see your profile."

"No, that's not what I'm asking. Does this side of my face look any different to you?"

"Different how?"

"Different than before. Different than before that night."

"Still not sure what you're asking."

"It's a *simple* question."

"Then what is the question?"

"*Max.* Am I me?"

He paused. "Are you you?"

"Yes. Am I definitely me?"

He leaned back in his chair and smiled. "Now that is a *deep* question. This just turned into the best session ever."

"No, that's not . . . Look, I know how I sound right now. I just need you to help me go over a few things. I just need to make sure."

"Make sure that you're you."

"Yes."

"And how do we do that?"

"Just ask me some questions."

"Questions about you?"

"Yes, questions about me, about us, about our history. Questions only I'd know the answer to. Like, ask me when we first met."

"Okay, when did we first—?"

"It was in the math lab in eighth grade. You asked me if I knew some math whiz dude named Theo, because this Theo guy was supposed to tutor you."

"Oh, shit, I forgot about that! And you played along for, like, ten minutes. You said this 'Theo guy' was a notoriously sadistic psycho who tutored with an iron fist."

"Right, and he weighed three hundred pounds, and he insisted all his students call him Keyser Söze."

"*Right,* right." Max sat up straight, laughing. "And I shouldn't be afraid when he brought out his bloodstained training hammer Petey."

"Yeah, and he ate entire wheels of smoked Gouda during sessions." I began to smile, too. "And he practiced 'enhanced interrogation techniques,' forcing his students to answer rapid-fire algebra questions while listening to Slipknot and Nickelback."

"Yes. See?" He leaned closer. "You're you. You're definitely you. No one else could have known about the Gouda."

I nodded. And in that instant, the day's fatigue took hold of my body, and I fell onto his pillow, flat on my back, head slipping back into the hood. I rested my hands on my stomach and closed my eyes like a corpse in an open casket.

"Give me another one," I said.

"Okay." The sound of his voice carried me through two more deep and easy breaths as he thought of his next question. "Okay, what was the first thing I asked you at our first tutoring session at your apartment?"

"Easy. Mom brought us bergamot tea, and you asked me if she'd ever tried to poison a boy who came over."

"Correct," Max said. "And what did you say?"

"I said I hadn't had a boy over since the fourth grade. Then I tested the tea for poison."

"See, you still have the best memory of anyone I know."

"Yeah, I'm not sure about that one." The pale blue ceiling was beginning to fade.

"Okay, last question. For the big money."

"Go," I mumbled.

"When you came to my last game, what was the final score?"

"It's a trick question," I said sleepily. "I've never been to any of your games. Can't take the stench of that many stools in one room."

"See?" He grinned. "I knew you were you. I even know you when you're pretending to be someone else."

My eyes snapped back open. "What are you talking about? When did I do that?"

"Sorry," he said. "We don't have to talk about that now. Try to get some sleep."

"No, I don't need sleep." I sat up so quickly that Max slid back in his chair. "Tell me. When did I pretend to be someone else?"

"Come on, Thee, it's just us here. You seriously want to tell me you had nothing to do with the letter?"

"What letter?"

He sighed, reached into his track pants pocket, and pulled out a wrinkled square of college-ruled paper. He unfolded it and began to read aloud. *"A Declaration of Romantic Intent. Dear, M. I really need to talk to you. Please don't be alarmed by the heading of this letter, but our time is running out here at Sherman, and I couldn't forgive myself if I didn't tell you how I truly feel . . ."*

I'D NEVER FELT SO stupid in my life. No, not stupid, ignorant. Too oblivious to see the blatantly obvious.

No. Stupid. I felt really stupid.

Dear M. I had written "M" for *Mike.* Hadn't Lou and I been writing that letter to Mike DeMonaco? No, apparently not. And the more Max read from Lou's—my—letter, the clearer it all became: those nine million urgent texts they'd sent me; Max so desperate for a session that he'd braved an hour of Beowulf Book Club with Mom and Todd; Lou's tired, angry eyes when she confronted me on the street. She wasn't afraid I'd ruined our five-year friendship with Max, she was *jealous.* She thought I was trying to steal him away right after I'd helped write her Declaration of Romantic Intent.

Max continued. "*I know you've only seen me as one thing for the past five years, and I know that people sometimes only see you as one thing, too. They see a dude's dude. They see another jock in a jersey who cracks a lot of jokes and has a strict cheerleader-only hookup policy . . .*" He looked up. "Okay, that's not fair."

He waited for me to provide an amen, but I remained silent. He frowned and kept reading. "*But I know there's a whole other side to you. A romantic side. A heroic side that you're too embarrassed to show anyone. I see the real you in little bits and pieces every day, even if no one else can.*

"All I'm asking is for you to wake up and see that there's another side to me, too. Sometimes I don't even think you see me as a girl. Who knows—maybe sometimes I haven't wanted to be one. But I swear, I'm not asking for some big romantic epiphany. All I'm asking is this: When you see me tomorrow, look again. Erase every single memory you have of me for the last five years and pretend you've never met me before. Look at me and pretend I'm a girl.

"If you follow these instructions—if you follow them just exactly as I've instructed—then I think you'll see it. I think you'll see what we could be.

"Love (not to be confused with IN love just yet),

Lou"

Max tossed the letter across the bed and stared at me.

"What?" I asked, unsure what I was even doing here anymore.

"It's a good letter," he said.

"I agree."

"But it doesn't really sound like Lou."

"I disagree. I think it sounds just like her. Why? What did she say to you?"

"I haven't talked to her yet. I've been avoiding her since she handed it to me. I wanted to talk to you first."

"Why?"

"Thee."

"What?"

"Seriously? I've been in the room at least twice when you've helped her with a Cyrano letter. This whole letter is you. It even uses all caps for emphasis."

"Okay, fine, so I helped her write the letter."

"And?"

"And what?"

"Dude." He jumped off the chair and flopped down beside me in our Freudian position. I let him; maybe I was too tired to protest. "I know I'm not the sharpest tool in the shed, but I did read that Cyrano play."

"You read a whole play?"

"Fine, the CliffsNotes helped, but I watched that Gerard Depardieu movie with you, and for someone obsessed with Cyrano, I think you're missing the point."

"Oh, really? And what exactly is the point, Max?"

He let out a caveman grunt, grabbed one of his pillows, and crushed it over his head. I had to strain to hear his muffled voice through the small opening under his pillow. "The point is, Cyrano didn't just write Christian's letters as a favor to his buddy—he wrote them because he was trying to say something to Roxane."

"Now I literally can't hear what you're saying. What are you trying to say?"

He ripped the pillow off his head and pushed himself up, putting us face-to-face. "That's what I'm asking you," he said, probing my eyes at close range.

"Max, what are you doing?"

"I'm not doing anything. I'm just asking if there's anything you want to say to me."

His eyes wouldn't let mine escape. They were bluer than neon blue. Bluer than the aqua blue walls and the digital fish tank. They kept getting bluer as they came closer, searching my eyes. Bluer and closer. Bluer and closer . . .

"OKAY, WHAT IS GOING ON TONIGHT?"

I howled it to the ceiling or to God, to nobody or to whoever was listening. I grabbed the drawstrings of my hood and pulled them as tightly as I could, nearly strangling myself. The hood shrank down over all but my eyes, nose, and upper lip.

Max jumped off the bed and backed away, almost tripping over his desk chair. "Jesus, what is *wrong* with you?"

"Why were you looking at me like that?" I shot back.

"You were looking at me, too."

"Yes, I was looking at you, but I wasn't *looking* at you. You were looking at me like—like a boy would look at . . ."

"A girl? Like a boy would look at a girl? Is that what you're trying to say?"

"No. You were looking at me like a boy would look at *her*. Everybody's looking at me the way they'd look at *her*."

"Who?"

"Sarah."

"Who the hell is Sarah?"

"Maybe *I* am. I don't know!"

"I thought we'd established that you were *you*."

"I *know* that."

I thought he'd take a step toward me. He always came closer when I was struggling. But tonight, he took two steps back.

"I was just trying to do the thing," he muttered.

"What thing?"

"The thing you asked me to do in the letter. I was just trying to do it. Trying to pretend it was the first time I'd ever—"

"*I* wasn't asking you to do anything. That was Lou's letter. I didn't even know we were writing it to you. I thought we were writing it to Mike 'Me Like' DeMonaco!"

"Oh." Max's entire body seemed to deflate. He drew in a deep breath and took another step back toward his TV. He examined its edges for nicks and scratches. "Okay. Can we just, like, strike this whole thing from the record? Can we just erase it and go back to the moment right before I said it?"

"Yeah," I said, looking down at my sneakers. "We can do that." I shouldn't have gotten into his bed with my sneakers on. That was rude. Why did I do that?

"Cool," Max said.

We looked at anything but each other until our eyes accidentally met again. I found myself searching for physical ways to recede farther into the sweatshirt. I wish I'd had six more sweatshirts to throw on, one after the other, till I looked like a puffer fish. This was supposed to be the safe place. But now I was drowning all alone on the bed. My mattress was sinking, and Max was the only tall ship for miles.

"Max," I said to my sneakers.

"Are you hungry?" He started walking quickly to the door. "Maybe I should make us some—"

"Max, do you think there is any possible way that I could ask you to hold me for a few minutes? But without it evoking any of the clichés of girls asking guys to hold them, and without it being sexually suggestive in any way, or implying that it might become sexually suggestive a few hours later after I've passed out, which I'm about to do, and we accidentally wake up face-to-face, or in some other entirely unintentional romantic configuration?"

Max took his time and considered my question. "Yes, I think I can do that."

"Okay," I said. I waited for him to come back to the bed.

"Oh, now?"

"Yeah, now."

I lay back down on my side and faced the window, shutting my eyes. I felt Max climb slowly onto the bed and reach carefully around my waist, searching for the least suggestive place to put his arm. He settled on cupping my shoulder with his hand, and we lay there in suspended animation for a few seconds.

"No, too weird," I muttered, sitting back up.

"Yeah, weird," Max agreed.

"Maybe just the hand," I said. We lay down on our backs, and he took hold of my hand at the center of the bed.

"No, still too weird," I said. He began to slide away. "No, stay close!"

He froze in place. "Like here?" he asked.

"Yeah, okay, there," I said. "Yeah, I think there's good."

I lay back down on the pillow. We were back in the Freudian position, both on our backs now, staring up at the ceiling—each with our own side of the mattress staked out, just like every other session we'd ever had. I fell asleep almost instantly.

Chapter Eleven

5:42 A.M. Max had kept his promise. He was still asleep when the sun opened my eyes, but the line down the bed had stayed intact. No accidental spooning or entangled limbs. I had slept so hard and so deep, I'd never even shifted onto my side.

I'd *slept.* I couldn't believe I'd *slept.* I hadn't slept for more than two hours in as many weeks, and that stuff had barely counted as sleep. Now I remembered what real sleep felt like. Maybe that was why my head finally felt a little clearer.

I watched Max's chest rise and fall, taking in his stubbly profile. Dawn was creeping through the huge windows, bathing everything in a pink-orange light. Yesterday already felt like a distant memory, like another life.

All except for my guilty thoughts of Andy.

I'd left him in my room, no doubt as freaked out and confused as I was. I wondered where he'd gone after I took off. I wondered what he'd done. I climbed over Max, careful not to wake him. Within seconds I'd snuck out of his apartment and was on the street, making my way home. If I could get back soon enough, I could make it into my own bed before Mom and Todd woke up and turned on NPR.

THE APARTMENT WAS LIFELESS. All the lights were out. The only sound in the kitchen was the hum of the refrigerator.

Todd's laptop was still asleep on the table, which meant they hadn't even gotten to the Huffington-Post-and-soft-boiled-eggs stage yet. I tiptoed through the dining room, watching for any sudden lamplight in the hallway.

On the third step, I somehow tripped the Complete-and-Utter-Chaos Alarm.

A horrid folk song filled my ears. It was a girl (maybe two?) and guitar: a poor woman's Joni Mitchell, but happy. Pop-Tart commercials/Disney Family Channel happy. The music stopped. Two spindly arms grabbed me from behind. I let out a strangled shriek as they swallowed me.

"Oh, thank God," Mom cried. Her body was shaking.

A door burst open, and I screamed again. Todd flew out of their bedroom, wielding a squash racket over his head, poised to strike. "What the—I heard screaming."

His Breathe Right nasal strip was still pasted over his nose. Aside from that, he wore too-short pajama pants puffed out like old-timey bloomers. I wondered if he'd seen a late night infomercial for "Pajoomers" and just gone for it. I'd say he was the third shirtless man I'd seen in less than twelve hours, but his chest and shoulders were covered in coarse white yak hair. He was, pretty much, wearing a shirt.

"She came back," Mom sniffled, not letting me go. "Todd, she came back."

My mother was hugging me. Not just hugging me, embracing me. Passionately, urgently. Maybe this still wasn't my life? She pulled back and shouted in my face, shaking my shoulders, "Where the hell *were* you?"

Okay, more like my life. Except that she had on these big, chunky headphones, the cord dangling down her flannel robe, pockets stuffed to the brim with used tissues. She must have accidentally pulled out the cord when she ran to me.

Todd exhaled and slumped against the wall, finally lowering his squash racket. "I told you she'd be back by morning, Meg. Welcome home, Theodore. I'm going to make us all some soft-boiled eggs. And how about some whole-grain Swedish limpa toast?"

I stared at him. "I don't know what that is, but okay," I managed.

"Coming right up."

Todd trotted down to the kitchen. Mom ripped off her headphones and tossed them on the dining table next to her laptop. She escorted me into my bedroom and shut the door behind us.

"Were you just listening to folk music?" I asked with disbelief.

"It was helping to calm me," she snapped. She must have finally gone haywire with fall semester stress because even with her blood boiling and her jaw clenched, there was . . . There wasn't another word for it. Love. There was love in her eyes. Actual, visible love. I suppose I couldn't be sure, given how seldom I'd seen it before. "Theo, you have to tell me everything. You have to tell me everything about him."

My spine stiffened. "Who?" I asked.

"The boy."

"What boy?"

"Theodore, there can't be any more bullshit between us. This is too important!"

My jaw nearly fell off its hinges. My mother just cursed. She must have found Andy. "It—it's not bullshit," I stammered.

"I see," she said, crossing her arms. "So you went to a semi-formal party last night and drank pink champagne all alone?"

"How did you know?" I saw the mop and bucket sitting in my bathroom doorway. The floor was sparkling clean now. She'd cleaned up my entire mess. Or maybe Andy had? There was a trash bag next to the bucket, which surely contained my puke-stained dress, reeking of champagne. Oh, God, was Andy's shirt in there, too? Had she spent the whole night interrogating him? Was she testing me to see if I'd confess?

"You *can't* drink on your Lexapro. You know that. It's not safe. How many times has Dr. Silver warned you about the side effects? Why do you think you got so sick?"

"You're right," I said. "I shouldn't have had that drink. I shouldn't have messed with my meds, but there's no boy, Mom." My eyes darted to the corners of the room, searching for signs of Andy—under the bed, behind the newspaper stacks. "I just went to Lou's second performance, and then I came back here to change. That's when I got sick, but I still wanted to meet everyone after the recital, so I went back out to meet them, and I ended up falling asleep at Lou's."

I knew she wasn't buying it. I wasn't even sure it made sense. But at least I knew she hadn't found Andy.

"I still feel pretty sick," I added. "And I'm so grimy. I've got to take a shower."

She shook her head. "Get yourself cleaned up. Todd will finish making breakfast. And then you're going to tell me where you really went last night and with whom, and we're going to set new ground rules that cannot be broken ever again. Are we clear?"

"Clear," I mumbled, trying to peer behind the bathroom door.

"Are we *clear*?" she repeated.

"Crystal," I said. "But I've *got* to shower, Mom."

I opened the door for her. She turned away, and I began to close it, but then she whirled around and wrapped me in her arms once more.

"I'm very glad you're back," she said, then let me go.

I locked the door as softly as I could and nearly collapsed. *Jesus Christ.* I needed to calm my nerves. I ran to the bathroom and swallowed down the pills I'd missed last night, along with a couple extra. I ran the shower for Mom and Todd's benefit. Then I flipped open my laptop and clicked on the Beatles' "Revolution 9," filling the room with just enough noise to reach the hall. The song picked up right where I'd left it nearly every night.

"Number nine . . . number nine . . ."

I felt a rush in my ears, a throbbing that I suddenly realized was my own heartbeat.

"Andy?" I kept my voice buried under the music, but loud enough for him to hear. "Andy, are you still here?"

I dropped down to the floor to check under the bed, and that's when I heard something rustling behind the closet doors. I jumped up, dragged open the closet, and found him lying between two towers of *The New York Times.* I wasn't sure if I felt relief or horror. He'd obviously slept there all night just to stay hidden from my mother. He'd turned himself into a closet-dwelling pretzel for me.

"Is she gone?" he said, his voice hoarse.

"Not for long."

ANDY'S MARATHON HIDEOUT HAD stretched the jagged holes of his T-shirt, which, combined with his messy hair, made him look like he was homeless, or a junkie, or in a band, or a homeless junkie in a band. I'd never seen his hair look anything but perfect, or at least perfectly *un*-perfect, but now it was dry and bushy—crushed into a sort of L-shape. And somehow he'd never looked sweeter or more innocent. It made me wish I could take back everything I'd said last night.

"I am so sorry," I said. "I don't know what happened to me—"

"No, it was my fault," he said. "I shouldn't have tried to kiss you. I don't know what happened to me, either. I think I just wanted her so bad that I went a little crazy."

"No, *I* went crazy. I shouldn't have accused you of keeping things from me—it was all just temporary insanity. No, you know what? Neither one of us is insane. Emma Renaux is insane. She's the one who thought I was Sarah when I am obviously me."

"But Theo, you were right. I don't think I've been totally honest with—"

"No," I interrupted through clenched teeth. "You said you weren't lying about anything else—"

"Wait, let me finish. I haven't been honest with *myself.* You were asking all the right questions. What do I really remember about that night? What do I really remember about *her*? It was all I thought about after you ran away. I was folded up in that freaking closet, staring into the dark for hours, and I finally had to face it."

I swallowed. "Face what?"

"There's just . . . My head is just like that closet. Dark. Some of it is darker than dead. I'm not just forgetting little pieces, I'm forgetting whole chunks."

"Like how much?"

I could tell he didn't want to say it out loud. Once he did, he couldn't take it back or deny it—even to himself. "Sunday morning," he said. "It's a total blank."

My stomach tied itself into a spiky knot. Because some part of me knew it already.

"I wasn't trying to keep it from you, I swear," he said. "I just didn't know. It's like the time I blacked out from drinking when I was sixteen. I didn't know I'd blacked out until I was walking around school the next day and people asked me what I'd done the night before. They had to ask me the questions before I realized I didn't know the answers. Hasn't anything like that ever happened to you? Haven't you ever blacked out or fainted, or lost a chunk of time somehow?"

I looked down at my sneakers, ducking under my hair. "Maybe," I replied.

"Theo, I don't even remember how I got to the café on Sunday. I mean, I was there by eleven forty-five, but before that . . . It's like everything just sort of stops before sunrise and starts again on the front lawn."

"A fugue state," I mumbled.

"A what state?"

The Beatles song came to an end, and then it began again. Always set to repeat. "Number nine . . ."

I dug my hands into my sweatshirt pockets, catching my gnawed-off fingernails on the fraying threads inside. "It's something my doctor has talked about. Sometimes, if a trauma is too acute, you can go into this state where you sort of erase the whole thing from your mind. It can happen to victims of abuse or violent crimes. Or to soldiers in combat. Even if you only witness something unthinkable, you can sort of . . . un-think it. Sometimes the cops will find a guy wandering around a bus station or by the side of a road, and he'll have no idea how he got there or where he was before. Not like he's forgotten his whole life—maybe just an hour or a day or a week. He doesn't know; he's just lost."

My mind began to race. Andy still had no idea what I'd called him before I knew his real name. He had no idea that I'd watched him for days, walking around the front lawn of the Harbor like—like what? Like he was in a fugue state. Not entirely sure what was missing or what had come before. He hadn't even known what day it was until I reminded him. He only seemed sure of one thing: when and where he was supposed to meet Sarah.

"Theo, I'm scared." He threaded his fingers through the holes in his T-shirt. "I think it might be like you're saying. I think something awful happened to her, and I think . . . I think I might have been there when it happened. I think it might have happened to us both."

I remembered the words I'd scrawled in my production book that morning. *What really happened to him? What kind of tragedy?* I knew it was something terrible. I knew it because I'd recognized the look in his eyes. I'd seen it in my own eyes whenever I accidentally glimpsed my reflection. Like some vital piece of code in our hearts had been deleted.

"I think you're right," I said. "I think you were there when it happened, and you've blocked it out—the places you went, the people you met. Andy, when Emma talked to me on that terrace, she said you were a saint. She said you were a good man, that you'd only ever tried to do good. You *know* Emma Renaux."

He shook his head, helpless. "I don't."

"But you do; you just don't remember. That has to be it. She has the answers. I'm telling you, she was weighed down by all this guilt. She said it wasn't your fault. That I shouldn't punish you, that she would fix it."

"Jesus, what is she talking about?" He pressed his palms deep into his eye sockets. He'd done this before, but only now did I know what that gesture really meant. It was a show of fear whenever he drifted too close to that gaping black hole in his memory.

"Have you ever heard of K.O.P.?" I asked. "Keeping Our Promise?"

He struggled for an answer. "I don't know. I don't think so."

"It's a women's shelter on Parker Street. Emma runs it with her fiancé, Lester Wyatt. It's less than five minutes from the Harbor Café and Battery Gardens. Less than five minutes from where you first saw Sarah and Emma together."

"A homeless shelter?"

"I think it could be, or maybe just a safe place for girls in bad situations."

He stared at me with wide, baffled eyes. "You think Sarah was living in a shelter?"

"I'm not saying it for sure, but I met this girl at the party—Helena—and she told me Emma and Wyatt weren't just celebrating their wedding, they were celebrating the shelter's anniversary. She said they'd invited six girls from the shelter as, like, shining examples, living proof of all the good K.O.P. does. She thought I could be the sixth girl because no one had met her yet."

Andy could only shake his head.

"What if Sarah was the sixth girl?" I pressed. "She could have been staying at that shelter. She could still be staying there. Do you have any memories of that kind of place? Groups of girls, dorm rooms, anything like that?"

His eyes drifted to the window, and I saw a glimmer of something.

"Maybe." He locked onto a thought. "A long hallway. It looks kind of like a dorm, a lot of doors on both sides. That fresh paint smell. Fresh white paint."

"We're going," I said. "After I deal with my mom, we're—"

I heard a faint beep from the floor.

My eyes landed on the trash bag by the door where Mom had stuffed the puke-stained clothes. The sound had almost gotten lost in the music. I crawled over to the trash bag, held my breath, and braved the stench to pull the phone from my jacket pocket. Andy's shirt was not in the bag; he'd been smart enough to remove the evidence. The phone was still connected to the button cam, but I tugged it free so he couldn't see.

Uh-oh.

LULUCELL: You said you'd be here at nine. You promised. I'll give you twenty more minutes, but I don't know why.

LULUCELL: I'd ask where you are, but I already know. He's not answering his phone, either. And please don't bother lying about it this time.

LULUCELL: So much for "ANDY," your fictional documentary subject and the Missing Persons Case of the Century. Did you and Max cook that one up just to throw me off?

LULUCELL: You know, if you had feelings for him, too, you should have just TOLD me when we were writing the letter. I guess "all bets are off," right? Anything can happen now. It's the big breaking story: Theo Lane Screws Over Best Friend For Other Best Friend.

LULUCELL: You're not the same person you were two months ago, you're not. You're not even the person you were last WEEK. I'm not trying to belittle what happened to you. I worry about you all the time. I think about all the terrible things that might have happened to you that night. But the Theo I knew would NEVER have used that to get Max's attention.

Those last texts hurt. Was I really doing that? Playing on Max's sympathies to get more attention? No. No way. Lou had so many things wrong, I didn't know where to begin. But how could I focus on her when the truth about Sarah was getting so close? Lou and I had the rest of our lives to straighten this out. The time to find Sarah was running out.

Unfortunately, Sarah would have to wait for as long as it took to placate my mother.

I COULD NOT, IN good conscience, ask Andy to spend another minute imprisoned in my closet, so I did what had to be done. I convinced my mother that we clearly needed a "Family Day" to help "bridge the divide" between us.

To my complete and utter shock, she went for it.

Todd was, of course, delighted.

I dragged them anywhere I could think of to keep them out of the house: a walk through Tompkins Square Park, a Billy Budd Browsing Bonanza at the NYU library, a late lunch at Todd's favorite macrobiotic dumpling house.

Again and again, I told my mother whatever she wanted to hear. That there were no secret boys in my life. That I wasn't sneaking out to parties. That I would keep her abreast of all my comings and goings and check in constantly by phone or text.

The plan worked to perfection. It not only gave Andy a chance to stretch out on my bed and catch up on sleep, but it left my mother exhausted by the time we got home.

The tears, my puke, her robe pockets filled with used tissues, her binge on syrupy folk music, the confusion, the interrogation, the dumplings—by five o'clock, it had all stacked up, and her body finally quit on her. She fell into a deep sleep on the living room couch, her mouth open and distorted like some cowering figure at the bottom of a Renaissance painting. And, as happened on most weekends, Todd fell into a snoring nap reading his weekend *Times.*

That's when we made our move.

Chapter Twelve

I must have walked by the Keeping Our Promise shelter at least nine times in my life; I just never noticed. Nothing about the building stood out. Plus, a scaffold had been built over the whole façade (from the looks of it, pretty recently); everything was drenched in shadow. Maybe the anniversary had inspired Emma and Lester to spring for a facelift.

I'm sure I'd seen a few girls smoking on the curb and thought it was a run-down public school. Underneath, it had that kind of look: bland and institutional. Tarnished metal letters—KEEPING OUR PROMISE—were nailed against a stone wall next to the door.

I pulled the iron handle. Then Andy tried. It wouldn't budge. There was a dusty, crooked intercom. I hesitated, trying to plan exactly how I'd announce myself, but when I reached for the buzzer, the door burst open, knocking me aside. I stumbled back, grabbing onto the scaffold.

"Don't even *think* about touching me!" a boy shouted.

He sounded frightened, and I saw why: a burly, hard-looking old guy with slicked-back black hair was shoving him down the steps. His dark windbreaker was tight around his gut, and three pounds of keys jangled from his belt loop. The boy was probably my age; he had that telltale fuzzy, failed mustache on his upper lip. His hair was short and spiky, buzzed on the back and the sides so you couldn't miss the three tattoos around his neck, the name *Victor* in red-and-white graffiti sandwiched between two sideways crucifixes.

Victor (I assumed he was Victor) puffed out his chest. His face was in Burly Man's face, but his feet told the real story: they were back-stepping, retreating toward the curb. "I swear to *God,* bro, I will *end* you!"

I shrank further into the shadow of the scaffold. My hand felt clammy on the cold metal. Andy stepped in front of me as a buffer.

"Let's stay calm, friend," Burly Man warned in an even tone. He spoke with a heavy Staten Island accent. "There are no boys allowed past these doors. I think you know that by now."

"This is *bullshit,* man!"

"Kid, you are violating an order of protection right now," Burly Man said. He'd clearly dealt with a Victor or two before. "Maybe you want to give me your probation officer's name so I can clue him in?"

"Yo, *eat* me, Tony Soprano! You don't *know* me. You don't know *shit* about me!"

"I do know this is a women's-only facility. And I know you can't be within thirty feet of her, so unless you'd like my boot in your ass, you better get it moving."

Victor hocked up a loogie and spat it at the steps near Burly Man's feet. *"Pinche maricón."* He raised his pained eyes toward the second-story window. "Helena!" he howled. "Baby, you gotta stop this! Come down here and talk to me. I'm sorry! I told you it won't happen again. I'm done with all that! Lena-Niña, *please.*"

My heart actually went out to him. He was repellent, but he loved Helena so much that he was calling to her balcony like Romeo. Where exactly did you draw the line between Hopeless Romantic and Psycho Stalker?

"Helena!" he called again. "BITCH, GET YOUR SKANK ASS DOWN HERE, GODDAMN IT!"

Okay, that's where you drew it.

Burly dropped his nonchalant cop routine and charged down

the steps, just far enough to launch Victor into a full sprint down the street. Once Victor had vanished, Burly huffed back up and threw the door open with all the frustration he'd kept in check. He didn't even notice us in the shadow. It was luck; the door swung closed slowly, and something in me jumped for the handle.

"What are you doing?" Andy whispered.

"I'm going in," I whispered back.

"After that? We should wait."

"I'll be fine," I said.

"No way. I'm going with you."

"Are you kidding? You heard Burly. No boys allowed. You want to start another scene like that one?"

"Theo, *please,*" Andy snapped. He sounded just like Victor. "I don't want you in there alone. This place is already creeping the hell out of me. No way Sarah is staying here. No way."

"Andy, don't worry. This is like the safest place a girl can possibly be. I'll be fine."

He took a deep breath and gave in. "Fine. Fine, I'll let you go in alone. But if she's really in there . . . if you really find her . . . then you've got to bring her out here to me. She might not want to see me after whatever happened that morning, but she's got to at least give me a chance to talk to her. You've got to convince her to talk to me."

I could see all the fear and anticipation in his silver-flecked eyes. "Andy, if she's in there, I will bring her to you. I promise. Five minutes. Just wait for me."

"I'll wait," he said.

I watched him watch me as the door swung shut between us.

THE LOBBY WALLS WERE bare all the way to the high ceilings. Dirty cloth tarps and paint cans were strewn across the floor, but only half of the room had gotten a fresh coat of white paint so far—

My toes clenched inside my sneakers.

Andy had definitely been here before. "*That fresh paint smell,*" he'd said. *"Fresh white paint."* It was one of the few details he'd remembered. Late Saturday night or early Sunday morning, he had been in this lobby. But how?

There was only one possible answer: Sarah had snuck him in. Jesus, she *was* here.

"Are you in any grave or imminent danger?" a woman's voice barked at me.

I jumped. I hadn't even noticed I was standing slack-mouthed right in front of a bulletproof plexiglass sliding window, like you'd find at the post office. Wrinkled paper signs and announcements were scotch-taped all over the office inside—a contradictory mix of inspirational messages (IF YOU DON'T LIKE BEING A DOORMAT, THEN GET OFF THE FLOOR!) and WANTED signs with dead-eyed sketches of rapists and murderers (HAVE YOU SEEN THIS MAN?).

"Young lady?" the woman pressed. Her voice was raspy; I could smell cigarette smoke. I tried to focus on her sour, heavily lined face. Her wig was an unfortunate shade of red. A nameplate on the desk beside her read, DELORES DANELLO. "Are you in any grave or imminent danger?"

"What?"

"Oh Lord, another one of these," she mumbled to herself. She began collating a stack of forms and placing them onto a clipboard, this time repeating the phrase as if I were mentally deficient. "Are *you* in any *grave* or *imminent DANGER*?"

"No," I said.

"Are you currently under the influence of drugs or alcohol?"

"No, wait. You don't understand. I'm not here for me—"

"Do not be nervous. You have found safe harbor." She had clearly read from this same invisible script every single day for years. "Gentlemen are not permitted past our doors, with the exception of Mr. Wyatt, our founder, security staff, and approved maintenance. No police presence is permitted without warrant or legal representation. If you are currently under the influence of drugs or—"

"No, maybe you didn't hear me. I'm here to find my friend."

She stared at me. "Are you sure about that?"

I caught her eyes darting over to the left side of my face. *Oh, God.* I draped my hand over my cheek, but it was too late. I hadn't reapplied my concealer. I'd been so wrapped up in our mission, I hadn't even thought about the scar. And now Delores Danello had sized me up as a textbook victim of domestic violence, one of those girls too ashamed to admit it, trying to hide injuries behind a hair curtain. The pity in her eyes—no, it wasn't just pity. It was condescension.

As far as Delores Danello was concerned, I was a tiny, battered flea, clinging to the itchy ass of the world. This was probably how every single girl who'd ever walked through the door felt. Maybe even Sarah. And it pissed me off.

"Delores," I said through clenched teeth, "I am just here to find a friend."

She sniffed and rolled back in her chair. "And who's your friend, sweetheart?"

"Her name is Sarah."

Something flashed across Delores's face. Like she'd swallowed a bug or choked on her own saliva. "Last name?" she asked.

"Last name?"

"Yes. Does this friend of yours have a last name?"

Andy, why didn't you get it? Why? No. Last. Name. Something came over me, a shaky, electric, *fuck-you* energy. I knew Sarah was here. I'd reached the finish line, and I didn't want any more questions; I just wanted to see her face. I was about to launch into a hysterical rant, but someone spoke up.

"Mac, is he gone yet?"

I recognized the voice. I turned and spotted Helena, peeking her head into the lobby. She was wearing her dowdy floral dress again, but her platinum hair was choppy—she hadn't flattened it into the good-girl ponytail. And she'd re-pierced: little silver hoops glistened along the side of her ear. "Mac" was Burly Man.

I hadn't even noticed, but he had taken a seat at a small table on the opposite wall, apparently his security station.

"I took care of him," Mac grunted.

Victor had a point; he did sound a little like Tony Soprano.

"You're the best, Mac," Helena said with a toothy smile.

"Helena!" I backed away from Delores and ran to her.

Her eyes narrowed. She seemed to be searching her memory banks. "Hey, I know you . . . Theo, right?"

"Right." I wished I hadn't given her my real name.

"What are you doing here?"

"I'm still trying to find—"

"She's looking for a girl named Sarah," Delores interrupted, her head poking through the office window. "No last name."

Helena stared back at Delores for a second too long, and then turned back to me. She sized me up, just as she'd done the first time we met. "What happened to you at the party? You ran out of there like the place was on fire."

"Yeah, I'm sorry about that. I'd had a little too much to drink. I got sick."

"Been there," she said.

Helena, Mac, and Delores were all staring at me now. Delores cleared her throat loudly. "Ms. Reyes," she said, "if you're done with your little chat, I'm going to have to ask your friend to leave. I can't allow visitors without authorization. Frankly, I'm not even convinced she knows—"

"No, *please*," I interrupted. I turned to Delores, then back to Helena. "Please, I just need to see Sarah."

"I'm sorry," Delores said, "I can't allow—"

"Nah, it's cool, Delores." Helena locked eyes with mine. "Theo's visiting with me today."

"You know this girl?" Delores asked dubiously.

"Hell, yeah," Helena said, searching my eyes. "She's a friend of Ms. Renaux's." Helena dialed up the attitude. "She's a guest at the wedding. You want to tell Ms. Renaux that you threw her out?"

With that, Delores's head disappeared back into her office. "Ten minutes," she called.

I almost hugged Helena in gratitude. "Thank you," I mouthed.

"Come on," Helena said, flashing a grateful smile at Mac, who buried his head back in his *New York Post.* "I'll show you my room."

IT WAS ALL EXACTLY as Andy had described: long, dorm-like hallways lined with metal doors. Maybe less like a dorm than a prison. The rooms were numbered, with a tiny pane of glass at the center of each door, just large enough to see inside, probably so Mac could check on the girls, make sure they were safe, make sure they'd made curfew.

I could feel Sarah behind one of those tiny windows. I could almost see her, even if the features were still a blur. How far away was she now? How many doors down? We passed Room Twenty-One, Room Twenty . . .

"You got to forgive Delores," Helena whispered. "A lot of these girls are running from something or someone, so they're real strict about who they let inside."

"Yeah, I saw what happened with Victor—" I clamped my mouth shut. *Ugh. There goes your clinical lack of discretion again.*

"Ay, Victor. You know, sometimes you just make really, really bad decisions, and then you got to keep paying and paying and paying."

"I know it," I said, though I really didn't. Past Room Sixteen, Fifteen . . .

"Well, there's no way Victor's getting his scrawny ass through that door again," Helena said with a sad little laugh. "Only way he gets another crack at me is if I'm dumb enough to go out there alone. See, the twisted dudes—the really twisted ones are always trying to lure us outside. And some girls fall for it. Some girls make whack-ass decisions like that and they end up . . . you know. Love just makes people really, really stupid."

I felt a sharp twinge in my stomach as Andy's words darted

through my mind. *If you find her, then you've got to bring her out here to me. You've got to convince her to talk to me.* It would be a pretty brilliant move. If he couldn't get in, then he could convince a clueless girl like me to do it instead. I could get past Mac without a problem, vouch for Andy's sweetness and undying love to Sarah, and convince her to come outside.

But I'd learned my lesson at the Magic Garden. I knew who Andy was. He wasn't one of the twisted ones. He wasn't Victor. I dumped the thought and moved on.

"So you're telling me there are never any boys in here, ever?"

"Oh, I didn't say that." Helena flashed a sly smile. "Nah, believe me, not every girl in here is 'keeping our promise.'" She pulled me into Room Ten and shut the door, lowering her voice to a cautious whisper. "Mr. Wyatt's got an office on the second floor. It's got a window in the back, near the fire escape, with one of those window gates on it. But he never locks the gate in the summer because he likes to keep the window open. So if a girl really wants to sneak a dude in, all she's got to do is tell him to meet her around back at the window. And if you tell anybody that, I'll break your face."

A second-story window around back.

Andy's half-assed memory had gotten it half right. Sarah did tell him to meet her at a back window, but it wasn't a brownstone on Bergen Street; it was an old, run-down shelter on Parker Street. Now it made so much more sense. She wasn't hiding him from her parents; she was hiding him from a three-hundred-pound security guard.

"Helena, are you sure you never met Sarah here?" I asked. "I know she was here last weekend. I know it."

Helena peeked back through her door, then stepped to the mirror by her bed. It was her entire room: a full-length mirror nailed to a bare white wall, a twin bed with a standard-issue brown blanket, and a wooden dresser.

"All right, look," she said, staring into the mirror, carefully removing each of the seven sparkling hoops from her ear. "I wasn't sure I could trust you when I first met you. I didn't know if you were one of us or one of them. If you weren't the sixth girl, then I thought maybe you were one of Ms. Renaux's cousins or something. That's why I didn't tell you about Sarah."

"Wait. You *do* know her?"

"No, I never actually met her. I just knew a chick named Sarah had been here for a night, and I knew she ran away, so I wasn't about to snitch."

"She ran away? She's gone already?" My chest felt brittle, like my lungs were turning to stone. "Why didn't you tell me?"

She glared at me over her shoulder. "Well, I didn't know how much you cared until I saw you in the lobby just now."

I dropped my head in my hands and massaged my throbbing temples.

"Look, Theo, you got to understand something." Her tone softened as she turned back to the mirror. "What you saw with Victor out there . . . I mean, yeah, that happens sometimes, but that's not the usual around here. We don't get a lot of visitors. Most of us either got families that want to forget we ever existed, or else *we* want to be forgotten. We only want people to see us when we want."

I nodded. "I understand."

She finished taking out her earrings and started brushing her hair. "I don't know if you do. We K.O.P. girls, we're kind of like ghosts. We want to stay invisible. A lot of the girls don't even give their real names when they come in here. Mr. Wyatt has to give them temp names like stray dogs at the pound, because you can only have so many Jane Does walking around one spot. Sometimes a girl will come in here so messed up, she doesn't even remember her name. But I don't always buy that one. I think it's just another way to stay lost. It's like Ms. Renaux always says . . ."

She left the sentence hanging. I know she was expecting me to confirm what Ms. Renaux always said. I met her gaze in the mirror. "Some want to stay lost," I echoed.

"A *lot* of us want stay that way. So I wasn't about to say shit to you about Sarah. If a girl doesn't want to get found, then she does not want to get found. Period. Besides, the whole Sarah thing freaked me out, so I wasn't going to say anything about it in front of Ms. Renaux."

"What do you mean, 'the whole Sarah thing'?"

She gathered her ponytail in a black elastic, glanced through the door again, and sat down close to me on the bed. She drew in a deep breath, and it was a little shaky as she blew it out. "Okay," she murmured. "I only told my girl Felicia about this. And I'm only going to tell you because you're Sarah's friend, but you got to *swear* you won't go making a scene about it to Ms. Renaux or anybody else. The girls feel safe here. We know how to ignore the creepy stuff, and I ain't about to mess that up."

"I swear," I said. Still, I forced the next logical question through my lips. "What creepy stuff?"

"I'm going to *tell* you." All her brash confidence had melted away. She sat on the edge of her spare mattress, suddenly looking much younger. "Ms. Renaux has this thing about keeping girls out of Room Nine."

I felt another twinge in my stomach, more painful than the last. For the briefest instant, I saw myself huddled in the corner of my bedroom, blasting the Beatles' "Revolution 9" on endless repeat. I could hear the voice on the track, repeating the words. The voice I'd always thought was John Lennon's. *"Number nine . . . number nine . . ."*

"Shit, I'm already freaking you out," Helena said.

"No, I'm fine," I said. I hadn't even noticed I was clutching her coarse blanket. I let it go. *Keep breathing. It's not what you think. It can't possibly be what you think.*

"Okay." Helena wrung her hands. "Okay, so the girls were all whispering at breakfast on Sunday about how Ms. Renaux put this Sarah chick in Room Nine. No one even wants to walk past Nine. It's got this energy. It's, like, too empty. I try not to look through the window when I walk by. I always come in from the other side just so I don't have to pass it. I didn't know Ms. Renaux put a girl in there, so when I heard those sounds coming from next door, I just about lost my shit."

There was that rush in my ears again. "What sounds?"

Helena bit her lip. "I don't really know. All I could picture was, like, a big rat clawing at the wall. Lots of little drags. So I got out of bed and peeked through my door, and I saw Ms. Renaux standing right in front of the room, looking in. She must have been staying late at the office. Maybe she heard the scratching from upstairs. She was staring through the door, and she had this look on her face. It was like . . . in those commercials for scary movies, when they show you the audience watching the movie? They get that look when something real sick jumps out, you know? That's what Ms. Renaux looked like. And she swung open the door and ran into the room, and I heard her yell, 'Stop it. Stop it!'"

"Someone was in there?" I choked out.

"I didn't even know it. I figured it was a new girl, freaking out on shrooms or H, scratching at the walls or whatever, 'cause we get those sometimes—girls who ain't even come down yet. That's what I told myself, and I slammed my door shut and hid my ass back under the covers."

"And then what?"

"Then I don't know. I didn't really see anything else. I heard Ms. Renaux come running back out to the hall, all agitated and freaked out, whispering to someone. It could have been Mac—it could have been anybody. All I know is, by lunch on Sunday, everyone was talking about how that Sarah chick ran away, and I thought, *Good for her.* If anyone tried to check me into Room Nine, I would have run for my life, too, and never come back here ever."

"So that was it? She never came back?"

"Well, that was the thing." Helena examined the folds in her frumpy dress, avoiding my eyes. "Even after Sarah was gone, I still heard the sounds sometimes. Only late at night, like, waking me up halfway. I think maybe it *is* the rats. There's got to be rats under these rickety old floors. That's probably why they're fixing it up, right?"

I tried to get her to look at me. "You really think it's rats?"

"Like I told you. The girls feel safe here. We know how to ignore the creepy stuff." Helena glanced at the digital alarm clock next to her bed. "Damn, we're going to be late for the rehearsal dinner." She jumped up and gave herself one last look in the mirror, redoing her ponytail, checking her ass, and frowning. "Shit, we're supposed to be making K.O.P. look good. You got to leave. Delores only gave you ten minutes." She finally looked at me. "Hey, how come you're not dressed yet? Aren't you going to the steakhouse?"

"What steakhouse?"

"Delmonico's Steakhouse . . . ? The rehearsal dinner? Aren't you going?"

I jumped up from the bed, trying to shake the dread that had consumed me, that had made me forget almost everything, even the wedding. "Yeah, I just need to run back to the hotel and change," I lied. "I might be a little late."

OUT IN THE HALL, Helena's door closed behind me, and I could feel the air change. It went sterile and cold. My legs began to quake, just as my whole body had when Andy first showed me Emma's picture. I forced myself to step next door. The number nine hovered right above that tiny window, daring me to peek through it. I heard the rush of my beating heart again, but now there was something else, a faint ringing in my ears, high-pitched and constant.

If I didn't know better, I'd swear the room was trying to sound a warning, trying to push me away. But I had to look. Would I recognize the furniture? The walls? Was it like one of those memories Andy described? Locked up in some story box in my head, with nothing but a song to remind me? I knew I'd blocked out The Night in Question, but what about last

Saturday night? How well did I remember that? I'd spent it in the corner of my room, listening to that Beatles song over and over . . . hadn't I?

I inched closer to the scuffed plexiglass and leaned forward, squinting into the darkness. I could just make out the black-and-gray outlines of a bed and a small desk, barely lit by the sunset through a barred window by the ceiling—

The shadow of a man bolted past the window. I buried my mouth in my hands to stifle a scream. Three more times, he flew past; he was pacing furiously, like a madman. I was afraid to look at his face, but on the fourth pass, I caught the profile of his perfect, ski-slope nose.

Andy . . . ?

Of course. He already knew the way in through that upstairs window. He must have snuck in while I was talking to Helena. I glanced down the hallway to make sure it was still deserted; I could hear Mac and Delores laughing about something. Drawing a shaky breath, I yanked the handle and slid through the door.

"What are you *doing* in here?" I whispered.

He didn't answer.

Bad idea to step inside. I'd attributed my tremors to fear, to some kind of post-traumatic stress after The Night in Question. But now I felt a weight. Like the ceiling was crushing me flat, and my bones were rattling from the resistance.

"Andy, I don't want to be in here," I said. It had been cold just outside the door, but inside it was sweltering and stale, like the hot air had been sealed inside ages ago, drained of all its oxygen.

Andy finally stopped pacing and froze by my side. The weight was crushing him, too; I could see it. He was cracking from the pressure, even though the room itself was nothing but an empty shell. A stained twin mattress on a frame. A battered desk and dresser. A grubby mirror on the wall. A mirror image of Helena's room, in fact, except for an ugly blue throw rug on the floor. He jabbed a finger toward the mattress.

"She was there," he said, his voice wavering like static. "She was crying on that bed. No, not crying. She was screaming. He wouldn't get off of her. He was so much bigger. He was crushing her flat against that bed. He wouldn't get off no matter how hard she squirmed, no matter how loud she screamed."

"Who?" I tried to get him to look at me. "Andy, *who* wouldn't get off of her?"

"I know him," he said. His cheeks turned as pale as the walls. His eyes darted from side to side like a camera capturing every moment. "I mean, I thought I knew him, but I don't. Not really. I don't really know him at all."

I'd made a promise to myself, but I couldn't keep it. I couldn't stop the doubt from creeping back in. "Andy, is it your face? Are you on the bed?"

He turned and focused on the door. "There were other men, too."

"What other men?"

"I could hear them running down the hall."

"Andy, look at me. Was it you on the bed? Was it you and me?" My chest was heaving—knots in my strangled throat. "Was I fighting you off? Was I scratching at the walls? Was it you and me?"

"No," he assured me. "But I could hear those other men shouting."

"What men? Maintenance men? Mac?"

"No."

I shook my head. He wasn't making any sense; maybe he'd distorted the memory somehow. How could a whole group of men have gotten in? How could a gang of men have sneaked in through that office window without anyone noticing? Helena said Emma was in the office all night. She would have seen them—she would have stopped the whole thing from happening. But then who? Who'd have the balls to allow a bunch of men through the front door of K.O.P. on a Saturday night?

I thought of Delores and Mac. Maybe I was asking the wrong

question. Never mind who'd have the balls; who would have the *authority*? That was the word Delores had used, *authorization*. And only one man would. The inkling landed like a mosquito, biting at my ear. A group of rowdy, shouting men . . . The Saturday before the wedding . . .

A bachelor party. A bacchanalian celebration of Lester Wyatt. *While his wife-to-be was here.*

"Theo, she was here," Andy said, as if reading my mind. "She saw it. At least, part of it."

"Who?" I murmured, even though I knew the answer.

"Emma. She was a witness."

Helena told me Emma had seen something through the window, but now I knew what she had seen. And I had the distinct feeling she hadn't told a soul about it. I backed away from Andy, pulled open the door, and ran from Room Nine. I didn't stop, and I didn't look back to see if Andy was behind me. I kept my eyes focused forward as I dashed past Delores and Mac, their faces twisted in surprise. I ran as fast as I could out the door because I didn't want Andy to follow.

I was going to Delmonico's Steakhouse, and I was going alone. No one would stand between me and Emma Renaux when I finally shook the fucking truth out of her.

Lou thought I was faster and meaner now? She had no idea.

Chapter Thirteen

"What *happened* to her?"

I didn't scream it. But I enunciated the question loudly enough to silence the chatter in the fancy dining room. I'd never seen so many adults shut their mouths at once. The buzz of conversation died a quick death, melting into the plush red-and-gold carpet. It hadn't been hard to spot Emma; she was right at the center table, under a candelabra-style chandelier, surrounded by, I guessed, Charles and Sally Renaux and a college-aged boy who was probably her younger brother. All of them in expensive formal wear. All of them seated on silver satin cushions, like a royal family.

"I know you were there," I said to Emma. "I know you saw it all, so just tell me what you saw." I wanted to stay calm and controlled, but I couldn't stop my voice from climbing. "Was it Andy? Because if it was Andy, then you have to *tell* me. I need to know what happened in that *room*."

Emma's manicured nails flew to her gaping mouth. Her eyelids fluttered in horror. A hundred eyes stared back at me. I was the party-crashing psycho in a sweatshirt and sweatpants, so I figured I might as well run with it while I could. It was too late to turn back now.

"Do *any* of you people know Sarah?" I swept the room with a steady gaze, picking out a pair of eyes every two or three mortified faces, trying to read their minds. "You think you can just sweep her under the rug? You think you can act like it didn't happen, and she'll just disappear from everyone's minds? Well, she won't disappear from mine!"

Emma burst into tears, breaking the silence. The next thing I knew, two powerful hands had latched onto my shoulders. They shoved me through the silent crowd. I tried to squirm away and caught a glimpse over my shoulder; it was Emma's brother, of course. A fratty-looking friend joined him. Together they lifted me just far enough off the floor to keep me from breaking free.

"No!" I growled. "NO! Somebody get them off of me!"

But I might as well have been invisible. It was like Helena said; I was a ghost. Nobody uttered a sound or moved a muscle. I writhed and kicked as the two forced me into the ladies' room and slammed the door.

I DO NOT RESPOND well to enclosed spaces. Especially after I've been manhandled by thick-necked frat dudes in lavender pants. The door wouldn't budge. They must have locked it. Or they were just blocking it with their steroid-pumped bodies. Either way they'd trapped me in here alone.

"Open it!" I shouted. "Open it, assholes! Open the door!" I pounded on it a thousand times harder than I'd pounded on the bathroom stall at the Magic Garden. "If you don't open this *goddamn*—"

But the door burst inward, sending me reeling back into one of the stalls. *Jesus, another bathroom stall.* Emma's brother charged at me, a sweaty blur of blond fuzz, thick lips, and rum-and-Coke-soaked breath.

"Shut *up*!" he hissed. "What the hell is the matter with you? Are you on drugs? You're scaring the crap out of my sister. You've just ruined the whole party."

"You think I give a *shit* about her party?" I pushed my face back into his. Then I hesitated. The next thought came quick.

He was there. Emma's brother was in Room Nine with all his repulsive fratty friends.

The groom had to invite the bride's brother to the bachelor party; it was an unbreakable rule. Even if Lester Wyatt thought Emma's brother was the douchebag he clearly was. But had Lester Wyatt invited all her brother's disgusting frat-bros, too? Had he brought them to a house full of damaged teenage girls in the middle of the night?

"I honestly don't care who you are or what's wrong with you," he said. "But you need to get the hell out of here now. Whatever happened . . . happened. What's done is done. And there's nothing any of us can do to change it now. So let it go."

My face shriveled behind my veil of hair. "Whatever happened . . . *happened*?"

"Fine, okay, I'm sorry, I get it." His skin reddened, fists clenching at his sides. "I get that you're upset. I just need you to be upset someplace else."

"Jesus, what kind of sociopath *are* you?"

"Will you *shut* it?" he whispered. "My sister has waited her entire life for this wedding, and I'm not about to let you fuck it up. Here's how it's going to go. You are going to walk out of here without saying another word to anyone. You're going to stay away from this wedding, you're going to stay away from my sister, and most of all, you're going to stay the hell away from Andy."

"Andy? *How* do you all know Andy? He's never even been to New York—"

"Tyler?" a slurred voice called, silencing me. Whoever it was, I could hear the fear in his voice. "Dude, where are you?"

"I'm in here," Emma's brother answered from our stall, his eyes glued to mine.

"Dude, we got one of the Motel Six coming. I mean, coming fast, like right—"

I heard the door burst open.

"*Excuse* me?" Helena's unmistakable voice. "I believe this is the ladies' room, no?"

"Yeah, we'll be out in just a sec," Boarding Stool growled.

"No, I think you'll be out now," Helena said.

"Okay, okay, chill, Mama."

"Mama?" I wish I could have seen her face in that moment. "How about you call me 'Mama' again, and we see what happens?"

A haughty sniff. "I was just leaving."

"Yeah, I thought so," Helena called after him. "Theo? Where you at?"

"I'm in here," I called out.

Tyler's eyes flashed in fury. Before he could move, the door exploded open behind him, slamming into his spine. He winced and collapsed ass-backward on the tile floor.

"Let's go." Helena grabbed his shoulder and spun him around. "Out."

"No," Tyler grunted. He shook his head, massaging his back, his flabby red features locked in a cringe. "We haven't finished our conversation—"

"I wasn't talking to you, white boy. I was talking to my girl."

"Fine." He snickered through his pain. "Your girl is all yours. Just get her the hell out of here."

IT WASN'T UNTIL WE were safely down the street that Helena finally let go of my wrist. "Girl, what the hell were you trying to do in there? What were you thinking?"

"I was trying to get the truth," I said, rubbing the tender skin where she'd seized and dragged me. "Helena, it was Emma's brother. He did something to Sarah the night of Wyatt's bachelor party. He practically just admitted it."

She arched an eyebrow. Her ponytail flopped limply over her shoulder. "Bachelor party? There wasn't any bachelor party."

"Last Saturday night at K.O.P. There must have been a—"

"You don't think I would have noticed a bunch of assholes having a party in the middle of K.O.P.? I told you, it was creepy quiet that night. Theo, all due respect, but you don't know what you're talking about."

"I'm talking about Tyler. You saw what he did. He cornered me in that stall. He could have done anything to her. They could have done awful, disgusting—"

"Theo, Sarah is *fine*," Helena groaned.

I stared at her. "What do you mean, she's fine?"

She glanced back through Delmonico's front doors. "Listen," she whispered. She eyed the noisy passersby, a gaggle of Wall Street tourists jabbering in French. "I just heard Mr. Wyatt in the kitchen. I heard him say Sarah was coming to the wedding."

I stood still, trying to process this. "Mr. Wyatt said that? You heard him say that for sure?"

"Yes," she insisted. She shifted on her feet, her eyes flitting back to the door. Something about her wasn't right. "Me and Felicia were in the kitchen when you went all psycho on Ms. Renaux. We were trying to get a break from all the richies. Her folks dragged her into the kitchen right where we were hiding, and Mr. Wyatt ran in behind them to calm her down. I heard him tell her that Sarah *wanted* them to have the wedding. That she was going to be there with them tomorrow."

"No, that's . . . maybe you weren't standing close enough. Maybe you misheard him."

"I didn't mishear anything," she snapped. "I told you. Sarah is fine, everything is fine."

"If everything's fine, then why are you so nervous? It's Tyler and those boys, isn't it? They're trying to intimidate—"

"Those *pendejos*?" she snorted. "With the purple pants?"

"Well then, what?"

She reached under the frilly collar of her dress, pulled a folded white envelope from her bra strap, and handed it to me. "It's because Mr. Wyatt wants you to have this."

I stared at the envelope. "Mr. Wyatt? Gave this to you for me?"

"Yes. Now just take it and go, all right?"

"No, I want to talk to him." I started back toward the restaurant.

"Not right now, you don't." She grabbed my arm and held

me back. "He wants to talk to you alone—as in, not in front of Ms. Renaux."

"About what?"

"Theo, if I knew, don't you think I'd tell you?" she murmured urgently. "This is the most Mr. Wyatt ever talked to me in my life. Someone must have told him you came to my room or something. Look, just take it and *go.* If Ms. Renaux sees me doing this, it's going to be on me. Just be there, okay?"

She jammed the envelope in my hand and turned to run. Before I could open my mouth to protest, she'd vanished back into the restaurant.

Be where? I wondered, ripping open the envelope.

CHARLES AND SALLY RENAUX

&

GEORGE AND LEONA WYATT

WOULD BE HONORED TO HAVE YOU SHARE IN

THE JOY OF THE MARRIAGE OF THEIR CHILDREN

Emma Renaux and Lester Wyatt

SUNDAY, THE EIGHTH OF SEPTEMBER,
TWO THOUSAND AND FOURTEEN
AT HALF PAST FIVE O'CLOCK
AT BATTERY GARDENS
INSIDE BATTERY PARK OFF STATE STREET
NEW YORK, NEW YORK.

R.S.V.P.

I WALKED BACK HOME with the wedding invitation dangling from my fingertips.

I tried to think, tried to latch on to one coherent idea, but I couldn't. None of this made any sense. Why would Lester Wyatt want me at his wedding? Why would he want to talk to me at all? I was the party-crashing freak. The girl who'd snuck into his shelter. Who'd crashed his fiancée's bridal shower. Who'd just screamed at his fiancée. And he didn't just want, he *needed* me to be at his wedding. What did that even mean?

I found Andy sitting on the pavement, leaning against the side of my building, looking as lost as I felt. As lost as he looked the first day I saw him.

"Where did you go?" he asked. He sounded tired, beaten down. "You ditched me in that place."

"I'm sorry. I kind of confronted Emma. At the rehearsal dinner."

"You went to the rehearsal dinner without me?"

"Yeah, lucky for us."

"Why lucky?"

"Because Emma's brother would have killed me if he saw me with you. I'm supposed to stay ten miles away from you."

"Emma's brother said that?" Andy looked baffled. "He doesn't even know me."

I sighed and sat down next to him on the ground. "Andy, he knows you. That whole family knows you, you just don't remember."

"Right," he mumbled, turning away. "Well, maybe Emma's brother is right. Maybe you should stay away from me." He refused to look at me.

"Andy, what is it? What's wrong?"

"You thought it was me," he said, staring down between his legs at the sidewalk.

"What?"

"In that room. When I was starting to remember things. You

thought I was remembering something *I* did. You thought I could do something like that to Sarah."

"No," I lied. "No, I never thought that."

"No, you're right, you didn't think I did it to Sarah, you thought I did it to *you.*" His head jerked up, his eyes finally meeting mine. "Like . . . like I did something so sick to you that we *both* blocked it out. So sick that we had to make ourselves forget. You thought I could do something like that to you."

My throat suddenly felt dry. My cracked lips struggled to form words. "I was in a panic. I wasn't thinking clearly. I've been that way ever since—"

"What if you're right?" he interrupted.

That was not what I'd expected.

"Not about the part where she's you," he went on. "I know Sarah is Sarah, but what if *I'm* the one that hurt her? What if that's why I don't remember? What if there's some horrible part of me that came out that night and—?"

I shut him up by shoving the wedding invitation in his face. His eyes quickly flashed over it. "What's this? Where did you get this?"

"Lester Wyatt gave it to me," I said.

"What do you mean, he gave it to you?"

"Well, he didn't actually give it to me. He had Helena give it to me."

"Why would he give you an invitation to his wedding?"

"That's the nine-million-dollar question. He says he needs me to be there. He wants to talk to me alone. And I think she's going to be there, too. I think Sarah is going to be at the wedding. Helena heard Wyatt say it." I almost took his hand. "Andy, I think she might be *fine.* I think maybe the stuff you remembered in that room—"

"Never happened?"

"All I know is, after everything we've been through this week, I trust Helena's ears way more than I trust your memory."

A distant light seemed to flicker inside him. "You think she could really be there? You think all the stuff I saw might have just been some shit I dreamed or something?"

"I honestly don't know. But I'm going to find out at the wedding."

"Well, I'm coming with you," he said.

I shook my head. "You can't. I can't bring you with me."

"Why not?"

"I just told you. Emma's brother practically threatened to kill me if I brought you anywhere near the wedding."

"Well, screw Emma's brother. I'll deal with Emma's brother."

"Andy, I'm serious."

"So am I." He pushed himself to his feet, looming over me. "Theo, you're not thinking this through. Lester Wyatt owns the shelter, right? He's the only guy besides Mac and a few janitors with a run of the whole place, the only guy who can go into any one of those girls' rooms whenever he wants. What if it was *his* face I saw? What if he was the one crushing her against that bed? What if everything I remember was real? I'll bet you anything if I saw his face, the whole thing would come back to me. All of it."

"If you saw his face," I echoed.

"What?"

A thought, an idea, an epiphany finally emerged from the sludge of confusion. "There is a way you could see it," I said. "Without actually being there."

Andy laughed shortly. "Do you *try* to confuse me, or am I just a dumbass hick?"

"Neither," I said. "Actually, I can boil it down to one very simple question. Do you have an iPhone?"

"Do I look like I have an iPhone?" he snorted.

"It's all right," I said. "We have a spare."

Chapter Fourteen

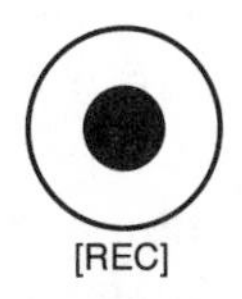

I can't describe how good it feels to be shooting again. I hadn't even realized what was missing. Now it's so clear: I was half myself without a camera; now I am whole. Like Sweeney Todd says, "At last! My right arm is complete again!" Or in this case, my collar. I have carefully sewn the button cam cable down the inner seam of my wedding dress and run it through an incision in the pocket, connecting it to my iPhone.

Yes, I am wearing my wedding dress. But there's a perfectly good explanation.

As my best friends love to point out, I own exactly two dresses. One is the rumpled, black ball of crusty puke that now resides in a trash bag on my bathroom floor. The other is the vintage wedding dress that, until now, I kept wrapped in tissue paper, creaseless and pristine, inside the cedar Glory Box at the foot of my bed. It's Sunday afternoon, nearly 3 P.M. The wedding is at 5:30, and all the dry cleaners are closed. My Ann Taylor puke dress is totally unsalvageable, so . . .

Yes. There are obviously a few problems with wearing a wedding dress to someone else's wedding.

For one thing, it's appalling and morally reprehensible. A full Boba Fett costume would be less offensive. Also, it's not exactly ideal if you're trying to lay low. But at least my "wedding dress," while being white, won't scream, *I'm a deranged wannabe bride.* It's a weird, funky, A-line thing from the late '50s/early '60s that I found at a vintage store and just knew would be my bridal gown. Not a wedding dress per se, but a wedding dress to *me.* More importantly, it has two features that are essential to Operation FaceTime:

1) The pockets. Ugly/beautiful pockets, one of which is the perfect vessel for my hidden iPhone.

2) A high, structured collar that flares out from either side of the V-neck, climbing toward my chin like two daisy petals. There's a buttonhole on the left petal, and a small onyx button on the right. They can be fastened over the neck to form a cutout on the chest, but I've left the collar open in the flared position and replaced the onyx button with my button cam. A button cam that is finally recording video again.

I am defacing my most prized possession with a button cam and white thread.

I'm committing sacrilege.

But for the potential answers to all our burning questions, and a potential happy ending to *someone's* strange and beautiful love story, it's worth it. All I need now is that second iPhone. I am ready to record some test audio and video before the big event.

WE WAITED UNTIL AFTER 8 P.M. to sneak back into the apartment last night. Emilio was done with his shift, and I figured correctly that Mom would still be crashed out on the couch. Todd never checked on me without Mom present—too afraid to barge in on me naked—so Andy and I made it back to my room without them ever knowing I'd gone.

The next bit of luck came this morning. Apparently Mom and Todd had to attend an NYU luncheon this afternoon. Mom was worried enough about me to offer to skip it, but I promised her I'd stay home all day safe and sound. Unfortunately, something was wrong with my phone, I lied. I'd get it fixed tomorrow, but in the meantime, could I borrow the one we kept as a fourth line in case anyone lost a phone and needed a temp? (Because Todd loses his iPhone every three to four weeks? I left that part out.) She agreed. Anything to ensure that I'd be in touch the instant I needed to be.

Now she's tapping lightly at my door.

"Bye, Mom," I call to her. "Thanks again for the phone!"

"The luncheon should only go about three hours," she responds, respecting that I've chosen to keep the door closed. "I've instructed Todd to forego his usual schmoozing of the dean so we can be home sooner. We should be back no later than six."

"Sounds great! Have fun."

"All right, then," she says.

I hold my breath, listening for their footsteps. There's only silence.

"All right, then," she repeats. "Just rest, sweetheart, all right? It's the most important thing." Another pause. "Theodore?"

Please just leave already! I squeeze my eyes shut. "Yeah?"

"Todd and I were having a discussion this morning, and I just wanted to clarify. You're aware that I love you, right?"

I feel another crack forming in my lungs. My eyes become damp. "Yes, I'm aware," I say. I was not, in fact, entirely aware. At least now I've got the proof on digital audio.

Only then do I hear the fading footsteps and the sound of the door closing.

I exhale, finally able to relax. But almost instantly, I tense again. I'd spent most of the morning convincing myself the wedding would be nothing more than a few mean looks from Tyler and a beautiful moment playing Cupid to Andy and Sarah. I can't dwell on the unknown, though. To paraphrase Tyler himself, whatever happens . . . happens.

Once I'm sure Mom and Todd are in the elevator, I yank open my bedroom closet, letting poor Andy, the budding yogi contortionist, back out of hiding.

"Okay," I say, "we've got the second iPhone, so I can walk you through Operation FaceTime for real."

"You're sure you want to stick with that code name?" Andy asks with a smirk.

"I admit, it sounded cooler in my head," I say. "But once you name an operation—"

"Hey, what are these?" he interrupts, peering into my Glory Box.

Stupid. I left it open when I took out the dress. Andy dunks his head in, clearly delighted he's discovered a treasure trove of my most personal secrets. All the sketches I've made of my dream wedding ring: the six little diamond daisy petals surrounding a gold center. A million sketches of me in my wedding dress, wearing my dream ring, wearing my dream wedding pearls, surrounded by dream wedding flowers. My face grows hot.

"Just some drawings," I mumble, slamming the box closed.

Andy flashes me a sly grin. "You really love daisies, huh?"

I ignore him by taking the iPhone from my dress pocket. (I made sure to leave enough cable so as not to disconnect the button cam.) I bury my face in the screen, tapping around, checking to make sure I've installed all the necessary software, hoping he gets the hint. Then I plop down on the couch, placing the second phone on the coffee table.

"Okay, check this out." I open FaceTime on my phone and dial Andy's loaner phone. When it rings, I accept the call, and then I show him the new image on his screen. It's a video image of my bedroom wall instead of my face. "See. I told you there was a way."

He sits down next to me for a closer look. "Wait. What am I looking at?"

"I found an app that makes the rear-facing camera the default video source for FaceTime calls. So now, instead of seeing my face on your phone, you're seeing my button cam feed." I stand up and do a slow twirl so he can see the pan around my bedroom on his screen. "Now I can keep the phone in my pocket the whole time." I slip my phone into my dress pocket and continue to twirl. "As long as our call stays connected, you'll be seeing and hearing whatever I'm seeing and hearing." I throw my fist out for a bump. "Come on now. Give me my propers."

I expect a full bump in return, and maybe even a hug, but Andy doesn't look impressed. On the contrary, his expression grows much darker.

"What's wrong?" I ask.

"This button cam thing," he says. "You haven't used this recently, have you? Like, on me or something? Because I told you how I feel about—"

"On *you*?" I interrupt. "Of course not. Andy, I made a promise."

He runs a quick visual polygraph on my eyes and thankfully buys the lie. "Okay, then it is a pretty freaking smart idea," he admits. "But if your phone is in your pocket, then how am I going to talk to you? How do I tell you when I spot Sarah or Wyatt?"

"Ah, that's what the IFB earpiece is for."

"The what?"

"The IFB earpiece. It's right here." I can't blame him for not seeing it; it's no bigger than a pearl, lost in the faded gold etching on my Japanese coffee table. I pick it up and roll it gingerly between my thumb and forefinger. It's a pale cream color and molded to fit right inside the ear, making it nearly undetectable.

"Sometimes we get to use them on location shoots for the *Sherman News*," I say. "I'm in charge of the gear. It's Bluetooth ready, so all I have to do is pair it with my phone and, *voilà*, I'll have you loud and clear in my ear. Okay, sorry about the 'voilà,'—I'm just a little excited. Dude, we've got to test it. I'm going to the kitchen. Stay here."

I'm more than just a little excited. I can barely contain it as I run to the kitchen, lodging the earpiece in my ear and pairing it with my phone. I do a slow walk around the kitchen, leaning slightly toward the collar. "Test, test. One-two, one-two. Can you hear me, Andy Reese? Tell me what you see."

"I see a kitchen." Andy's voice pipes into my left ear with perfect clarity.

"Hell, yeah, you do!" I take a moment to do a small fist-pumping dance. He can hear me, and I can hear him. He sees everything I see. Everything works. "So what do you think?" I ask eagerly. "Are we ready for this wedding, or are we ready?"

"I guess," Andy says. "Just remind me why we're doing all this? Do we really need this fancy setup?"

"Andy, there's nothing fancy about it. Earpiece, button cam, FaceTime. I can't walk around Battery Gardens shoving my phone in people's faces till you recognize Sarah or Wyatt. Tyler would see your big face on my screen and go apeshit on me again. No, this is the way to go. Quick, quiet, and under the radar. The Renauxes will never even know I'm talking to you."

"Okay, fair enough."

"Good. So, you're in, right?" There's a long silence on the line. "Andy?" I press my finger to the earpiece, making sure it's securely in place. "Andy, can you hear me?"

"Yeah, I'm right here."

"What just happened? Where did you go? I thought there was a glitch."

"I didn't go anywhere."

"Then what? Are you ready to do this or not?"

"Theo, I can't," he says. "I'm sorry, but I can't let you go in there alone. It's too risky. Between Tyler and this Lester Wyatt dude, you need someone there to watch your back."

I lean against the fridge. "You can't go with me. How many times do I need to explain this?"

"No, I get that. But can't you at least bring someone else? You could pass him off as your date. Don't you have some friend who'd go nuts if he knew you were walking into this weird-ass wedding alone?"

The answer is quite obvious, so I have to lie. "Nope. No, I don't know anyone who fits that description."

"What about that dude who came over the other night?"

"No, Andy. Forget it. I've been avoiding his texts and calls for the last thirty-six hours. I can't suddenly call him up and invite him to a wedding with two hours' notice."

"Why not?"

"I just can't, all right?"

"Oh, wait." I can practically hear him grinning through the earpiece. "I get it. You like him. You don't want to ask him on a date because you're afraid he'll say no. Theo, we don't have time for that stuff right now."

"No, I do not *like* him. We're not like that. He's like my goofy older brother."

"Then asking him to hang with you for twenty minutes should be no sweat."

"I don't . . ." My heart starts racing. I press my palm to my chest. "Okay." I sigh. "Okay, I'll call him. But you've got to wait in the kitchen while I make the call."

Andy laughs. "Of course. Those goofy older brother calls always need to be made in private. Everybody knows that."

MAX ANSWERS BEFORE THE second ring.

"Seriously?" He barks it instead of *hello* or *what's up.* Then he repeats it minus the question mark. "Seriously."

"What?"

"Thee. Seriously?"

"*What,* Max?"

"Seriously?"

I pull the phone from my ear and let him get it out of his system.

"You come to my house in some deep existential crisis, bordering on losing it completely, not totally sure that you are in fact *you.* Then you sneak out the next day while I'm asleep and don't answer my calls for two days? You can't do that. You can't make a power forward feel like a Jewish grandmother. Like I need to sit in my rocking chair with an afghan on my lap, worrying all day that you've been kidnapped by Cossacks or hobos."

"I only understood about half of that," I say. "What is a power forward, and why are you wearing an afghan?"

"Jesus, what's the difference? Just tell me what *happened.* Where have you been, and how hard is it to answer *one* call? See, I'm already speaking in Grandma! That's what you do to me, Thee."

I knew this was what it would be—Max yelling about what a bad friend I'd been, having every right to do so. I park myself on the bedroom floor, leaning against the side of my bed, in it for the long haul, pillow tucked between my chin and knees as protection from his general pissed-offness.

I regret not stopping the recording before I made the call. I'd figured all drama was good drama—at least on film. But not so much in real life, I'm learning. Anyway, I won't be able to hear his side of the conversation in the footage, so this scene won't even make the final cut.

"Theo, are you there?"

"Max, do you have a suit?"

"What?"

"A suit. Do you own a suit? You know, like a suit that people who wear suits wear."

"Yeah, I know what a suit is. I don't wear track pants twenty-four hours a—"

"Max."

"What?"

"I'm going to say something, and it's going to take a while, so just let me finish before you interrupt. Can you promise you'll do that?"

Silence. Then a deep breath. "I'm all ears, Thee. Whatever it is can't be any weirder than the last session."

"Do you think there is any way I could ask you to go with me to a wedding today? As a favor? A friend favor? Without it evoking any of the clichés of girls asking guys to weddings, or being confused in any way with me asking you out on a date, and without it being romantically suggestive in any way, or implying that it might become romantically suggestive later on, like—to—"

"Wait," Max interrupts.

"No, you promised you wouldn't interrupt me."

"I said I was all ears. But let's back up a second. Did you just ask me to a wedding?"

"Yes."

"And the wedding is today?"

"In less than two hours."

"And whose wedding is it?"

"Not relevant. A friend. A friend of a friend."

"And how do you know this friend of a friend?"

"Not relevant. Can you go? I mean, given all my conditions, can you go?" I don't hear any nervous fumbling on the other end.

This was a terrible idea. I should never have listened to Andy. "Max, I'm going to hang up now. Please, if you can just forget we ever had this conversation—"

"I'll go."

I blink several times. "You will?"

"At least I'll know where you *are*," he groans. "Just give me a time and place."

I blink rapidly again and realize my eyes are moist. But I'm smiling. It's the generic effect of weddings—all weddings, any weddings—that's what it is. "Five thirty. Battery Park. Meet me in front of the Harbor Café."

ONLY ONE THING REMAINS to be done before I leave. I'd avoided it for as long as I could. But now the time has come.

I step into my bathroom, lock the door, and look in the full-length mirror.

I'd always imagined I'd look like Audrey Hepburn when I finally put it on. That was before I was disfigured. I thought I'd look like Audrey Hepburn in that white Givenchy dress from *Sabrina.* But once I finish concealing the scar and applying the lipstick and dusting on the blush and rolling on the mascara and gelling the curtain, I take in the dress.

I do not look like Audrey Hepburn. I look like Elvis.

I am '70s Elvis in drag. No, I'm a '70s Elvis impersonator in drag. All I need are some giant rhinestones down the neckline, and it's straight on to Vegas. And the ass . . .

Let us not speak of the ass. Let us just call the dress a "tragic epiphany," and leave it at that.

Chapter Fifteen

I am a Theo-Cam. A walking, breathing camera. The impartial observer I was born to be. I am Andy's eyes and ears, his remote-controlled drone. I'm keeping my distance, hovering in front of the Harbor Café, zooming in on the entrance to Battery Gardens, scrutinizing the guests as they stroll through the ivy gates, framing each young brunette in my crosshairs.

This is it, Sarah. This is the day we meet. Operation FaceTime is a go.

"Anything yet?" I murmur into my collar.

"Nothing yet," Andy's voice replies in my ear. "You know what? I'm not worried about finding her. That'll be cake. She's so much more beautiful than all these girls. She'll stand out like a Disney princess. It's him, Wyatt. I need to see his face."

"I know."

It's a bigger wedding than I'd expected. Probably more than three hundred guests. I take a seat on a stone bench on the Harbor's front lawn. How many times have I shot this scene? How many Sundays have I spent shooting the newlyweds coming in and out of Battery Gardens? And it's always a variation of the same themes: the bride with her smile frozen and her bridesmaids shuffling alongside her, guarding her hair and dress from the elements. Then the groom, silent with his groomsmen, his smile tinged with terror. And then without fail, one or two hours later, they emerge from that second-story balcony overlooking the water, posing for classic, windswept photos that their children and grandchildren will admire.

I glance around for Max, nervously tapping my heels. Andy was wrong; this is not cake. If Tyler spots me before I make it inside, the whole thing could be blown. Or maybe I'll make it inside just fine, only to be cornered by the mysterious Lester Wyatt. Will he answer all my burning questions, or will he chloroform me and drag my limp body down to the basement? Maybe Helena will step in and protect me again. The problem is, I haven't spotted her yet, either.

"Theo!"

It's Max's voice. And someone is hurrying toward me across the lawn. I squint, not trusting my eyes. This clean-cut, dapper stranger is not Max Fenton. This person in the tailored black suit, spotless white shirt, and silver tie is *not* Max Fenton. But it is. And he has shoes. Actual shoes.

"What?" Max asks, stopping in front of me. He does a quick examination of himself for stains and/or bird poop. "What's wrong? You don't like the suit?"

He even got a haircut. Short, but not enough to lose those trademark dark ringlets.

"What? The hair?" Max asks. "I told the guy I only had fifteen minutes."

"Okay, wait, wait, wait!" Andy's voice pipes into my ear. I flinch and nearly fall off the bench. "*This* is the goofy older brother? Are you kidding me right now?"

"Shit, it's the hair, isn't it?" Max runs a hand through it, annoyed. "Too short, right?"

"I mean, he is a good-looking dude," Andy says. "And I don't even like dudes. Not even a little."

"Okay, shut *up*," I mumble into my collar.

Max frowns. "What did I say?"

"I said, shut up, because your hair looks fine," I mutter, lamely fighting to recover. "You really didn't need to get a haircut. At least let me pay for it."

Max laughs. "Okay, I knew Theo Lane was hiding in there somewhere."

Andy laughs, too. "I like this dude. All right, I'll shut up now."

I begin to wonder if Operation FaceTime was the best idea. But we're committed now, and once I have my answers, I can go back to my old life, writing love letters for Lou and lying in Freudian position with Max. I stand and take my first steps toward Battery Gardens, but Max doesn't follow. I turn back, and now he's staring at me.

"What's wrong?" I ask.

Max's blue eyes cloud over. "It's . . . you're wearing your dress. That's the Dress, isn't it?"

It's not until he says it that I realize how monumentally bizarre a decision it truly was. To wear the dress that's supposed to stay enshrined in a cedar deep-freeze until that very special day when I awaken it from its slumber, to wear it once and only once.

"We're not eloping, are we?" Max asks. "Because I should at least call my mom."

His straight face does the trick. I giggle. For the first time that day, I relax. If only for a fleeting second. "I told you to shut up, Max. This is literally the only dress I own right now. The other one was destroyed in an unfortunate . . ."

My voice trails off. Someone has pressed the PAUSE button on Max Fenton. Like a victim of Medusa, he has seen his first full-length view of '70s Elvis in drag and has turned to stone. Did I screw up my concealer? My hand flies up to my face. "Let's just go, all right?"

"Right behind you," he says stiffly.

I turn away, feeling ill.

"Keep your boy close," Andy whispers. "Keep him real close."

SOMETHING IS WRONG. I can feel it as we climb the winding white staircase and enter the main hall.

"This is weird," Andy murmurs, as if reading my mind. "Why is everyone so quiet? And why's the band already playing?"

There's a twelve-piece orchestra at the end of the hall, playing Glenn Miller's "In the Mood." A few uncomfortable-looking guests dance halfheartedly on the parquet floor. The center of the room is so empty that the band's blaring trumpets echo like a coach's whistle in gym class.

This is not what the pre-ceremony is supposed to be. There should be a charming violin quartet welcoming us in with prelude music. People should be hugging and laughing. *"Oh, darling, it's been too long! Why do we have to wait for occasions like this to get together?" "Well, look at you! You know, I haven't seen you since you were* this *tall!"* But there is no laughter. It's more like one of those morbid concession parties when a candidate loses an election.

I'm two parts disturbed and one part disappointed. I never would have admitted it to Andy, but some part of me has been dying for this moment. The moment I would finally step through those ivy gates into Battery Gardens—not as a distant observer, but as a real-live guest. Granted, I'm the real-live guest of a total stranger who may be a vicious psycho, but beggars can't be choosers.

It's too bad, because the place really is beautiful. A timeless kind of beautiful. Wide-open spaces, cream-colored walls, luxurious curtains that sway and flow in the breeze from the river. It reminds me of those huge, airy beach houses that the stars own in East Hampton, the kind I only see in the *Times* real estate section. A view of the Statue of Liberty, even, right across the water.

Max leans in and whispers in my ear. "Why did you bring me to the most depressing wedding ever?"

"Let's find out." I grab his hand and pull him through the sparse, uneasy crowd. I catch a few double takes as I scan their faces. It's the dress. I'm not just the Mystery Guest no one knows; I'm the '70s Elvis impersonator no one knows. Why did I wear my wedding dress again? Oh, right, because *I don't own another dress, assholes.* It's a concept people with walk-in closets wouldn't understand.

Of course, for some here, I'm also the raving tweaker who crashed their rehearsal dinner and accused them of rape and collusion. I guess I might steer clear of me, too.

I finally find someone who doesn't cower from me when I draw close, a twenty-something girl, alone, with a dark brown shag haircut and a half-drunk clueless gaze. She clutches an empty beer bottle. Definitely not one of the Renauxes' inner sanctum.

"Do you know what's going on?" I ask quietly.

"I'm not really sure," she says, breathing beer into my face. "Someone came out and told us there were delays and that we should all drink and be merry. I think it was Emma's dad, but I honestly don't know." Her eyes flicker over Max, and her voice drops to a scandalous whisper. "I don't know if anybody else heard it, but I thought I heard screams downstairs. I think that's why they had the band start playing so loud. Just to drown out all the screaming."

"*Jesus,*" Andy hisses. "Get down there. *Go.*"

I back away from the girl and Max, searching for the way downstairs. "It's not her," I whisper, trying to calm Andy down. "I'm sure it's not her."

"Not who?" Max asks, trailing after me.

"No, nothing," I mutter. "I just . . . I need to get downstairs."

"Are you kidding?" Max says. "You can't go down there while they're fighting. And by the way, *who* are they again? And what are we doing at this weird-ass wedding? I think I deserve an answer now." His voice takes on an edge. "Seriously."

"Theo, *GO.*" Andy's voice crackles, reverberating through my skull. I cup my left ear and stumble back two more steps from Max.

"I'll—I'll explain it all to you in a minute," I say. "I just to need to find the bathroom." I'm still backpedaling. Suddenly there's a burst of static in my ear, and I bump into a middle-aged couple on the dance floor. I freeze in place, straining to listen to Andy.

"Theo, I can't . . . something hap—Just keep . . ."

"Theo, what the hell is going on?" Max demands, staring at me along with the couple I've just bumped into.

I turn and bolt for the stairs. The music from the orchestra fades as I clatter down the steps, and I can hear something else now, a kind of wailing. A woman sobbing. Static crackles again in my ear, and I grab the sides of my dress to keep from falling.

I leap down the stairs in twos and threes on my never-before-worn wedding shoes. The banister saves my life twice before I spill into a long white hall with doors on both sides.

Now the wailing fills the air. There is no worse sound in the world.

"Oh, God, that's her," Andy says, suddenly loud and clear again. "That's Sarah's voice. Theo, hurry."

I force myself to run—around a corner down another hall and through an open doorway. And then I see them.

Emma Renaux is in a strapless Vera Wang gown, a long train bunched around her feet. She leans tearfully on her brother's shoulder as he comforts her with a hug. She spots me and looks up. Then Tyler looks up, too, and the three of us freeze.

I have made a mistake. I've made a terrible mistake.

"How did you get down here?" Tyler snarls.

"Theo," says Andy, "I think I remember . . ."

I shake my head. I can't focus on Andy right now.

"Who let you down here?" Tyler demands. "Who let you in?"

Emma takes one last look at me and rushes into a dressing room, slamming the door behind her. Tyler starts to advance. His beady eyes blaze with the same rage I saw last night.

Oh, shit. *Shit, shit, shit.* I whirl around and launch myself back down the hall, swinging around the corner and racing up the stairwell.

"Hey!" he barks, breaking into a run. "Hey, psycho!" His gruff voice echoes up the steps. “I told you to stay the hell away from here!”

“Mr. Wyatt invited me!” I shout back pointlessly.

I reach the top and bolt out into the deafening *rat-a-tat-tat* of a drum solo. The horn section hits its final chord to “In the Mood,” and they start right up with the next song. A slow ballad this time, which just makes it easier to hear Tyler’s heavy stomping. Two of Tyler’s Boarding Stools are hanging by the entrance, my escape route, nursing beers. They see me, so I turn back around, but Tyler is already on the dance floor, snaking his way through the crowd.

Without thinking, I take off for the circular hall that runs along the perimeter of the ballroom, bumping my way through a flock of guests who shower me with hateful glances. I’m ruining this wedding more than it’s already been ruined, but for no justifiable reason, some tiny part of me is, I don’t even know what to call it, relieved? Why am I relieved?

“Andy,” I pant into my collar, cupping my ear. “Andy, are you still there? You said you remembered something? What did you remember? Talk to me.” All I can hear is heavy, labored breathing. But is it in my head, or is it coming through my left ear? Is it me, or is it Andy? “Please, Andy, if you—” I slam into someone and let out a yelp.

“Whoa!” Max catches me in his arms. “It’s just me, just me.”

“Max.” My muscles go lax.

“Did you find a bathroom?” he asks suspiciously.

“I . . . did.” My eyes dart around the hall and spot possible salvation: a pair of glass terrace doors. I drag Max after me without looking over my shoulder. Blinding sun and a gust of wind hit us as we step through the doors to an outdoor patio. I quickly close them, grab Max’s lapels, and place him directly in front of the glass, hiding my body behind his tall frame. Then I flatten myself against him like a human shield. My arms cling to his waist under his jacket, chest pressed against his stomach, face pressed against his chest.

"Theo, what are you doing?" Max asks. I can almost feel his fingers hovering over my back, trying not to touch me. "Is this a test?"

"Shhh," I whisper. "Just be quiet."

The seconds tick by. I strain my ears, listening for Tyler and his bros. Nothing. The seconds stretch on, marked by the gentle rise and fall of Max's chest. Andy is silent. The sun warms the back of my neck, and the wind cools it down. I can hear the clarinets crooning faintly from the ballroom. It actually brings me some peace. I open my eyes just a crack, peek over my shoulder, and realize for the first time where Max and I are standing. I can see the entire front lawn of the Harbor Café.

This is the balcony that overlooks the river. We're standing at the very spot where all those newlyweds posed for their classic shot. I'm in my wedding gown, and Max is in his suit. He's pressed against me, and somewhere along the way, he'd let his long fingers rest on my back. And somewhere along the way, I guess we'd begun to sway to Glenn Miller's "Moonlight Serenade."

And I let us stay that way. At least for a few more seconds. Because Max understands something that very few guys understand. He knows when not to speak.

But he's not the only one. Andy has gone silent, too. I picture him at home—waiting, impatient. I pull away from Max, and then . . . the horror.

There's a beige stain running down the center of his silver tie. All of my concealer. *All* of it melting down his tie like a glob of wet putty.

I'm bathed in sweat from all the running I did up and down those stairs. All that running from Tyler and his friends.

"Oh, God." I rip myself from Max's arms and cup the left side of my face in my palm.

"Thee, what's wrong? Why do you keep doing that?"

"Doing what?"

"Holding your face like that. You're kind of freaking me out."

"Just give me your tie," I say with a crack in my voice. "I'll clean it off."

He looks down at his tie. "Whoa, what is that? Makeup?"

"Just give me the *tie,* please." I hold out my right hand, keeping the left pressed to my face.

"Thee, your makeup doesn't bother me."

"Don't, Max. Don't do that."

"Do what? Please don't get so upset."

"Oh, right, because what's the big deal? Because I look *fine,* right? What could possibly be more stunning than a giant gash on your—"

I go silent and strain to listen through the wind.

"Theo . . ."

I press my hand over his mouth.

There's been a sudden change in the music. The band has stopped playing Glenn Miller, and a new song has begun.

The prelude music.

A string quartet is playing the opening prelude to the bridal processional. They're starting the ceremony.

"Shit, we're missing it," Max says.

But I'm already running.

HOW CAN THEY BE starting? How can they possibly be going through with this wedding after all that crying and screaming? No, this is all wrong.

I'd raced back to the ballroom and found the guests piling into the lofty chapel room next door, rushing to take their seats. Now the processional music wafts over my shoulders as the priest enters from the archway at the back. He's pudgy, white-haired, and cherubic. He reeks of happiness. Am I the only one that sees through his forced smile?

He walks down the aisle, stepping carefully onto the altar in his unassuming gray suit. Wedding etiquette dictates that he should have entered from the side with the groom and his best man, but something tells me Emma and Lester want to make a statement. Something tells me they'll be marching in together now.

It's all wrong. All of it.

"Crap. Now *I've* got to go to the bathroom," Max whispers.

I nod. Maybe he wants to bolt. I can't blame him if he does.

Once he's gone, I sweep the crowd and whisper quietly into the button cam. "Andy? Do you see her yet? She has to be here; this is our best shot."

No reply.

I spot Helena and the four other K.O.P. ambassadors seated on the other side of the aisle. Helena waves a hand to beckon me over. She saved a seat for me, but I shake my head and mouth, "I can't. I'm with someone."

Her eyes narrow. She clearly has no idea what I'm trying to communicate.

I turn away from her.

"Andy?" I whisper again.

Nothing but that heavy breathing in my ear.

A seemingly endless supply of groomsmen and bridesmaids enter two by two, arm in arm. It is so long and slow and painful.

I hear footsteps behind me. Max's return.

I can't talk to Andy with Max glued to my side. I try to think of a polite way to shake Max off, but a collective "Awwww" from the crowd snaps my attention back to the processional.

The flower girls have begun their trip down the aisle. Two of them, no older than six, a blonde and a brunette. Each wears a silvery princess dress; each sneaks a smile at the adoring older faces on either side, taking care to do what she practiced, walking slowly.

The blonde pulls red rose petals from her basket and sprinkles them across the runner like fairy dust. The brunette follows behind with white petals, but it feels as if she's scattering ashes. Something breaks loose in my stomach. It's not a pang or a twinge this time; it's a spasm, an excruciating cramp, like I've swallowed a shard of glass.

That piercing tone fills my ear again—high-pitched and constant like feedback. Is it in my head? Is it the buggy earpiece? I crush my palm to my ear and turn away from the flower girls. This wedding is all wrong. Why am I the only one that sees it?

I hurry away from Max, leaving him baffled and angry for the thousandth time—but I stop dead in my tracks when I hear Andy's voice. "Theo, I remember now."

"Andy?" I whisper, crouching down in the corner.

"I'm here," Andy says.

"You're at the wedding?" I whisper in shock.

"I'm at the shelter. I'm in Room Nine."

"What are you talking about? You were supposed to stay in my—"

"I remember everything now. I remember them lying together in that bed. I remember him crushing the life out of her, choking her till she couldn't breathe."

Now *I* can't breathe.

"He just ripped them apart," he says. "He ripped them all to pieces, and no one's ever going to find them. They've fallen through the cracks. They're all buried under the floor, burning."

"Who's burning?"

"We can't let it happen to another girl, Theo. Do you understand? Tell me you understand."

"No, I *don't* understand."

"We can't let it happen to another girl. That's why it has to burn."

In panic, I rise up from the floor. "Andy, whatever you're doing, *stop*." I'm done with the whispers. They don't matter if he's doing what I think he's doing.

"It's what has to happen, Theo. You know it, too. You know this is what happens."

"Andy, listen to me, don't! Please, just don't!"

He's gone silent. So has the processional music. I spin around and see three hundred pairs of accusatory eyes. Emma has stepped out into the chapel room. And of course, there's that other pair of eyes—closer, uncomprehending, deep blue—trying to figure out what has happened to his friend.

I wish I could explain it all to Max, but now is not the time. Right now, I need to do what I've always done. I run.

ANDY IS SILENT ON the cab ride over; the line of communication appears to be severed. But there's no smoke billowing from K.O.P.'s windows, thank God. I smack the dusty buzzer five times—

Delores opens up. She looks alarmed and opens her mouth to say something, but I push past her, sniffing for fumes in the lobby. Nothing yet. Just the pungent odor of fresh paint. Mac isn't at his security station. Maybe he's at the wedding? It doesn't matter—it gives me a straight shot through the lobby without breaking my stride.

"Helena forgot her glasses!" I holler at Delores. I doubt Helena wears glasses, and I doubt Delores cares, but I'm through to the dorms. The rooms fly past as if in a countdown: thirteen, twelve, eleven . . .

"Andy!" I shout. "I'm here!" I give my deadened legs one last push and burst through the door of Room Nine. "Stop it!"

The room is empty.

I'M NOT SURE HOW long I stand there. My lungs are heaving; I'm dizzy; my feet are killing me in these shoes. But Room Nine hasn't changed since the last time I was here. It's the same dismal, empty shell: stained twin mattress, desk, dresser, mirror on the wall, that ugly blue throw rug on the floor. A mournful excuse for light trickles in from the tiny barred window by the ceiling.

There are no signs of Andy, no signs of any fire.

But I feel that weight again. First in my chest, then in my head, then in my quivering legs. The ceiling is threatening to come down, to smother me and everyone else here.

They're all buried under the floor, burning.

I turn to the floor, and my eyes fix on the blue rug—the one thing that made this room different from Helena's.

I bend over to take a closer look. There are thick metal staples all along its edges. It's fastened to the floor. I drop to my knees and dig my fingers under the edges, using the strength I have left to rip it loose, staple by staple. The feedback grows louder in my ear with each violent tug. It is a deafening assault by the time I toss the rug aside.

I almost expect to find a trapped door.

I don't. But I see why someone wanted this patch of floor covered. It is pockmarked with tiny stains—messy droplets, almost black. Dried blood? There is a sea of wild scratches in the wood, vicious and unhinged. But floating in the middle of that sea is a group of scratches clear enough to form words.

MY NAME IS NOT SARAH. MY NAM

I remember what Helena said. She said some of the girls didn't even give their real names when they came to K.O.P. She said Mr. Wyatt gave them temp names. Like stray dogs at the pound . . .

"Are you pure?" Andy whispers in my ear.

I stiffen. "Andy!" I shout. "Where are you?"

"Are you *pure*?" he asks again.

"What do you mean? Andy, if you're here, just tell me what the hell is going on! Who is Sarah? What happened to her?"

As soon as I'm done yelling, I hear shuffling in the hallway: doors opening, the sound of murmuring female voices. That was not smart.

I hear a man shouting from the lobby. "Which way did she go, Delores?" his deep voice demands. It isn't Mac.

"To Helena's room, I think?" Delores calls back, uncertain. "I thought she was authorized, no?"

"It's fine." The voice is closer now.

"I'm sorry, Mr. Wyatt," Delores calls to him.

Mr. Wyatt? He followed me here from his own wedding?

"Down that hall," Wyatt calls out. "Room Ten."

"This way?" another voice asks.

The color drains from my face. That voice I know. It belongs to Tyler.

"Yeah," Wyatt calls back. "I'm right behind you."

I pull off my shoes and scurry out of the room, away from the lobby, past two more wide-eyed girls peeking through their doors, past a dilapidated TV room, and mercifully find a back stairwell. *The office,* I think desperately. Wyatt's office is on the second floor. If Andy can get in through that window, then I can get out.

"She's taking the stairs," Wyatt calls out. "This way."

Shit, shit, shit.

They're gaining on me, and all I can think about is that disgusting phrase. *Are you pure?* It makes me so nauseated and dizzy that I trip on the landing between the two floors and double over. I'm going to puke all over the steps.

Breathe, I tell myself. *Keep moving.*

I straighten up and try to climb the second story, but pain seizes my stomach like I've swallowed another shard of glass. I collapse on the landing, shrinking into the fetal position as my eyes tear up. The stairwell door opens beneath me. Determined footsteps come pounding up the steps. And then I can feel him hovering over me.

"Jesus, Theo, what happened?"

Lester Wyatt's deep voice. Talking to me as if I know him. I look up through watery eyes. His face . . . I know it, but I don't. I swipe the tears away, but he's still a blur. Alien but familiar. Like someone I once knew. Like if I were beamed into the past, I'd know every inch of his face by heart.

The room grows brown around the edges, flickering out like a dying bulb.

"Theo?" His voice calls to me from further away, cutting in and out with the light. "Theo, can you hear me?"

I try to force myself to stay conscious for one last look. I take in his crow's-feet, the creases in the forehead . . . and that's when the face clicks.

His name falls from my lips as I watch him fade to black. "Andy?"

Chapter Sixteen

The rumble of the road wakes me before I open my eyes. I slowly pull my eyelids apart and see lights of the city race past through a car window. I'm in a car. A nice car. The seats are plush leather. A Mercedes, maybe? In the front passenger seat.

I catch a fleeting glimpse of a street sign. East Houston. I press my palms deep into my aching eye sockets. Then I turn and see his hands on the steering wheel. (Yes, it is a Mercedes.) I follow along the sleeves of his tuxedo jacket, past his broad shoulders, past his black bow tie, and finally to his face.

The ski-slope nose, but with fewer freckles. The blond hair, but shorter and darker and more conservative. The perfect skin, but not so vibrant and smooth. The chestnut eyes, but housed inside lids that have taken more stress and strain. Eyes that have since lost their boyish beauty.

The boy is gone. Now there's only the man. Andy Reese, nine or ten years into the future.

Is that where I am? Is that what this is?

"Is this the future?" I'm in such a fog I actually ask the question aloud—to myself or to him, I don't even know.

"She finally wakes," he says, keeping his eyes on the road. His smile is the exact same, even with those faint little lines around his mouth. But the voice is deeper now, with less of the Texan twang. "How's your head?" he asks. "I think you took a pretty bad bump when you hit the floor. What were you doing there? Why did you run to K.O.P.?"

A bump on the head? Could that explain it? I'm Dorothy, and the black interior of this Mercedes is my Oz? East Houston Street is my yellow brick road? Strange Future Andy is my Scarecrow, scaring the shit out of me? But why? Why would I dream Andy as an older man? Why would I turn him into Lester Wyatt?

No. Never mind all that "am-I-dreaming?" crap. People know when they're awake and they know when they've been dreaming. Confusing the two is just an excuse for David Lynch movies and stoner conversations at a late-night Denny's.

"Theo?" He shoots another glance at me, his grip tightening on the wheel. "How are we doing over there? You want to tell me why you ran back to the shelter? You want to talk about it?"

"Back?" I mumble. I rub my throbbing temples. "I'm sorry, I don't . . . I don't understand what's happening."

"It's okay," he says. "It's okay. I know there's been way too much drama today. It's been a hellish day for us all."

"No, I mean *you*. Who are you? Delores called you Mr. Wyatt, but you look just like . . . Why are you so old?"

His eyes widen. "I'm *thirty*," he says, sounding offended. "That is not old. Anyway, you look a hell of a lot older than the last time I saw you."

"When was that?"

His laugh dies off. "You don't remember?"

Static suddenly invades my left ear. "Theo . . . Theo, can you . . . me?"

It's Andy. The *real* Andy—I think? Finally speaking to me again. Our FaceTime call never dropped. My earpiece is still lodged in my ear. I didn't lose it when I hit the floor. My button cam is still feeding video to Andy's phone. He can still see what I see.

"Theo, you need to get out of that car. You need to get out right now. That's him. That's the face I couldn't remember. Lester Wyatt, just like I told you. He's sick in the head."

"Andy?" I press down on the earpiece. "Andy, where are you?"

"I'm right here," Wyatt says gently. "I'm right here, Theo."

"No, not you. *Andy.*"

"I'm Andy," Wyatt says, half amused and half concerned.

I shake my head and try to back away in the seat, but I'm strapped in. The back of my head bumps the window. "No, you look like Andy, but you're Lester Wyatt."

"Right. Lester Andrew Wyatt."

"Lester Andrew . . . ?"

"You think I would have made it through puberty if I'd gone by Lester?" he says. "No way. My life would have been at least twenty percent shittier."

"Theo, listen to me—"

"Shut up, Andy!" I yell into my collar. "You're the one who was talking about burning the place down!"

Wyatt slams on the brakes, veering to a screeching halt on Elizabeth Street. My neck nearly snaps as I'm thrown forward against my seat belt and back against the seat.

For an excruciating moment, all is still. I stare at Lester Wyatt or Future Andy or whoever the hell he is. He turns off the ignition and closes his eyes. His jaw twitches. He takes a deep breath, opens his eyes, and turns to me. "I wanted to talk to you alone, because I really thought we could share something today. Just you and me. But you're obviously not well. You're obviously having a problem separating reality from fantasy."

"No, the only problem I have is you," I whisper. "I can't explain you."

"You can't 'explain' me?" He squints. "You mean, like how old I am? Is that what you can't explain?"

My silence is the only answer he needs. A layer of sweat dribbles down my neck, dampening the back of my dress.

"Theo, what year is this?" he asks.

I know the answer. It's 2015. Of course, it's 2015. But I still have a seed of doubt. No, it's more than a seed. There's a whole cloud of doubt drizzling rain into the cracks and the gutters in my head. I can see it in his haughty, silver-flecked eyes: If I give him the wrong answer, he'll think I'm crazy. He'll think *I'm* the one that's sick in the head. It's almost like he *wants* me to give him the wrong answer.

"Jesus, just answer him!" Andy pleads. "Answer him and get out."

"Theo, I'm not trying to upset you, all right?" Wyatt forces my eyes to meet his. "Just give me a year."

"Just tell him it's 2003 and get out of the car!"

"What?" I breathe into my collar.

"Just tell me what year it is," Wyatt repeats.

"Jesus, Theo, how far gone are you? It's 2003. The year is 2003."

"No, Andy. No, it's not."

"What's not?" Wyatt asks. "You know what? Let's forget about the year."

He reaches for his seat belt. Dread overcomes me, and I take my chance. I flip up the lock, tug the lever and swing open the door.

MY BARE FEET CAN only last until Mulberry Street. I find an alcove under a front stoop and climb down the steps, balling myself up, hiding myself away—from Andy, from the world at large. For the very first time in my life, I think I might be legitimately insane. Is Andy so far gone that he thinks it's 2003? Or am I so far gone that I don't know it's 2003? Or maybe . . .

Crouched in this damp corner, rocking back and forth, I can't help but think of all those nights in my room, huddled in the exact same position, listening to the Beatles over and over. *"Number nine . . . number nine . . ."*

I think of all the overwhelming emptiness in that room, the bone-rattling pressure, the lack of oxygen, like some kind of black hole. But maybe not a black hole. Maybe a wormhole? Maybe I'm the one who's fallen through the cracks? I've fallen through a crack in time, a tiny crevice where two timelines overlap—where eighteen-year-old Andy and thirty-year-old Andy coexist. Because he *is* Andy—the man I just escaped,

Lester Andrew Wyatt. He's not a dream, he's not the Scarecrow, he's not an impossibly identical older brother or anything other than the same man. The boy and the man: two separate people, but one and the same.

I pull my phone from my dress pocket, but gently, keeping it plugged into the button cam. "Andy? Andy, are you still there?" No reply. "Andy, you saw his face, I know you did. You keep saying he's the one that did it, but he's *you,* can't you see that? Help me understand it."

Dead silence.

I open my browser and type in "Lester Andrew Wyatt."

The first hit is a website for K.O.P. The second is Wyatt and Emma's wedding announcement. The third is something I very much wish I'd seen seven days ago.

HEROIC TEEN LOSES GIRLFRIEND IN FIRE

It's an article from *The New York Times,* dated Monday, September 2, 2003.

Heroic teen . . .

I remember something Helena said about Mr. Wyatt at the bridesmaids' party: "It's totally true what everyone says about him. He really is an honest-to-God *hero,* you know?"

The article's microscopic text starts at the bottom of the page, but the near-full-screen photo tells me the whole story.

It's a photo of Andy Reese, perched on the back of an ambulance. An EMT is draping a gray blanket over his shoulders as he stares into a sea of black smoke. It's my Andy Reese, the Lost Boy. In a picture from twelve years ago. Even on a four-inch screen, the look in his eyes breaks my heart. It's like I'm there with him, feeling all his pain as he stares at that burning building.

That fire must have taken her life.

Sarah is gone. Long gone. She died in 2003, I know it in my heart. But Andy doesn't know it. He still hasn't let her go. He's still trying to find her.

Never mind all my time-traveler nonsense. I think I know what he is now.

I scroll down to pinch open the article, but droplets of water splash across the screen. I cover it and look up to the sky for signs of rain, but it's a clear and cloudless night. Of course it's not rain. I should know that by now. It's not the thick layer of sweat on my face, either. The droplets are my tears. I wipe the screen and my eyes with the hem of my dress.

"*There* you are."

Lester Andrew Wyatt stands over me, at the top of the tiny staircase. He's taken off his bow tie and unbuttoned his collar. Aside from that, his tux is as crisp as ever. He must have ditched the car and chased after me on foot.

I stare at all the changes in his face. This man has seen so much more than the boy I know. His eyes have lost all of Andy's innocence. In that moment, I know I believe Andy. *My* Andy. But then, wasn't he the one I heard whispering those nauseating words?

Are you pure?

My brain is beginning to fry. This is all too much. There are too many pieces that don't fit, too many pieces that break the rules of logic and reason.

Wyatt reaches down to me. "Come on, Theo, let's get you back in the car, okay?"

I nod and allow him to help me out of the hole I've crawled into.

Then I whirl and kick him, barefoot, in the crotch.

As he doubles over, I sprint down the street. I'll find a bus. I'll find a cab driver who won't be scared off by a scar-faced, barefoot Elvis impersonator in drag. I'll tell him to take me to the only safe place I know.

WHEN MAX OPENS THE door, I fall right into his arms. If my incessant pounding (not to mention another disappearance) bothers him, he chooses not to show it.

"Oh, God, *Thee.*" He tightens his embrace as I bury my scarred cheek in his chest. He's still wearing his dress shirt and pants, but the tie with half of my face on it is thankfully long gone.

"Max, I need a session. Like, real bad. And a bed. Or a couch. Or a crib."

He pulls my arm around his neck like he's dragging me from battle. My feet don't even touch the ground as he carries me swiftly to his room.

"What happened to you?" he asks as I float.

"Too much," I say.

He sweeps up my legs and cradles me, and I don't even resist. I just want to be lowered onto my rightful spot on his bed.

"Max, I'm sorry," I mumble. "I'm sorry about the way I ran off. That was very unprofessional of me. I can explain in the session."

"It's okay," he says, "but this might not be the best time for a session."

"Why? No, I don't even care. I just need to close my eyes for a minute. Just put me down on my spot."

But when we get to the foot of his bed, I see that my spot has been taken.

By Lou.

She pops up to her knees on the bed, her face slack with shock. I'm drenched in sweat, there's street soot all over my dress, my feet are blackened and blistered, and I have a generally unconscious demeanor. I don't blame her for being frightened. "What the hell happened?" she asks, her eyes flashing to Max.

"Too much," he replies, gently laying me down at the foot of the mattress.

I lie back. Max and Lou lean in; their faces hover overhead like two pessimistic surgeons. Lou is fully clothed in one of her New-Lou floral skirts and a form-fitting black tank top, but despite all the insanity and confusion swishing around my brain, I can't help asking. "Were you two just in bed together? Not that I have any problem with—"

"No," they bark in unison.

Lou looks at Max and nods.

"I called her because I was worried," Max explains.

"We *both* were worried," Lou stresses.

"We just needed to clear some things up," Max says. "Lou told me what she thought was going on with you and me."

"And I owe you a big apology, Thee," Lou says.

"I told her you thought the letter was for Mike—"

"Mike DeMonaco!" Lou laughs incredulously. "You must have thought I'd lost my mind! But then I remembered our talk about how stripper-pole obvious I was being. I thought you meant it was obvious that I was trying to make Max jealous by draping myself all over Mike."

"The point is, *no*," Max says. "No, we were most definitely *not* in bed together. I mean, we were physically *in* the bed, but not—"

"Forget it," I moan to the ceiling. "I'm just glad you're both here. I need you both here." Summoning what little energy I have left, I reach out and grab their hands, squeezing firmly, feeling for one fleeting moment that glorious sensation of not being alone. But like I said . . . fleeting.

"Thee?" Lou leans closer. "Are you crying?"

"Probably," I say. I blink. I feel wetness on my cheeks. So yes, I am crying.

Max drops down on his knees next to me. "Okay, that's it," he says, wiping away my tears with his thumb. "You have to tell us everything. For real this time, Thee. Everything. I told Lou about your freak-out at the wedding, and she told me about this Andy guy—this new documentary subject. Was that Andy's wedding we were at?"

I try to smile through my tears. "Yes and no," I say. "It depends on which Andy you mean." My eyes move from side to side, watching their expressions.

"Are there . . . two Andys?" Lou asks hesitantly. Her eyes flash to Max again.

I hold my breath, waiting. I just need Andy to say something in my ear. Anything. I've kept my earpiece. I've kept my button cam feeding into my phone, but I haven't heard a peep since I bolted from the car. I just hope he can hear my next question and maybe begin to understand.

"Do you guys believe in ghosts?" I ask, forcing my eyes to stay open.

They share another inscrutable glance. "Maybe," Lou says.

"Better question: do you think you have to be dead before you can be a ghost? I mean, do you think a younger version of someone could be a ghost, even if his older self is still alive? Because I think that's what's happening. I think I've been with the ghost of Andy's younger self, and we've spent all this time trying to find someone he's never going to find."

This elicits no response. No answer, not even an attempt to try to maybe look for an answer.

I stare up at them. They stare back.

My body is shutting down—demanding sleep in return for everything I've put it through. I ride that fine line between mumbling to my friends and mumbling in my sleep. "He still thinks it's 2003. He knows something happened to her, but he can't remember what. He can't let go of her. So he just keeps waiting. Every day, waiting and waiting for her to come back. And isn't that really what a ghost is? A spirit who refuses to let go, who refuses to stay in the past?" I allow my eyes to close. "Andy, if you can hear me, please say something. Do you understand what I'm telling you? You have to let her go."

"Theo," Max's voice chimes in gently, "it's going to be okay. You just need to sleep. Just let yourself sleep for a while, okay?"

Warm darkness begins to carry me away. But I can still hear them. They think I'm already asleep, but I can still hear their voices.

"God, you're right," Lou mutters. "She's hallucinating."

"I know," Max says. "It's bad. She needs help."

"I knew something was weird when she told me about the

Andy thing," Lou says. "Jesus . . . ghosts," she adds sadly. "She thinks she spent the last week with a ghost."

But I did. Lou, you know me. You have to trust me. Just check the footage. Check the footage on my phone, and you'll see him. You'll see he's the same as he was in 2003. He hasn't aged a day in twelve years.

"I wasn't sure until she said that thing about the gash," Max says. "I'm telling you, she thinks she still has some kind of cut on her face. Or a scar or something."

What are you talking about? Of course I have a scar.

"Oh, God, that's why she got her hair cut like that," Lou gasps. "To cover her face. That's why she's been wearing all that makeup. That's why she keeps pulling her hair down like that."

What are you guys talking about? You know I have a scar. Why are you pretending? I need to force those words from my mouth, but I can't. I'm fading. It's like counting backward from ten when they prep you for an operation on the surgical table. You don't remember losing consciousness; you just . . . slip away.

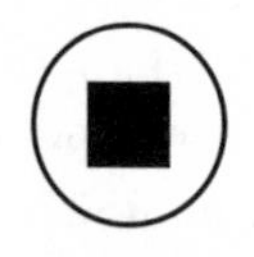

Chapter Seventeen

I woke to the sun burning my eyes. My throat was parched. I could hardly swallow. I pulled the sheet up over my head and caught a familiar whiff of Tide detergent.

This is my bed. How did I get back to my bed? How long did I sleep? Is it the next day?

I threw the sheet off my head and sat up, scowling in the glare. My mouth felt cottony.

I was still in my wedding dress, now gone the way of the funeral dress: stained with dirt and sweat, crushed in ugly folds, the collar drooping down like two withered daisy petals. All that was missing was the puke. I was '70s Elvis impersonator in drag after a night in prison.

Who brought me back home?

I looked over at my coffee table and saw Andy's loaner phone, right where I'd left it before the wedding. Had he come back to my room last night? Was he the one who brought me home?

Closet. Check the closet.

I felt so many kinds of unpleasantness when I stepped out of bed. The sting of my blistered feet, shooting pain in my shins, dizziness from standing upright. But I shambled to the closet door and threw it open. Nope. Nothing but stacks and stacks of Sunday *Times*. Andy had abandoned his nest.

I sat down on my couch to get a better look at his phone,

but when I landed, I saw *my* phone next to his, propped against a stack of composition notebooks. A Post-It was pasted to the screen.

PLAY ME IF YOU WANT THE TRUTH.

I knew the handwriting; it was Max's. Had he brought me here? He must have had a very good reason for swiping the phone from my dress pocket while I'd been passed out. Maybe Andy . . .

Oh, please don't let it be some kind of final message. Don't let this be Andy's last goodbye.

I could sit there for another hour speculating, or I could just press PLAY.

The jittery white screen comes to life. It's blank, white. A shade of white I can't recognize at first. Not white paint, not a cloud, not a ceiling, not a piece of paper. It's as pale as tissue paper, but with pink undertones. It's not flawlessly smooth like paper, but imperfect and textured, almost like . . .

Flesh. Oh, God, it's human flesh.

I shrink farther into the couch as the camera zooms out. I don't want to see any more. I want to press STOP. I know it's a body. I can tell by the skin that it's female. Hairless, smooth, female flesh. How old is this video? Is this Sarah? Some dreadful swath of her body, stripped naked?

No, it's a cheek. A pale white cheek.

The camera pulls out farther to reveal an ear, and then strands of dark hair pulled behind the ear, and then finally a face.

I know the face, but I don't.

It's my face. It's the left side of my face, couched in my

pillow, lit up bright white by the sun as I sleep. But it can't be the left side of my face. There's no scar. There's a tiny pink nick just below the ear. That's the only blemish. Not even a zit. Just smooth, sunlight-deprived skin. *My* skin. This must have been taken before I was disfigured, before The Night in Question.

The shot zooms out farther still.

I stop breathing. I'm wearing my filthy wedding dress. This was filmed this morning. The camera swings over to reveal Max and Lou. Lou holds the camera as they stare into the lens together.

"Thee, I hope this works," Lou whispers, careful not to wake me.

"If it works," Max says, "then please come out into the living room. And remember, we all love you. I mean, not like—"

"Ugh, Max, you're a nightmare." Lou slaps his shoulder. "Don't make me shoot another take."

"Sorry," Max whispers. He looks back into the lens. "Sorry."

"Thee, we all love you," Lou says. "We just want to talk to you and make sure you're okay. I hope this helps you see things a little more clearly."

Her finger dives into the lens, and the clip ends.

I SAT THERE, MOTIONLESS, feeling just like Andy had so often looked. But I felt more than just lost. I felt behind. Like I was stuck on a satellite delay.

I stuffed the phone in my pocket and bolted for the bathroom mirror, half sick at the thought, half praying for it to be true. Could I wake up from a two-month nightmare and have the slate of horrors wiped clean? Like Dorothy clicking her heels? When I grasped the edge of the sink and leaned into the mirror . . .

It was still there. As huge and gory as ever. Maybe even worse than before. It was punishing me for even entertaining the notion. I couldn't understand it. I believed in video nine times more than I believed in myself; Lou knew that. She knew the words would have meant nothing to me, but the image meant everything. So why the hell was there no scar in the video? Who was the girl in the video? Who was the girl in the mirror? Something inside me roared to the surface, and I cried out. "Lou!"

There was a patter of footsteps, and she was through my bathroom door in seconds, her arms wrapping tightly around me. "I'm here," she said. "I'm right here."

"It's still there," I whimpered, clutching her back with one hand, pointing at the mirror with the other. I touched my face and felt only that smooth skin. "I mean, it's there, but it's not *here.* It's not . . . I don't understand what's happening."

Lou gently shushed me and caressed my matted hair like the mom I'd always wanted. "Thee, sweetie, it's okay."

Max appeared in the doorway but didn't cross the threshold. I waved him in urgently; I needed him, too. He swept us both into an embrace, and I rested my head between their shoulders. He was the one who'd carried me home. I was sure of it.

"Max, why is it here but not there? I don't understand."

"Thee, this happens," he said. "This happens to people all the time."

"What happens?"

"People get sick. They take too many meds, they stop sleeping, they see things, they hear things."

I lifted my head.

"Don't be scared, okay?" Lou said, her voice breaking. "You're just having a little problem separating reality from fantasy right now."

I swallowed. I'd heard those words before. I'd heard them out of Lester Wyatt's mouth. "Who told you that?" I demanded, shaking free of their dual hug. "Who said that to you?" I backed out of my bathroom.

Lou watched me back away, her eyes bleary and pleading. Her right hand was clenched in a fist. "Thee, please," she said meekly. "Please don't get mad at us."

If she didn't want me mad, then she shouldn't have quoted Lester Wyatt. I began to stammer. "You—you're saying I'm just 'imagining' the scar. I'm just dreaming it up out of thin air."

"Among other things," Max said.

"What is *that* supposed to mean?"

Lou held out her right hand, unclenching her fist. "This."

In her palm was my earpiece.

I brought my finger to my left ear. It was gone. It must have fallen to the floor in my sleep, and Lou must have found it.

"Was Andy talking to you through this?" Max asked. "Is that why you kept holding your ear at the wedding?"

"Yeah, I wired us for two-way com—"

"Thee, it's completely dead," Lou interrupted quietly. "I tested it. The circuitry is shot. I'm not sure if it ever worked. It's a piece of plastic. Unreliable junk, like Schaffler always says."

"No, it probably broke last night," I said. "There was static . . . It probably shorted out. You have no idea what I went through last night."

"No, I do," Lou said. "We watched all the footage."

"What footage?"

"All of it," Max said. "All the footage for your new doc. All the scenes."

"Ugh, thank *God*. Then you know I'm not crazy."

Both of them looked down at the bathroom floor.

"Stop that," I said. "Stop it." I ripped the phone from my pocket and searched the cloud drive for all my Andy files, picking one at random. Wednesday, September fourth. I hit PLAY . . .

A shaft of sunlight illuminates an empty chair. I recognize it instantly as one of the chairs from the Harbor Café.

"Andy," my voice says from behind the camera, "not that I saw you crying, but . . . why were you crying?"

There's no response from the empty chair. It is a long, boring, static shot. It's like watching one of those awful experimental Warhol movies. *"Chair,"* he might have called it.

"Who?" my voice asks the chair.

Beyond the silence, there's only the ambient sound of chitchat. At tables. On cell phones. Or on their Bluetooth headsets.

It was "Bluetooth or Psycho?" *One of Max's favorite games.* Three seconds to decide if the annoying dude yammering to himself is an asshole talking hands-free on his phone or a raving lunatic.

Everyone in that café thought I was the asshole. They assumed I was talking to my friend Andy on the hands-free. But they all had it wrong. I wasn't the asshole. I was—I am—the raving lunatic.

"Well, come on. She's not even an hour late," my voice tells the empty chair. "I'm assuming she's a 'Pretty Girl'?"

I can't take it. I mash my finger down on the STOP button.

I BEGAN SCROLLING WILDLY through my video gallery, scrolling up and down, mumbling, "No, no, no . . ."

"Thee," Lou said, stepping closer.

"No," I snapped. "No, just give me a . . . Just wait."

"Thee," Max said.

"*NO*, Max! Just . . ."

I picked another clip from the next day. Thursday, September fifth . . .

Another Warhol movie. *"Rainy Street,"* he might have called it.

The camera bounces up and down, left and right, but the star of the movie is rain. Pounding droplets, a shower drenching brownstones and leafy trees.

"That's ridiculous," my voice says from behind the camera. "There is no possible way you're camera shy."

I can't watch anymore. There's no need.

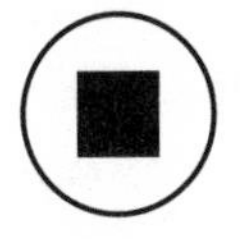

Chapter Eighteen

It's a unique moment, knowing that the two people whom you know best are scared shitless that they don't know you at all. And I loved them even more for letting me freak out in silence. Both of them. We stood there for I'm not sure how long. I glanced back toward the open closet. Andy's empty nest.

I wouldn't have seen the footage for days. Maybe even weeks. Not until it was time to edit. But I didn't even need the phone anymore. I had the playback in my head:

The way Emilio stared at us—at me—from across the street. He wasn't being a protective father figure; he was watching me, baffled, as I talked to thin air.

The bouncer at the Magic Garden who refused to acknowledge Andy's presence no matter what he said. The club rejects in the back alley who laughed as I talked to myself, swinging punches at no one. The way Max didn't see Andy when he ripped open the closet that night, even though he should have been impossible to miss.

No one had ever seen Andy Reese. Only me. I thought Emma and Tyler had seen him, what with the way they kept warning me to stay away. But they weren't talking about my Andy, were they? They were talking about Lester Andrew Wyatt, Emma's thirty-year-old fiancé. All this time, I'd been hiding Andy away from my mother and my friends for so many different reasons.

But there was really only one reason. I didn't want Andy to be seen because somewhere deep in the recesses of my brain I knew there was nothing to see. "Can I ask you guys something?" I whispered.

"Of course," they said at the same time.

"Was there even a Night in Question? Or did I make that up, too?"

Max put his hand gently on my shoulder. "Just come out to the living room," he said. "You need to talk to your mom."

"My mom?" I pulled back from him. "Why my mom?"

"We won't leave your side," Lou said. "Not for a second. But she has to be the one to tell you."

"Tell me what?" Anger simmered inside me again. Not at Max or Lou, of course. Anger at the notion that my sanity might depend in any way, shape, or form on my mother.

I was already three feet ahead of them, marching to my living room. But I stopped dead in my tracks when I saw the man in my stepstool's chair.

It wasn't Todd. It was Lester Andrew Wyatt.

HE'D LOST THE JACKET and tie, but he was still in his tuxedo shirt, unbuttoned at the collar, as if he'd never gone home last night. Finding him here, of all places, was a slap in the face. His expression was grim, matching that of my mother's, who stood beside him. Then I realized that the room was quite crowded, a virtual sea of grim faces.

Dr. Silver stood by the coffee table. Todd sat on our black leather couch, hand stretched out to my mother's. I'd never seen so much sadness in my mother's face, not even that morning when I'd come home to her tears and folk music. Her eyes were visibly swollen from crying.

Anger slowly gave way to fear. "Mom, what's going on?"

"I'm the one who asked Andrew to be here," she said, trying to hold back more tears. "We spoke last night after your friends brought you home. He thinks you're in trouble, and he thinks it's my fault. They all think it's my fault. And they're right. I've done something unforgivable. I thought it was the right thing. I thought . . . I don't know what I thought."

It was in my ear again: not so much feedback as a distant, wailing siren, warning of some approaching disaster. It was hard to hear my own words as I spoke. "What are you talking about?"

"I'm talking about Sarah," she said. Her voice cracked at the end in a choked sob.

Strange—at this moment, I missed the Ice Queen. I would have done anything to bring her back. But the Ice Queen was gone forever, like Andy.

I don't even know why I asked the next question, because the answer was dawning. Slowly at first, but quicker now, clawing its way up from under the floorboards in my head. "You know Sarah?"

Mom nodded again, sniffling, avoiding my eyes. "She's all I think about. She's all I've thought about every day and every night."

My mind flashed to those headphones. The big, chunky headphones I'd never seen Mom wear before. I thought of them coming loose from her MacBook as she rushed to hug me that morning, letting that syrupy-sweet folk song erupt in the dining room. How quickly she must have slammed the laptop shut to stop the music.

I bolted for her bedroom.

"What are you doing?" she called out. "Theodore, where are you going?"

Todd and Wyatt jumped to their feet, but I don't think they even knew why. They only knew what I knew: that there was something my mother didn't want me to see.

Her laptop was asleep on her bedside table—the clunky headphones lying next to it, plugged in. I flipped the laptop awake, tugged out the headphone cable, and plopped down on the bed. I went straight to iTunes, but there were no recently played files.

Not a music file or a video file. Then what?

A *slideshow.* It had to be a slideshow.

"Theodore, don't," Mom called to me as they all came rushing to the room. "Not like this."

I checked the recent slideshow files, and there was only one. A file simply titled "C." I clicked on it and thrust out my palm. The simple gesture somehow froze them all at the doorway. I slammed down the spacebar and played file "C."

The first image fades up slowly as that saccharine folk song fills the room. It's more than a snippet of the muffled song. Now I can hear every picked string of the banjo and every word those bubblegum Joni Mitchell wannabes are singing.

This is the garden of make-believe
A magical garden of make-believe
Where flowers chuckle and birds play tricks
And a magic tree grows lollipop sticks

It's not a folk song. It's a children's song. About a magical garden. The longer it plays, the more familiar it becomes. I know this song. The singers aren't wannabes at all. They're a pair of radiant, heartfelt voices singing to kids. So why does this song makes me physically ill?

The first picture floats across the screen. An old photo of my mother in a hospital bed. She's barely recognizable at first, so young, elated, and chubby-cheeked. She holds me, all pink, mushy, and newborn. A rugged individual with a stubbly, square jaw leans in next to her, his wide hand resting on one of my minuscule shoulders. He grins at the camera like a proud father.

Because he *is* my proud father. Probably no older than twenty. So handsome and so young, just like Mom always said. I've had exactly two images of his face to hold onto my whole life, but now I add a third and a fourth and more. As the photos travel across the screen, zooming and panning and cross-fading, my father shows up time and again. He and my mother are flushed with bigger and bigger smiles, as I grow older from slide to slide.

There's a shot of them holding my tiny hands as they walk/lift me through my earliest steps. A shot of them laughing uproariously in freeze-frame as I splatter his face with mashed peas from my high chair. A shot of me in a tiny ballerina tutu, twirling safely under his strong fingers. (When did I ever own a tutu?)

I know I should feel waves of joy seeing myself as a happy-go-lucky child with a bright and innocent smile. A child who still hasn't read any Dostoyevsky or Eugene O'Neill. A child with a father. But as I pass the age of four or five in the pictures, my features take an unexpected turn. I grow uneasy as the song plays on.

If you sing for me (la la-la-la-la-la)
I'll sing for you (lu lu-lu-lu-lu-lu)
If you cry for me (hu hoo-hoo-hoo)
I'll cry for you (boo hoo-hoo-hoo)
If you scream for me (Ahhhhhhhh!)

The girl in the pictures . . .

She's me, but she isn't me. She's another me. A me from an alternate universe. She has my dark hair and Cupid's-bow lips, but a sharper nose. My pale cheekbones, but better defined. She's the Pretty Girl version of me.

I watch her turn seven or eight, and my father is still in the pictures. There's a shot of her proudly presenting him with a colorful drawing, then a close-up of her artwork. It's a classic child's rendering of a nuclear family—father, mother, and daughter all lined up side by side, holding hands on a tree-lined street under a blue sky and a quarter yellow sun. She has signed her art in childlike print at the bottom right corner:

Cyrano Lane.

That was my sister's name. Cyrano Lane. The sister my mother never mentioned in my presence. The sister who only exists in a slideshow full of photos I have never seen until this moment. Cyrano—my obsession, my favorite character of all time, a character I've tried to portray all my life. Cyra for short. I know that instantly. Not Sarah, *Cyra.* I couldn't remember her name, but my mind had done its best to sound it out. *Cyra.* Because what girl would want to go through life named Cyrano? No, that's not true. Cyrano is a beautiful name. An unforgettable name. At least, it should have been.

I watch the slides as Cyra turns twelve or thirteen, and then a newborn baby makes her debut appearance, wrapped in a hospital blanket. There's a new pink ball of mush in my delighted mother's arms—a gift for my elated father and my older sister.

Cyra holds me up proudly to the camera, and we become the stars of all the photos. She holds me swaddled in a blanket in front of a colorful wall of old books. She pushes me down a long street of brownstones in my stroller. She holds a daisy out for me to sniff as we sit in a vast field of overgrown grass. She shows off her glistening blue-green Little Mermaid costume as I reach gleefully for one of her crepe-paper fins.

The song's final two lines echo through the room, and it sparks a memory. Not a distant memory, but a recent one. It's the couplet I saw at the bottom of that club's webpage:

So come on in without a fuss
'Cause the Magical Garden is waiting for us!

"The Magic Garden." Mom's voice drifts in from the present. "That show always stopped Cyra's crying when she was a baby. I think it was the way those two girls sang in unison." I don't want my mother to speak, but I need every word. "Cyra got so excited when they reran the show on Nickelodeon," she goes on. "She was too old by then—sixteen or seventeen—but she wanted to share it with her baby sister. She sat you down for every episode, tried to teach you all the songs. God, it always made you so happy, Theo."

The next song begins with a bouncy guitar. My head is spinning too fast—my whole body vibrating.

You don't need a key, so follow me
There are no locks on Story Box, on Story Box, on Story Box
The stories are here. They're all in here
From Crafty Fox to Goldilocks on Story Box, on Story Box
There are no locks on Story Box, on Story Box, on Story Box . . .

"You'd act out the stories together," Mom says now. "You *always* loved making up stories, Theodore. I think you got that from her."

Brain running too hot. I glance at my mother, but I miss some of the pictures. When I turn back, the whole family is posing for graduation photos. There are barely any shots of us from Cyra's high school days, and the next two pictures show me why.

Decked out in a beautiful white strapless dress, Cyra proudly holds up her diploma. Close-up of the diploma: it's from Phillips Exeter Academy. My sister went away to boarding school. The same boarding school as Emma Renaux and Lester Wyatt.

And right on cue, his photo appears. Andy Reese wears a totally uncharacteristic blue blazer and khakis. Cyra's arms are wrapped around his waist. Then all three of them are posing arm in arm: Cyra in the middle, Andy on her left, and a spritely little eighteen-year-old Emma Renaux on her right.

They were a threesome. Just like Lou, Max, and me, only not like us, because Cyra and Andy are so plainly in love.

The final Magic Garden song plays.

See ya, see ya
Hope you had a good, good time, da-dum
Hope you have a good, good morning, mm-hmm
Hope we get to see you again

The slideshow ends on a final image of Cyra, radiant in her white graduation dress, her diploma tucked safely under her arm. My gut tells me it was the last picture of her ever taken. Before the fire. Because there was a fire, wasn't there?

Heroic teen loses girlfriend in fire.

AFTER I RETURNED TO the living room, they waited. Six people standing there, wondering what I'd do. Encircling me.

I felt a hand on my back. Lester Andrew Wyatt's hand. I whirled around and saw a tear rolling down his cheek.

"That's the first time I saw any of that," he said, his voice choked with some sort of emotion, though I wasn't sure what. He leaned closer to my ear. "This is what I wanted. This is the moment I wanted us to share. Just a moment for you, me, and Cyra."

I couldn't believe he was crying and I wasn't. I had an overwhelming impulse to bat his hand away. I still wasn't sure what he was to me—not sure what was real or what I imagined or what I remembered.

I turned to my mother. "Why did you hide these from me?" I asked.

She brushed a crumpled tissue over her quivering lips. "I hide them from myself, too," she said. "I only take them out twice a year, on her birthday and on the anniv—I've never even put them on the computer before. I only kept prints, and I kept them hidden in my closet. But Todd found them. He made this slideshow for me and gave it to me on her birthday. I think he was hoping the music would do for me what it did for Cyra. September is always so hard."

The fall semester stress.

Todd didn't say a word. What could he say? He'd broken my

trust in a way that could never be mended. He'd gone all these years keeping my mother's secret.

I didn't feel shaky. I didn't even feel angry anymore. I mostly felt pity.

"Those pictures should have been in frames," I said to my mother. "They should have been in frames my whole life. I should have passed them in the hall every day. We should have looked at them together on every one of her birthdays."

"I know that now," Mom said, hiding her face behind the tissue.

"You erased her."

"No." She shook her head, knowing that was exactly what she had done.

"You did. You just . . . crossed her out."

"It was the only way I could function. It was a mistake."

I blinked slowly, still without a hint of tears. "Forgetting your umbrella at the restaurant is a mistake. Forgetting to say 'please' and 'thank you' is a mistake. But forgetting . . ." It got harder to find the words I wanted, but at least I found the words I needed. "You made me forget my sister. I see her in these pictures, but I don't remember her at all. I don't remember a thing about her."

"I don't think that's entirely true."

Ah, that weaselly voice could belong to only one man: Dr. Silver. It was perfect that he'd chosen that moment to finally chime in. "I think you may have recently begun to remember her, but you're having difficulty processing the trauma."

I glanced at my mom, at Todd, at Max, at Lou. All of them kept their eyes on Dr. Silver. "What trauma?"

Dr. Silver's eyes were on me. "Theo, do you have any memories of the fire?"

I frowned. Funny, I'd never seen him in anything but a striped dress shirt and khakis. Now he was wearing jeans and a red zip-up fleece. Nothing but the closely trimmed salt-and-pepper beard and glasses to prove he was the shrink in the room. He appeared to be waiting patiently. He'd have to wait until the end of time, because I had no memory of any fire.

On the other hand, I did remember something Andy had said to me. (Imaginary Andy, that is.) He said sometimes we don't even know what we've forgotten until people ask specific questions. Doctor Silver had asked a specific question. Maybe that was why I could feel the heat burning the lining of my stomach, making my face sweaty and flushed, making my (nonexistent) scar burn.

Andy had lost Cyra in a fire on September 1, 2003—that much I knew. But now I understood the missing piece.

I'd been there, too.

I dashed back into my mother's room, back to the laptop. Nobody said a word as I Googled Lester Andrew Wyatt again. I'd been such a harried basket case the first time. I'd been running barefoot through the streets, reeling from the discovery of two Andys, not even sure of the year. Tears had blurred the microscopic text on my iPhone screen, and Wyatt had been so close on my tail, I'd let a photo of the fire tell me the whole story. But now, I could actually read the text of the *Times* article.

Now I understood what made Lester Andrew Wyatt such a hero.

IT WAS JUST FOUR paragraphs. Four paragraphs that could have saved me from the past four days. Four paragraphs in the classic *Times* font that told the story of Sunday, September 1, 2003. The story of two eighteen-year-old do-gooders who were deeply in love.

Andy and Cyrano had just graduated from Exeter and had spent the summer helping to build a women's shelter on Parker Street called "Keeping Our Promise." It was a passion project funded by George Wyatt, Andrew's father.

Cyrano had simply wanted to give her five-year-old sister a tour on a beautiful Sunday morning. But the electrical work hadn't been fully completed, and a fire broke out in one of the rooms (I didn't have to guess which room). The three of them were trapped.

Wyatt spoke from behind my shoulder as I read the article. "Do you remember now?"

The answer was no. I knew this was the part where I was supposed to surrender to suggestion. *Yes, I remember now.* But I wouldn't. The fire was only part of what I'd forgotten. I'd forgotten my own sister. And some of the people hovering around me now were responsible for that.

"There was so much smoke," Wyatt said. "Everything was crumbling down. The walls, the ceiling . . . There was no way I could have gotten to both of you in time. "

I realized what he was trying to say and shut my eyes.

"Cyra knew," he said. "She knew it had to be you, Theo. She wouldn't even let me try another way—all she cared about was getting you out. By the time I went back for her, it was too late. The fire department was there by then. They tried to go back for her, but . . ."

I forced my eyes back open.

"Half the building was gone by the time they put it out," he said. "We kept what we could, but it took us two years to rebuild."

If half the building had burned to cinders, I couldn't imagine what had happened to my sister's body, and I didn't want to ask.

"Theo, we've all had a talk this morning," Dr. Silver said quietly. "Your mother and Andrew and Max and Louise and I. And I think I've pieced together what happened here."

Have at it, Dr. Silver. God knows I'm in the dark.

"You were only five," he said. "When a child that young endures something so traumatic, sometimes her only way to cope is to repress the memory—maybe even to repress all of her memories before that age. That surely could have been addressed in counseling. Someone could have helped you process those feelings, allowed you to grieve, but your mother . . ." He turned to Mom. "I'm sorry, Margaret, but I can't overstate this. You made a deeply misguided decision. Never to speak of

Cyrano again, to remove all her pictures, to move away from your home, to cut all ties with Andrew, and with Cyrano's father."

I could see the real story taking shape. She'd cut ties with *my father*, too. No doubt because he refused to go along with her "reset" approach. I bet he'd tried to contact me a bunch of times, but she'd shut him out at every turn. He must have given up at some point and just let her build our fictional little world without him in it. Maybe that's why she was always so afraid when the doorbell rang? Afraid my father would come back to wreck her fake, Cyra-less life with the truth.

Mom, of course, refused to look at me as Dr. Silver spoke. She couldn't look at anyone now.

"Cyra went off to boarding school when you were only a year old," he said. "You only saw her for summers and holidays, which I think made it that much easier for you to forget. But repressed memories tend to reemerge at some point. Usually there's some kind of trigger. It could have been as simple as a scent on the street, or a significant location, or a song."

"The slideshow," Mom said, nearly under her breath. "I played the slideshow the night of Cyra's birthday. That was the night Todd gave me the disc. I didn't even know what it was. I played it with the volume all the way up, but when it was over, I heard Theo screaming from her room." Now she finally looked at me. "I ran to your bedroom and found you writhing in your sleep. It was the worst nightmare I'd ever seen you have. You were thrashing around so violently that you fell out of bed before I could get to you. You rolled off the bed and knocked your face into that damn coffee table. You woke up for a second after the fall, and I asked you if you were all right, but you shooed me away and fell right back to sleep."

"Which night?" I asked. "Which night was that?"

"Cyra's birthday," Mom said. "June seventeenth."

June seventeenth. The Night in Question. I couldn't remember where I'd gone because I hadn't gone anywhere. I couldn't remember what had happened to me because nothing had really happened. Just a very bad dream that had shaken me out of bed and knocked me on my ass, leaving me sore as hell.

"I bought headphones to make sure you'd never hear the songs again," Mom said. "I swore to myself I'd never even look at the pictures again, but then I found your dress covered in sick that night, and I thought I'd lost you, too. I was sure of it—"

"Why didn't you *tell* me, Mom? Why didn't you talk about my dream the next day?"

"I was afraid. I didn't know if you'd wake up remembering the songs, remembering her. I was afraid we were about to have the conversation. I was waiting for you to say something. I saw that tiny nick on your face from when you hit the table. I thought for sure you'd ask about it, but you didn't say a word." Mom shook her head. "If you thought something terrible had happened to you, why didn't you tell me?"

Yeah, right. Like I was about to tell Meg Lane that all her years of overprotective insanity were justified. But at least I knew where the Ice Queen had come from. It was why neither one of us had said a word that morning. Because that was us. A few polite, disinterested questions at breakfast.

"For the record, it's not a tiny nick," I said. "It's huge. It's disgusting. Why am I seeing it if it's not there?"

Dr. Silver stepped toward me. "I found at least part of the answer in your bathroom." He reached into the pocket of his jeans and pulled out a prescription bottle. My bottle of Lexapro. "Theo, there's not even a quarter of the pills that should be in this bottle. Have you been taking more than I prescribed? Even more than twice as much?"

"I've been doubling up," I said defensively, ignoring the sudden attention from Max and Lou. "And I took some extras when I was anxious. To help calm me down."

He let out a sigh. "Theo, I made it clear that you had to take this medication strictly as prescribed. That much Lexapro wouldn't calm you down—if anything, it would do the opposite. Have you been feeling speedy? Agitated? Snapping all the time?"

Faster and meaner.

I stole a glance at Max and Lou. Their accusatory glares softened.

"Yeah," I admitted.

"Do you remember me telling you that one potential serious side effect of Lexapro is hallucinations? Both visual and auditory?"

I almost snapped, *I remember a list of potential side effects that pretty much amounted to everything.* But snapping didn't seem like the best move right now.

"Your friends also told me you'd stopped taking your Ambien," he continued, "which I had given you specifically to counteract the insomnia from the Lexapro. Theo, sleep deprivation alone could cause hallucinations."

I hung my head. It was ironic: after his lecture, all I wanted to do was take a nap. If sleep was the cure, bring it on.

"It'll be okay," Lester Wyatt chimed in. "You're sick, but you'll get better." He looked to Dr. Silver. "She just needs some psychiatric care, Doctor. And she'll get better, right? She'll come back to reality, and we can put this all behind us?"

Dr. Silver nodded. "Yes. It'll take some time. Now that we have a clear picture, we can begin some targeted therapy. First, we need to decrease the medication and wait for the side effects to subside. I think that would be best done in a hospital environment."

Fear gripped me. "You're locking me up?"

"No," he reassured me. "I don't think you're a danger to yourself or others. I just need you safely monitored while we lower the dose. I'm checking you into the medical wing."

I opened my mouth to argue, but couldn't. I'd made myself sick, and I needed help. Lester Wyatt was right. Everything he'd said to me was right. I couldn't separate reality from fantasy. It was just like my mother said, just like I'd told my imaginary friend Andy Reese: if there was one thing I was good at, it was making up stories.

Chapter Nineteen

Every hospital room looks the same. Ugly white walls, a bed with bars on either side, fluorescent lights that make everyone look like shit, and a TV on the wall that is inexplicably twenty years too old. Every hospital room feels the same. Depressing as hell.

I had a laundry list of things to be depressed about. Where to begin? The sister I'd lost and still couldn't remember? The scar I'd been hallucinating for months? The boy I'd been hallucinating for a week? The mother who'd purposely robbed me of the chance to grieve, robbed me of the chance to be totally sane for the last twelve years? I was just beginning to understand the extent to which that fire and the loss of my sister defined me.

Maybe the most depressing thing was the company. Not Lou and Max, of course, but my mom, always in the chair at my side, never leaving. I was so sick of her guilty expressions, her attempts to apologize a hundred different ways. Now that the secret was out, she couldn't seem to shut up.

She said she'd never wanted Cyra to date Andy in the first place (big surprise!). She said she never liked him, that she blamed him for taking us to K.O.P. that morning. She'd been secretly happy that high school was over, and that Cyra and Andy would finally have to break up.

I could have endured it, though, except for one problem. There was still a physical remnant, a nagging sensation.

Not a blaring siren, not even a buzzing, more of a steady quiet blaze. It was still there, burning a tiny part of me from the inside. How long would it take to come down from my Lexapro trip? How long until it stopped? Maybe it was embarrassment. I'd spent a week of my life falling for a hallucination. I'd launched us into that pathetic "investigation." Why couldn't I just *remember* Cyra and Andy like a normal person? How could I have forgotten that Andy rescued me from that fire? Why did my unconscious have to torture me with all the psychodrama? All the madness with Unhinged Andy the Arsonist, and the "claw marks" under the rug. I was clinically compelled to make up stories.

At the very least, that provided an answer for some of the insanity. A depressing answer, yes, but at least I'd hit my depressive rock bottom. Or so I thought until day three, when the nurse told me I had a visitor.

I was certain it would be Andy Wyatt. I wasn't ready for that visit yet, but when I saw her walk through the door, I wished it had been him. That would have been easier.

I'd been so busy reeling from epiphanies, I'd nearly forgotten about her. I'd nearly forgotten the one person in this godforsaken mess that I'd actually tortured more than I'd tortured myself.

"Hi, I'm Emma," she said quietly, shaking Lou's hand. She shook Max's hand and then my mother's. "You might not remember me, Ms. Lane. Emma Renaux. Cyra and I were—"

"Yes, of course, I remember you." Mom's voice hitched. "Emma. Cyra adored you."

Emma's eyes began to tear up, but she kept her polite smile intact. "Well, I adored her, too."

There was a painful silence before she finally turned to me. "Hello, Theo."

I hadn't been expecting a smile. I couldn't help but smile back. I began to tear up, too. I'd ruined her wedding—the most important day of her life—and here she was in this awful place, forgiving me. Her hair was combed more simply than I'd ever seen it. I'd only seen her dolled up for wedding events. Now there was just a small diamond barrette holding back her bangs. Her outfit was simpler, too. A cropped black jacket, designer jeans, and flats. The only complicated thing was that smile. It was a muddy mix of sadness, longing, good manners, and a whiff of sincere happiness. Then, of course, there was the fear. She was a little afraid of me. How could she not be, after that all-out assault I'd launched at Delmonico's Steakhouse?

"Hi," I managed, trying to sound as un-scary as possible.

Lou scooted toward the door. "Maybe you guys want a minute," she said. Before I could argue, she led Max and Mom out of the room, leaving me alone with Emma for the first time since our encounter on the terrace of the Ritz-Carlton.

Silence stretched between us. My smile gradually faded.

Emma spoke first. "Theo, I want . . ." she began. "No, I *need* you to forgive me."

I stared at her, unsure how to respond. "You want . . . me . . . to forgive *you*?"

"If you can," she said quickly. "I know it can't happen overnight."

"No, it's not that, it's . . . Why are you apologizing? I should be the one apologizing. I ruined your wedding."

"No." She pulled a chair up next to my bed. "That was just an event. It's just a symbol. It doesn't mean anything. What happened between us is real. It is so much more important. I'm so ashamed of myself."

"Why?"

"I don't know where to begin," she said. She leaned closer. "Theo, do you believe in ghosts?"

I nodded. "I do."

"I do, too. Andy made fun of me about it for years, but Cyra and I always believed. The thing is, when I saw you on the terrace at the Ritz, I thought . . . Well, I thought you were a ghost.

I thought you were Cyra. You're almost the same age she was when we lost her. You're so much alike . . ."

I struggled to sit up in bed. In all my Mom's wailing and self-flagellation, she'd never once told me what Cyra was really like. "You think I look like her?"

"That's part of it. But it was eerie. It was hard to look at you. The truth is, I'd been waiting for her. From the second Andy proposed to me, I'd been waiting. I thought she would hate me so much for taking him away that she'd come back, just to remind me that he was hers and hers alone—that he belonged to her. Because he did belong to her, Theo. I may have loved him first, but Cyra beat me to it. And he loved her *so* much more than he could ever love me. More than he loves me now, I know that. Who wouldn't love her more? She was Cyra."

I tried to swallow, but my throat was clogged. I nodded as if I understood, but how could I really? I didn't know her.

"I tried to convince myself that twelve years was long enough," Emma went on. "We even decided to get married on the K.O.P. anniversary in her honor. So when I saw you that night, I wasn't myself. I thought she had come back to punish me. That's why I told her—I mean, told *you*—not to blame Andy, that it wasn't his fault. I was the one who'd pushed for the wedding."

"I'm sorry," I said.

"Don't be. I went right to Andy that night and told him the wedding was off, that I'd seen Cyra's ghost and we had to call it quits. He said I was being crazy. He convinced me it wasn't a ghost, but then we couldn't figure out who it was. Who could look and sound so much like her? Then Helena told us about the girl she'd met at the party. A girl named Theo. How many girls are named Theo? I can't tell you the *joy* I felt. The closest thing to Cyra on earth. Here you were walking back into our lives after twelve years of nothing—"

"That wasn't my fault!" I protested, tossing my blanket aside. I almost leapt off the hospital bed to grab her hands.

"I know, I know. Andy told me the whole story. But when you

stomped into the rehearsal dinner, you were so angry. Everything you said about Cyra, about how I knew what had happened to her, how I was trying to sweep her under the rug and forget her, how you could never forget her . . . it wasn't wrong. It was like you knew all my greatest fears, all the guilt, this huge weight I carried. I should have just talked to you then and there. I should have put my arms around you. But I panicked. I hid. I told my brother to ask you to leave."

I almost laughed. "He took you pretty seriously," I mumbled, lying back against the pillows. "He did a little more than ask."

Emma crossed her arms. "Oh, God, what did Tyler do? He can be a bit of a bully sometimes. His friends are idiots. Was he rude to you?"

I thought about what Tyler had said. *"Whatever happened, happened. What's done is done. Let it go."* He was talking about my sister's death. He knew more about my sister than I did. He just happened to be an utter asshole.

"Never mind," I said. "We just had a misunderstanding."

Emma leaned close in her chair. "Can you forgive me, Theo?"

"Why do I have to forgive you?" I pressed. "I mean, I'll forgive you, sure, of course, but I should be asking you to forgive me, right?"

She shook her head. "Andy explained it all. About how your mother hid Cyra from you. Whatever you were going through, I made it worse. I wasted all of our precious time thinking your only mission in life was to destroy my wedding."

I reached for her hand. "But I did," I said. "I did destroy your wedding."

"You did nothing of the sort." She smiled, sniffling, and clasped her hand over mine. "We went to the courthouse this morning and did the deed. I mean, not *the* deed; we haven't done *that* yet." She laughed and wiped a tear away. Her face turned bright pink. "Okay, *that* was an overshare!"

I laughed along to ease her embarrassment, but I couldn't help wondering if she was even more of a traditional Southern belle than I'd thought. Saving herself for marriage, no matter how many years it took? Could I wait that long? I could barely wait for a fully toasted Pop-Tart.

But then I thought about what Tyler had said to me in that bathroom stall. *"My sister has waited her entire life for this wedding."* It was so true. Emma had only ever loved one man. She'd been saving herself for him ever since she saw him across that crowded room at the freshman Winter Formal. Because she knew before she'd even asked him to dance. She knew she was going to marry him.

The nurse stepped back into my room. "Ladies, I'm afraid visiting hours are over. I'm going to have to ask you to say your goodbyes."

"No," I said. I squeezed Emma's hand tightly. "Don't go."

"Oh, honey." She grew misty again and squeezed back. "I've got to go. We're doing a little makeup wedding night with the family at the hotel. But I'm going to come back and visit you every single day, I promise."

"Sorry, ladies," the nurse insisted. "Rules are rules."

"You don't have to listen to her," I said. I didn't know why I was so desperate to keep her. Maybe because I had finally made my first real connection to Cyra. I didn't want to let it go.

"Theo, I know," Emma whispered, extricating herself. She drifted toward the door. "I feel the same, but I promise I'm not going anywhere. We're going to be friends, you and I. There is so much I can tell you about her, about how much she *adored* you. Tomorrow, okay?"

She blew me a kiss as the nurse escorted her out, and I realized what a mess I truly was. I barely knew Emma Renaux, but as she walked out that door, I felt like I was losing Cyra all over again.

I MUST HAVE DOZED off, because the next thing I knew Max and Lou were at my side, shaking me awake.

"*Jesus,* come on, Thee," Max was saying. "Did you see it? You saw it, right?"

I yawned and rubbed my eyes. "Saw what?"

"The *ring*." Lou tried her best to whisper, but she was too revved up. She glanced back at the closed door. We were alone. I wondered if Mom had gone home.

"What ring?" I asked. "What's going on?"

"*The* ring," Lou said. "Your dream ring. The wedding ring you've sketched a zillion times? The one you supposedly dreamed up in your imagination? It was on Emma's finger."

Now I was awake. I sat up straight. "What? No, it wasn't."

"Yeah, it was," Max said.

Lou gripped my wrist. "Six little diamond daisy petals with a gold center? Who else has a wedding ring that looks like a daisy? Who else would dream of a wedding ring that looks like a daisy? Thee, it was your ring."

Not only was I awake; I was afraid. Three days, and I was still so far gone that I'd missed the ring on Emma's finger. I had missed the *wedding ring*. Apparently, I was in no condition to notice anything at this point. "Wait, slow down. When did you see it?"

"Five minutes ago," Max said breathlessly. "Not even. When she left. She hugged us all goodbye. It practically dug a hole in my back."

Lou dragged a chair over as Max sat down next to me on the bed. "Listen, Thee, it's not just the ring," Lou added. "I've been thinking about this all night. I just didn't want to mess with your head any more than it's been messed with."

"I don't even think that's possible," I said.

"Well, then, here's the thing." Lou leaned in. "All anyone talks about is the stuff you made up. But no one's talking about the stuff that might have been real. Like that ring. If you didn't make it up, then it's something you've seen before, something you remember, something from your past. What if there's more like that?"

"Like what?"

"That's what we're asking you," Max said. "I mean, Dr. Silver's smart, and yes, he's got the beard on me, but what about *us*? I've been in sessions with you for over three years. I think I'm pretty freaking qualified to assess your overall sanity, and my verdict is: Not Crazy. I mean, yes, you're crazy, but you're not *crazy*."

Really? Then why do I feel crazier than ever right now?

"Thee, I was wrong," Lou said. "I was wrong about your iDoc."

Forget crazy; now I was frightened again. My eyes darted between the two of them. "What the hell are you guys talking about?"

"Remember we were talking about Schaffler?" Lou said. "About how you were breaking the rules? About how you were 'tainting the narrative' by putting yourself in Andy's story?"

"Yeah."

"Right, but Thee, you *are* Andy."

"I'm Andy?"

Lou exchanged a glance with Max. She rested a hand on my shoulder. "I mean, not the real Andy, but you're Andy Reese. You've been Andy Reese this whole time. You've been writing all his lines. Every time Andy remembered something, it was really you remembering, and every time he couldn't remember something, it was because you couldn't remember it. I think Dr. Silver is right. Something triggered your memories of Cyra, but I think the only way you could deal with the memories was to turn them into a movie, to turn them into your new iDoc. Thee, you never broke the rules, because you never put yourself into Andy's story. It has always been your story. You've been trying to tell your own story."

I wedged my palms deep into my eye sockets and tried to shake off the confusion like Andy always—

Like *I* always do.

It's true. When I'm confused, I shake my head like a wet golden retriever and I press down on my eye sockets. It's what I do when I'm trying to remember.

"Okay," I said, feeling an unexpected surge of energy, "Okay, so every time Andy told me something, I was really trying to tell myself something. So what was I trying to tell myself? That Cyra existed? That she died in that fire at K.O.P.?"

"That's what we need to figure out," Lou said. "We can't see anything in your footage. You're the only who knows what Andy said. We've got to start at the beginning—the first time you saw him."

The "beginning" was long before I saw Andy. I'd been trying to tell myself this story for years, starting with the Cyrano de Bergerac obsession (something my mother never acknowledged, of course). Hearing those Magic Garden songs in my sleep had sent me tumbling into a nightmare, but at least I'd woken up from The Night in Question with one more clue in my head: the number nine. Still, Lou was right. Something much bigger had triggered Andy's arrival. Something changed last Sunday. Something set me off on this insane journey . . .

"The *blurb.*" I slapped my thighs. "Emma's picture in the *Times.* I'd just read about her wedding when I first saw Andy through the window. That's when I started making my new movie."

"That's good," Lou said. "That's when you started telling the story. Okay, so remember, you were writing Andy's lines, so what did he tell you? Where did he take you? We're looking for other stuff like the ring—stuff that's real, stuff that had to come from your memory."

My mind went straight back to Room Nine. I knew I'd been trying to tell myself about the fire, but what about all that horrible stuff under the rug? Was that real, like the ring? Or hallucinated like Andy Reese?

"All those claw marks," I muttered.

"Claw marks," Max repeated. I recognized the tone; the nurses and Dr. Silver used it with me. He was clearly ready to dump "claw marks" in the hallucination bin. I was seconds away from agreeing with him, but one thing about those claw marks was different from every other experience I'd had. *I* wasn't the one who'd heard those sounds in Room Nine. Helena had heard them. And Helena also told me that someone named Sarah had run away from the shelter . . .

"I think the claw marks might be real," I said.

"Where are the claw marks?" Lou asked.

"At K.O.P. In Room Nine."

"Well, then, that's where we're going," Max said. "Do you still have your sweats here?" He stepped to the wooden cubby with my clothes.

"Now?" I asked. "You'll really go with me now?"

Max turned to me. "Thee, if you think I can wait till tomorrow to see if the 'claw marks' are real, then maybe you are crazy. Nobody waits to see if the 'claw marks' are real."

I almost smiled. Almost. "Okay," I said, jumping up and grabbing my sweats from Max. "We go now, but Lou, I need your help."

"Name it," she said.

"You've got to stay with my mom. When we walk out, we'll tell her that Max is walking me to the vending machine. But you need to take her home and keep her company tonight. I don't want her to feel any more alone than she already does."

Lou nodded. "I'll do it," she said. "But you've got to let me know what you find *when* you find it."

"Done," I said.

"So we don't hate Mom, then?" Max asked.

"We don't hate Mom," I echoed, and saying the words freed some invisible weight from my shoulders. "How could I? She needs more help than I do."

"What about this K.O.P. place?" Max said. "Will we have trouble getting in?"

"I'm not sure," I said. "We just need to hope that Andy Wyatt went to his office today, and that his room got really stuffy."

Chapter Twenty

Having a basketball stool as a best friend comes in handy when dealing with fire escapes. It only took one graceful jump for Max to grab the ladder and pull it down into the alley. We scaled our way to K.O.P.'s second floor. Max's keychain flashlight barely lit the way. I held my breath as I stepped up to Wyatt's window.

The Fates, having been exceptionally cruel for days (weeks? Months? Twelve years?), finally did me a monumental favor. They provided a heat wave. They made Wyatt uncomfortable and distracted enough today to leave his window gate unlocked, just like Helena said he often did.

Max helped me through, and we snuck down the stairs toward Room Nine. Being back here, I realized just how much I'd been hallucinating. Everything looked duller, more dismal—difficult for such a dull, dismal place. Clearer, but less vivid. I checked in Helena's room, but it looked like she'd stayed out for the night. Two more steps and we were standing right back in front of my least favorite spot on earth.

Then it all came back.

First, the piercing siren sound, then all of it the same as before: the emptiness, the pressure, the airlessness. But this time, there was a difference. There was Max. And Max was real. He swung open the door to Room Nine like it was any other room. I stood there frozen like the five-year-old child I'd been when whatever happened . . . happened.

"Aren't you coming?" Max whispered, holding the door open for me.

I nodded. Even if Lexapro and sleep deprivation were still having their way with me, Max was here to help. I took his hand. The door fell shut behind us. We were alone in the dark with nothing but a narrow wand's worth of light from Max's keychain.

Someone had stapled the blue throw rug back to the floor.

I felt sick.

"Where are the claw marks?" Max whispered.

I couldn't bring myself to speak. I just pointed at the rug beneath my feet.

What had taken every last ounce of my strength took Max less than five seconds. He ripped the rug from the floor, staples flying out on all sides, and tossed it to the corner. Then he aimed the narrow beam where the rug had been.

The floor was blank.

No . . .

It seemed blank in the dark, but as my eyes began to adjust, and his flashlight steadied, I saw them, those chaotic slashes, the unnerving words still carved at the center.

MY NAME IS NOT SARAH. MY NAM

I felt a crippling mix of terror and relief. Relief that it was actually there, that it was at least one thing I hadn't imagined. Unless . . .

"Max," I whispered nervously. "Do you see it? Is it really there?"

"You think a *girl* did that?" he asked bluntly. I almost laughed. Only Max could have made me laugh in that moment. "Like, with her nails? You can't seriously believe that."

I became hyperconscious of my own gnawed-off fingernails, still catching on the loose threads in my sweatshirt pockets. It was too dark for him to see those tiny droplets of dried blood on the floor. "I don't know," I said. "I really don't know."

"Dude," he said, "she *really* wanted someone to know her name."

Her name. I hadn't even thought of it until Max said it. Sarah was the name my battered brain had conjured up. It was the name I thought everyone had been saying, but it wasn't her actual name. *Is that what she's trying to tell me now? That her name isn't Sarah, it's Cyra?*

No. That was crazy talking again. There was no way she had carved out those words, because she had died in a fire twelve years ago—that was real, that was true.

Max drew closer to me. "Is this the part where we start talking about ghosts again?"

"No. No ghosts. But Helena said she heard most of the scratching late at night. I think if we really want to know who did it, then we need to wait."

He waved the light over the mattress, the bare walls. "Wait in this creepy-ass room till the middle of the night to see who's clawing these creepy-ass marks in this creepy-ass floor?"

"Max." I dug my fingers into his arm. "You brought me here because you know that I need to know the truth. I'm telling you, I've had this panicked feeling clawing at my chest all day like something is still wrong—like I still need the answers to all the questions now. Not tomorrow, *now.*"

"Clawing?" Max flashed the light in my face. "Seriously? You had to go with 'clawing'?"

I squinted, shielding my eyes. "Please. Will you wait with me? I can't wait here alone."

He took a deep breath and flicked off the flashlight, blanketing us in darkness. "Okay, we're waiting. I'm going to wait on this creepy-ass mattress over here." He lay down on his side, then flicked the light back on, fixing it on me like a night watchman.

I parked myself next to him at the edge of the bed. "Max . . . ?"

"Yeah?"

"Do you think there's any way I could ask you to share this twin bed without it evoking any clichés of—?"

"Just get in." He held up his arm.

I jumped down and spooned myself against him, wrapping his arm securely around my waist. We lay there in silence for a moment. I began to feel the adrenaline wear off as the deep exhaustion of Lexapro detox kicked back in.

"Hey, Thee," Max whispered. I could feel his warm breath on the back of my ear. "Can I ask you a question?"

"Okay," I answered tentatively.

"When you invited me to the wedding. Was that your idea or Andy's?"

"Definitely Andy's," I mumbled.

"But Andy is really just you, right? Your subconscious."

"Let's not talk, Max. Someone might hear us."

"Okay. I was just wondering if Andy said anything about me. Like, if he had any strong opinions pro or con."

My body twitched when I thought of the embarrassing things Andy had said about Max.

"He had very strong opinions," I said. "He also wore the same T-shirt for seven straight days and slept in my bedroom closet."

"Okay, but opinions pro or con?"

I couldn't muster the energy to answer. I had to close my eyes for a moment. If only to escape the conversation.

I DREAMED OF FIRE. It spread across Room Nine in a bellowing tornado roar. It was a giant beast of black smoke, hovering over the ceiling, wings spread wide, talons made of jagged glass. It breathed out blue rings of flame that forged a fiery circle in the center of the room. Caged inside that circle was my sister Cyra, her raven hair even longer than in the pictures. She was on her knees, digging at the floor with her bloody fingernails, each piercing scratch dragging me further and further from sleep . . .

My eyes slowly fluttered open.

I knew when I was dreaming and when I was awake. I knew

the flaming beast was a dream, but those scratching sounds—the ones that had woken me up—they were real. And so was the girl making them.

"Cyra . . . ?"

Max woke with a start and punched his keychain flashlight on.

We weren't alone. *My God, it's her.*

I wasn't hallucinating, because Max leapt off the bed. The girl gasped and snatched up her own flashlight, aiming it straight at our faces, momentarily blinding me. I caught a brief glimpse of her eyes, but her dark hair fell over her face as she jumped up from the floor and ran out the door.

"Cyra!" I called out, stumbling after Max. "Cyra, wait!"

I got to the door just in time to see her turning the corner at the end of the hall. Max was already chasing after her. I pumped my legs for all they were worth. At least I was wearing sneakers this time. I heard her feet skittering up the stairs as we got to the end of the hall.

"Cyra!" I called again. "It's me! It's Theo!" But she wouldn't stop. "Max, she's going through the way we came!"

Max took the steps in threes and fours. He was through the window by the time I got to Wyatt's office. I ducked my head out and reached for the fire escape bars, watching from overhead as Cyra dropped from the ladder, hair swaying in the wind as she landed on the pavement and bolted for Parker Street.

Shit, shit, shit.

Max was already leaping down after her. I followed as fast as I could. Once his feet hit the ground, he reached for my waist, lifting me down to the sidewalk. He was off again, but my lungs were on fire.

"Max," I gasped, "I take back everything I ever said about basketball. You have to stop her. She still doesn't know who I am. Go."

"On it!" Max raced out ahead of me. I watched him draw closer and closer to her as she neared the entrance to the West

Side Highway. He reached for her hand and latched on, snapping her back toward him. He had her.

She struggled to break free, harder than I had even struggled against Tyler. I stumbled toward them, clammy and woozy. I could finally make out the details of her face under the streetlights. I doubled over, hands on knees, trying to catch my breath.

I'm an idiot.

It wasn't Cyra. Of course it wasn't Cyra. There were similarities in her face and hair, but she was definitely not my sister's ghost. And we'd run her down. We'd freaked the shit out of her. We'd made her cry. I wasn't just an idiot; I was a very bad person.

"I'm not a thief," she said between sobs. "I'm not. Here, take them back. Please just take them." Max loosened his grip on her. With her free hand, she reached into her jean jacket pocket and handed him something so small I couldn't make it out. We both leaned closer. Two tiny, pearl-shaped orbs sat in his wide palm. One black and one white. The white one was an actual pearl, but the black? A black pearl?

I picked them up and held them to the streetlight. "Where did you get these?" I asked, amazed.

"In the floor," she said between sniffles. "They were buried in the cracks. I wasn't trying to steal anything."

My mind sailed back to the sound of Andy's voice in my ear. *They've fallen through the cracks. They're all buried under the floor, burning.*

Pearls. Not women, *pearls.* That's what he'd been trying to tell me. No. That's what I had been trying to tell myself.

I knew a little about pearls. I knew jewelers sometimes held them to a flame to check if they were genuine. Because real pearls didn't burn.

It wasn't a black pearl in my hand. It wasn't a black pearl in my hand. It was a pearl that had been charred in a fire, but survived.

"You can keep them," she said. "Just please don't turn me in."

Max finally let her go. "We won't," I promised. "Please don't cry."

"We didn't mean to scare you," Max said.

"I thought you were someone else," I explained.

"Well, I'm *not,*" she said, swiping at her tears. "I'm me."

It sounded like something I might have said. The faster, angrier me. I studied her face again. Girlish, but jaded. She couldn't have been much older than nineteen, but she looked like the world had already trampled her to the ground. Or if not the world, then at least a guy or two.

"Is your name Sarah?" I asked.

"No," she barked. "My name is not Sarah. That's the name *he* gave me. *I* just wanted a bed and some sleep. That's all I wanted. But he saw me in the lobby filling out the paperwork, and he started talking to me and smiling at me and interviewing me like he *liked* me, you know? Like I was his girlfriend or something. He just creeped me out."

I nodded, that uneasy fire burning inside me again. She had obviously been waiting a long time to tell someone this story. It was a grievance or a confession or both. I think it had been quite a while since she'd had anyone to talk to.

"The way he kept staring at me," she said. "Like he knew me. He asked me my name, but I wouldn't tell him, so then he just says, 'Well, let's call you Sarah for now.' Like it's that easy? Like this asshole can just give me any name he wants?"

Sometimes he gave them temp names. Like stray dogs at the pound.

He'd named her Cyra, not Sarah, I was sure of that. But who wouldn't hear that as "Sarah"?

"He told the old lady at the desk to give me Room Nine," she said, "and I was, like, fine, Room Nine, good night. But then he *follows* me into the room. He would not leave me the hell alone. He wanted to talk more. He said I reminded him of some girl he knew when he was a kid. He said my face had this 'purity' that he really admired, and he wanted me to be his 'ambassador' or something. Everything was 'Sarah' this and 'Sarah' that. 'There's something special about you, Sarah. We're going to take good care of you, Sarah.'"

"Did you even know who he was?" Max asked, jaw clenched. He was finally getting a picture of the real Lester Andrew Wyatt.

"Oh, I found out *real* quick," she said. "He was '*Mister* Wyatt.' All the girls called him that. But the more he called me 'Sarah,' the more I wanted to punch his perfect little teeth out. He finally left me alone and told me to go to bed, but I seriously thought he might try to sneak in and cop a feel. Plus, that room was giving me the heebie-jeebies. No way was I going to stay. I just wanted that freak to know something before I left. I wanted him to know my name. So I took out my pocketknife and I started carving my message into the floor, just to be sure he wouldn't forget it when I was gone."

I reached into my pocket and dug out a crumpled Kleenex, handing it to her. "It's clean," I murmured. I was liking this girl more and more.

"Thanks." She dabbed at her eyes. "Anyway, my knife hits something hard while I'm carving. It was a freakin' *pearl.* All charred up, trapped in a hunk of old soot, but a *pearl.* It had to be a miracle, right? A real one. Like some guardian angel up there was looking out for me for once. A pearl in a homeless shelter, and I found it fair and square."

I lurched forward and wrapped my arms around her. I couldn't help it. She had no idea what she'd found, no idea what she'd just given me. Cyra's pearls. My sister's pearls. They had to be. Half the building might have burned down, Cyra might have burned away, but she had refused to fall completely through the cracks. Despite all my mother's attempts to erase her, she had still left a piece of herself buried in the floorboards for me to find.

"Were these all you found?" I asked, pulling away. "Just these two?"

"I tried to find more," the girl said, her arms rigid in my grip. She looked a little taken aback by my sudden show of emotion. "After I found the first two, I started digging all over the floor with my knife. Then that chick, Ms. Renaux, spotted me through the window and got all super-freaked. She started screaming at me, and then that big security dude 'escorted' me out."

I nodded. "Mac. Yeah. He's scary."

She sneered. "He tried to be. But I've been sneaking back at night, through that window upstairs, scraping around for more till my freaking fingers bled. I just wanted to find enough to buy a plane ticket home. I swear, I wasn't trying to rob anybody."

I placed the two pearls in her palm and closed her scraped-up fingers around them. "I want you to take them," I said. "They were my sister's, but now they're yours. And take this." I reached into my pocket, pulled the last sixty dollars from my wallet, and stuffed them in her jean jacket. Then I stepped to the curb and held my hand out for a cab. "I want you to take this cab to the diamond district on West Forty-Seventh Street. Find a late night shop where you can pawn those pearls, and go home."

She stood there, clutching the pearls, her jaw slack.

A taxi pulled up, and I opened the door. "Come," I said, taking her hand and helping her in.

"I don't know what to say," she said.

"You don't have to say anything," I replied. "Well, maybe just one thing. What *is* your name?"

"It's LeAnne," she said. "LeAnne Stemson."

"Well, it's nice to meet you, LeAnne. I'm Theo."

She smiled, her hard eyes finally brightening. "Theo," she said. "What a cool fucking name."

I closed the cab door and watched her ride off.

"The pearls," Max said, trying to put the pieces together. "That's the other thing you've sketched a million times."

My nagging panic returned. "I tried to tell myself about the pearls," I said. "I knew they were buried in that room."

"The ring and the pearls," Max said. "Thee, it's all the stuff for your dream wedding. All that's missing is the dress."

"Oh, *man*." I clamped my palms on my head. "The *dress* . . . Max, it was the very first place he took me. I mean, the first place I took myself."

"Where?"

I grabbed his hands, then let them go and waved for another cab. "He said she'd needed to change into 'something fancy' at her house for their date. But when we got to her house, it wasn't her house, and we got all confused. I mean *I*—I got all confused. Because I knew it was the right house, but Sarah didn't live there."

"Okay, now I'm confused," Max said.

"Max. She didn't live there because it's 2015. She lived there in 2003. 224 Bergen Street. It was *my* house, Max—our house. I tried to take myself home."

THE WOMAN I STILL only knew as "the mother" cracked open the door. She was dressed in a white robe and slippers. She kept the chain lock fastened. Her hair was pulled back, and her face was stripped of makeup, eyes staring at Max and me like zombies who'd come for her brains.

Yes, it's me! The freaky, homeless tweaker who was skulking around your house on Thursday night! The one who scared the crap out of your daughter. And I've brought a really tall, imposing friend with me! Oh, and yes, it's midnight!

Once she got a good look at me, she tried to slam the door shut, but I held it open.

"No, please wait," I begged. "I know it's late. I know I scared you and your daughter before, and I am so sorry about that, but if I could just have two seconds of your time to explain? Please, it's incredibly important."

"It's really important," Max echoed.

She looked at Max. Thank God I'd brought a relatively normal-looking person with me this time instead of a hallucination. With his shave and his haircut, Max looked even less like a potential vagrant than he had before.

"My name is Theo," I said.

"I thought your name was Emma," she snapped.

"Um . . . I sometimes go by my middle name," I pathetically

suggested, "but my first name is Theo. Theo Lane. My mother is Margaret Lane. My sister's name was Cyrano Lane."

All at once she dropped her defensive scowl. She placed her fingers to her heart and a hint of pity flashed across her eyes. She remembered. She remembered the second I said the name. The *right* name this time. "She was your sister?"

I'd been so busy frightening her, it hadn't occurred to me that she might, in fact, be a kind person. I nodded, swallowing the lump. "This was our house," I said, knowing it to be true whether I recognized it or not.

"I remember your mother," she said. "She told me what happened to her daughter when I bought the house. But I never met you."

Of course not. Because Mom never brought me back after that day, did she? We'd probably stayed at a hotel while she went about the business of selling our life away.

This could have been my house. Right now. This beautiful brownstone on this beautiful, tree-lined block on Bergen Street. It *had* been my house until I was five, but it could have been the home I grew up in.

Who would I have been then? If I'd known about my sister? If my mother understood grieving? If I'd grown up in Brooklyn like I was supposed to? Would that girl have smiled more? Would she have quoted Nietzsche in her eighth-grade yearbook? Would she have had a more peaceful mind?

"I need to see my old room," I said, plain and simple. "Would it be all right with you if I looked at it really quickly?"

"Oh, no," she said, shaking her head apologetically. "Not now. It's after midnight. My daughter is fast asleep upstairs—"

"Mommy, what's going on?" The tiny peep of a voice came from the top of the stairs inside the house. I could see her through the front door. Her dark hair was ruffled from sleep. She wore a Little Mermaid nightshirt down to her knees and held a stuffed Little Mermaid doll in her right hand, rubbing her sleepy eye with the left. I realized now that she was probably closer to seven or eight than five.

"It's nothing, Josie," her mom whispered, shooting me an annoyed glance. "Just some friends paying a visit."

Josie finished rubbing her eyes and then took a better look at me. "Emma?" she asked.

"No, I'm sorry. My name is Theo."

Josie's little ruby lips dropped open in shock, the kind of pure shock only children under ten could manage. "*You're* Theo?" she said, letting her Little Mermaid doll drop to the floor. "Theo Lane?" she squeaked. "Why didn't you say that on Thursday?"

My brow furrowed. Her mother and Max stared at me.

Before I could answer, she shot past her mother, grabbed my hand, and began dragging me up the stairs. "I can't believe you're finally here," she whispered. "What *took* you so long?"

I shook my head. There was no use trying to answer or make any sense of this. I just had to go with it. At least I knew that I wasn't hallucinating. I glanced over my shoulder. Max and Josie's mother gaped up at me as we climbed the carpeted staircase with its polished wooden banister.

Josie pulled me toward her room. The door at the opposite corner of the hall swung open, and a beefy man in a T-shirt and pajama pants stepped into the hall.

"Carol, what is going on?" he grumpily shouted down the stairs.

"Nothing, Daddy," Josie answered, as if this were perfectly normal. As if her nonchalant tone might throw him off the scent.

"I have no idea, Dale," Carol shouted back. She and Max thundered up the stairs. Josie pulled me to her room, flipped on the light, and my hand went limp in hers.

Daisies. Four walls covered in bright, daisy wallpaper.

"It had flowers everywhere," Andy had said. *"Daisies."*

White on yellow on white on yellow. On and on. Petals

everywhere, except for the ceiling, which was covered in old Little Mermaid stickers. They'd been there so long that they'd blended into the paint.

The window facing the alley was open, but the window facing the street was shuttered closed, just as I'd seen it from outside, hiding the big crack in the window.

"We loved the wallpaper," Carol said from behind me. "We decided to leave it for when we had kids. Honestly, the only thing we really moved was the bed. We never got around to those stickers, but it sure made Josie love that Little Mermaid, huh, sweetie?" She patted her daughter's back.

"Theo," Josie said, taking charge, "only you can come in. Mom, Dad, Cute Giant, you have to wait outside." She pushed at her mother's waist until Carol was in the hall and then shut us in quickly.

I stared at all the flowers, willing myself to remember this place. But I couldn't. "How do you know my name?" I asked.

Josie pulled me down to the floor with her and whispered, "I didn't tell anyone else. Not even Mommy or Daddy. Just like it said."

"Like what said?" I whispered back.

"The box," she replied.

"What box?"

"Your Magic Story Box, silly."

She slid herself under the bed as I flattened myself down to see what she was doing, heart racing, literally floored. I heard the music fade up in my head.

The stories are here. They're all in here
From Crafty Fox to Goldilocks on Story Box, on Story Box
There are no locks on Story Box, on Story Box, on Story Box . . .

Josie carefully placed her fingernails between the planks of the wood under her bed and removed three of the floorboards. "I only found it last year," she breathed. "We are *super* lucky I could read it."

She handed over a hinged wooden photo box about the size of a shoebox. There was a large, dusty, yellowed label on top. The neat handwriting was in all caps:

THEO'S MAGIC STORY BOX

Under that, in smaller writing, it read:

This is Theo Lane's secret story box. No one else can open this box but Theo Lane.

A story box. Under the floorboards. Her pearls and my box, all buried.

I'd been trying to lead myself to this box for days. Now I could only stare at it like it was wired to explode. I brought my hand to the lid, but couldn't bring myself to open it.

"What are you waiting for?" Josie whispered, propping herself on her elbows under the bed. "Is it really magic?"

"I don't know," I whispered back. My throat was bone dry.

"Well, *open* it," she said. "No one else can open it but you. Okay, I *might* have peeked. But I don't get what's in there. They aren't stories."

I held my breath and lifted the lid.

Digital videocassettes. Old mini-DV cassettes. Of course Josie didn't know what they were. They were obsolete. They were all lined up in the box like files in a drawer, except for one. One had been tossed on the top, facing up. The label stared back at me in red marker:

September 1st, 2003
THE BIG DAY!

LEAVING 224 BERGEN STREET was a blur. I think I kissed and hugged Josie more than I should have. I know I thanked her for keeping my secret, and I promised her I'd be back soon. I think I hugged Dale and Carol even though they wished I hadn't. I think I dragged Max out to the street, feeling dangerously wobbly, and told him to call Lou because my hands were too shaky to dial. It's possible none of those things happened except the Josie part.

I do remember my three-sentence exchange with Lou. "Do you have the keys to the editing room at school?" I asked.

"Yeah, why?" she said. "What's the story?"

"I think I might have the whole story in my hands."

After that, I remember the emotions. Gratitude: that all of Mr. Schaffler's video equipment was crap from the late '90s. Comfort: sitting down at the editing bay with Max and Lou on either side of me. Fear: in their eyes and mine, as if they were spotting me as I stepped onto a mile-high tightrope.

I inserted the tape, glued my finger to the control keys, and pressed PLAY . . .

Chapter Twenty-One

The screen flickers to life. So, finally, does she.

My sister. Cyrano Lane. No longer a still image, but a living, breathing, stunning creature in a glorious close-up. Her face is made up to perfection, her hair tied crisply in an elegant French braid. She holds a red marker in her mouth like a cigar. The frame swivels and shakes, tilting left, then right, then half obscured in darkness.

"Damn," she complains, dropping the marker from her mouth. "I think I need to make the buttonhole just a little bigger for the lens. Thee, you won't be mad if I rip your peacoat buttonhole just a teensy bit, will you? I'll buy you a new one tomorrow, but this is, like, the biggest day of my life. Cool?"

"Mm-kay," a tiny voice replies from off camera.

My tiny voice.

"Cool, thanks," she says. The frame pulls back from her face, revealing her bare, slender shoulders and clavicles, then the string of white pearls dangling from her slim, delicate neck, the largest pearl hanging at the center of her chest. And then the sunny wall of daisies in the background. This is our room.

She reaches out of frame and brings back a silver mat knife. She plunges it toward the lens, cutting into the dark wedge that obscures the frame until the shot is whole again. Then she looks off to the side and smiles. "Now *that's* what I'm talking about.

Okay, if I sewed this thing in right, it should tilt up perfectly to see everything we want to see. It's wired into the camera in your pocket, so it might be a little hot against your side, okay?"

"Mm-kay," I reply again, jovial and eager to please.

"This little spy-cam cost me about a billion dollars, so let's not go slamming into any walls."

"I won't," I promise.

"Okay. Let's try this sucker on."

The shot goes into a wild blur, flashing past Cyra's face, across a sea of Little Mermaids on the ceiling, past flares of sunlight, past a TV screen that shows a mirror image of the shot, past the quickest glimpse of my five-year-old face and my arm slipping into a navy blue sleeve—all of it set to the rumble and boom of the jostling microphone. And then finally back to Cyra's beautiful face.

She peers off to the side again, checking the TV monitor. "Aha! Ha, ha! We *have* Theo-Cam, ladies and gentlemen."

I giggle. "Yaaaaay," I sing.

"Yaaaaay," she sings along. "Oh, shoot, *shhhhhh.* We have to stay real quiet, Thee. We can't let Mommy and Daddy hear us. We're on a super-special secret agent mission today that they can't know about, remember?"

"Right," I whisper. "Super-secret mission."

"Okay, let's check the frame." She moves farther back, revealing herself head to toe. I can practically hear the glissando of harp strings as she floats into the wide shot, holding the bottom of her strapless white wedding dress like she's preparing to curtsy.

She looks like Audrey Hepburn in the Givenchy dress from *Sabrina.*

She checks herself in the TV monitor and twirls. "What do you think?"

"Pretty," I swoon.

"Why, thank you. Okay, let's button you up. He's going to be here any minute. We have to be at the Harbor Café by eleven forty-f—"

"I *know*," I sigh. "Eleven forty-five. You've said it, like, a ga*jillion* times."

"Well, I don't like to be late. And someone very important is meeting us there." She jumps back into extreme close-up and buttons up the rest of my peacoat. "It's not too hot, is it? Because you cannot take off this coat no matter what. You understand that, right?"

"Yeah, I'm okay," I say.

"Ugh, I am so sorry to make you do this, Thee, but you know Andy is super-duper camera shy. I can live with that any other day, but if he thinks I'm not going to record this day for our children and grandchildren to see . . ." She slips into a nasal cartoon voice. *"Then he don't know me very well, do he?"*

"Hee, hee," I giggle. "Bugs Bunny."

"I love that you're five and you get my references. Okay, so you remember the plan, right? We go out on our super-secret mission, and then we come right back here and hide the cassette in the Magic Story Box."

"Duh."

"Okay, smarty-pants. Just making sure."

There's a gentle tapping off camera, and Cyra has a quick panic moment ducking out of frame. I think she's unplugging the TV monitor. Theo-Cam swivels to the window that faces the alley, and there, standing atop a metal ladder in all his golden glory, is Andy. He's wearing a tuxedo, carrying a big, overstuffed backpack on his shoulder. He waves at Cyra with his devastating smile. She does a little happy dance as she runs to the window and lifts it up high for her Romeo to enter.

"Oh, *man*." He grins, taking in his bride-to-be. "When you change into something fancy, you really change into something fancy."

"Andy Reese's!" I squeal with excitement, a toddler with a massive crush.

"Well, *hey*, Snuggle Bear!" he says. He climbs in through the window, revealing the black Chuck Taylors that match his tux. He drops his overstuffed bag on the floor, reaches into his pocket, and hands me a Reese's peanut butter cup.

"What do you say?" Cyra prompts me.

"*Thank* you, Andy Reese's," I dutifully respond.

"Well, you know I've always got the hookup for my Snuggle Bear," he says.

"What's in the bag?" Cyra asks.

"You're just going to have to wait to find out," he says with a grin.

"Is that a Speed Stick in the pocket?" she teases. "Are you *that* nervous?"

"Come here," he says. He wraps his arms around her, and they melt into a passionate kiss.

"Ew," my little voice mutters.

But the kiss goes on and on as they begin to twirl across the room. Twirling and twirling until *smack,* Andy's back slams into the window that faces the street, leaving a long crack right down the center.

"Oh, *shit, shit, shit,*" Cyra gasps. "*Shhhhhhh.*" She presses her finger to her lips as they both stare at the crack. And then they fall into silent laughter.

"Oh, man," Andy whispers. "We got to get out of here."

"Let's go, let's go." She grabs hold of my hand.

"Wait," Andy says, freezing in place. He keeps the smile tacked on his face, but it grows faint.

"What?" Cyra asks.

Andy turns his back to me, the camera. "She's coming?" he murmurs.

"Andy, this is my wedding day," Cyra says. "I only get one, and my sister is going to be there."

"But what about, you know . . . the after-plan?"

"Don't worry, I have that all figured out," she says. "We'll make it work."

Andy lets out a long sigh.

"Or we could just call the whole thing off," Cyra says. "We could just plan another—"

He shuts her up with a kiss. "Okay, come here, Snuggle Bear," he says, holding out his hand to me. "We're going to have to get you down this ladder. What do you say you and Andy Reese's go strutting down Burger Street?"

I hear myself break into massive fits of laughter behind the camera. "Burger Street!"

"She never gets tired of that one," he marvels.

"Wait, I almost forgot." Cyra grabs a small brown paper bag from the desk and hands it to Andy.

"What's in here?" he asks with a sly grin.

"It's not for you." She giggles.

"Damn," he sighs, disappointed, stuffing it into the front pocket of his backpack. He reaches for me again and the "Theo-Cam" becomes a shaky blur.

Max, Lou, and I watch as Andy lifts me safely down the ladder, walks me down the alley, lifts me over the iron gate, and hails us a cab.Then an endless static shot of the inside of a taxi. My eyes stay riveted on the screen, but some instinctive, almost autonomous part of my brain begins to control the playback buttons, making decisions about what needs to be seen.

FAST-FORWARD . . .

Theo-Cam sits at the marble table closest to the door of the Harbor Café. The camera looks out the window, across the front lawn, all the way to the tall ivy gates of Battery Gardens. The river and Lady Liberty melt into an ethereal blue-green blur in the background.

Andy and Cyra sit together on the right side of the frame, feeding each other pastries, handing me a chocolate croissant that rises in and out of the shot as I eat.

Cyra looks out the window and gazes up at the Battery

Gardens balcony, sighing as she watches a couple (two black and white dots on the screen) pose for photos.

"Someday," she says, "when our parents get over all their issues and realize we weren't too young, we're going to renew our vows in a *humongous* wedding at Battery Gardens." She turns back to Andy. "Promise me?"

"Promise," he says. He looks down and checks his watch. "Oh, man, come on now," he complains. "It's eleven forty-two. The Justice is meeting us at noon. She's *got* to be here by eleven forty-five."

"There she is!" Cyra bellows, delighted. "My maid of honor!" She pops up from her seat and flies out the door to greet a young and vibrant Emma Renaux on the front lawn.

Emma rushes to meet Cyra, a white purse strapped to her shoulder and a big bouquet of daisies wrapped in white deli paper. They embrace on the lawn.

"Okay, Snuggle Bear," Andy says, rising from his seat. "It's time to tie the knot."

Theo-Cam rises as Andy hoists on his backpack and walks out into the wind to give Emma a hug. The hug lasts too long—Emma won't let go at first, but as Theo-Cam runs at her, she finally releases Andy and greets me.

"Well, don't you look as snug as a bug in that adorable coat," she says.

"Thanks," I reply.

"Come on," Andy says, pushing the girls along. "The Justice is meeting us in front of K.O.P. at noon. Let's move."

We travel the short walk to Parker Street and approach the immaculate, brand-new façade of Keeping Our Promise. Bright, gleaming letters are set against the bright white stone wall.

The Justice of the Peace waits at the top of the front stoop—short, bald, and pleasant. Andy and Cyra thank him for meeting them.

"And this is your witness?" he asks, turning to Emma.

"This is our witness," Andy says.

A witness. Emma was the one and only witness to their

wedding, with the exception of five-year-old me. That's what I'd been trying to tell myself when Andy (I) was falling apart in the crushing pressure of Room Nine. *Emma was a witness.*

She was *there.* Emma was there on their secret wedding day. Why didn't she tell me that in the hospital?

FAST-FORWARD . . .

They move in fast-motion. Andy unlocks K.O.P.'s front door and heads into the lobby with the Justice of the Peace. But Emma waits out on the stoop, and her face momentarily fills the frame.

The look on Emma's face . . .

It's the first time the camera has gotten close enough to really see it. The weighty sadness behind that pasted-on smile. The tiny creases of mourning in her furrowed brow. And something else. An ugly tension in the corners of her eyes and mouth. Visible veins in her neck. It's not just sadness, and it's not just jealousy.

It's anger.

It may be masked behind that Southern belle smile, but it's as plain as day for anyone bothering to look.

Emma rips the white deli paper from the flowers with too much force. She hands Cyra the bouquet but keeps three daisies for herself. She begins to tear off the petals, one by one, with taut fingers. It looks like a violent game of "He Love Me, He Loves Me Not." She finishes shredding them and takes a deep breath. Then she turns to me and marches toward the camera. She leans in too close to the lens and drizzles the loose petals like ashes into a tiny pile in my outstretched hand.

Of course. I'm the flower girl.

Cyra takes my free hand and guides me through the front door of K.O.P. "Go on," she says from behind the camera. "Just like we practiced."

Emma's and my voices begin to sing in unison.

"Dum, dum, da-dum . . . dum, dum, da-dum . . ." An a capella "Wedding March."

I become a slow dolly shot through the freshly painted white lobby of K.O.P. I move in gradually on Andy and the Justice of the Peace. My left hand holds the shredded white petals in front of the camera as my right hand takes them in pinches and sprinkles them across the floor, creating a sad excuse for an aisle.

Theo-Cam reaches Andy and then pivots back around to Cyra and Emma, who are walking up slowly from behind, arm in arm.

Emma is still trying to sing "The Wedding March," but the closer she gets to the camera, the more her voice begins to quaver, and the lower her head begins to droop. Tears begin to roll down her cheeks as they grow more and more flushed, the veins more visible in her neck. And then she abruptly stops singing.

She stares, stone-faced, at Cyra, her gaze drifting down to the string of pearls on her neck. I've seen that gaze before. I saw it through Emma's gauzy veil the day I ruined her wedding.

"What's wrong?" Cyra asks.

Emma doesn't answer.

"Em, what's wrong?" Cyra repeats.

"Sorry, nothing!" Emma says, recovering her fake smile. She hands Cyra over to Andy, robotically, but hovers too close to them. She can't take her eyes off the pearls wrapped around my sister's slim neck.

The Justice begins the ceremony. "Dearly beloved . . ." He recites the usual script right up until "the ring, please." And then dead silence again.

"Em," Andy murmurs. "Em," he repeats. "The ring."

I can see it in her eyes: Emma has left her body. Her hands take over, reaching for Cyra's neck, latching onto the pearls.

Cyra jerks her head back. "Em, what are you doing?"

"I'm sorry," Emma says. "I just can't . . ." She rotates the pearls ten degrees on Cyra's neck so that the largest one hangs dead center down her chest again. "I'm sorry, I just had to do that."

"It's okay," Cyra assures her. "Um, the ring?"

"Right," Emma says. She lowers her head, reaches into her white purse, and presents my dream ring to Andy. Little diamond daisy petals glowing around a gold center. Cyra and Andy both smile with relief, and the Justice returns to the script.

"Do you, Lester Andrew Wyatt . . . ?"

"I do," Andy says, sliding the ring on Cyra's finger.

"And do you, Cyrano Sylvia Lane . . . ?"

"I do," she says.

"Then by the power vested in me by the State of New York, I now pronounce you husband and wife. You may kiss the bride."

They share a passionate kiss. But without any violins, or a crowd to applaud, the only sound left in the lobby is the sound of Emma's crying. She steps forward and reaches around both of their shoulders. "That was beautiful," she weeps. "I am so happy for you both."

They thank her and share a long three-way embrace. Cyra's hand reaches toward the camera and pulls me into the hug.

Then Emma turns around and begins a painfully slow walk back to the front door, shrinking smaller and smaller into the background.

"Emma," my squeaky voice calls out. "Emma, where are you going?"

But Cyra crouches down to me and whispers, "Leave her be. Just leave her be for now."

"Okay," I say as the door slowly swings shut.

Now I know why Emma was so racked with guilt. I know why she feared revenge from Cyra's ghost. She hadn't just married Cyra's boyfriend. She had married her husband. Did anyone but Emma and Andy know that?

FAST-FORWARD . . .

I watch in fast motion as Andy and Cyra shake the Justice's hand and say their goodbyes. Andy picks up his backpack and then me, and we travel into the halls of K.O.P., passing all the untouched dorms, until we reach the common room with the TV, where he sets me down. The TV flips on, and SpongeBob races around the screen at high speed until Cyra crouches into frame, holding Andy's backpack.

Cyra unzips the front pocket of Andy's backpack and opens the brown paper bag she handed him earlier. She pulls out four items, placing each one on the floor in front of Theo-Cam: a sandwich in a plastic baggie, two Tropicana juice boxes, and an apple.

"Okay, Thee." She smiles. "Andy and I are going to take a little bit of grown-up time to celebrate, just the two of us, and you can watch all the SpongeBob you want. We won't be far away—just down that hallway, so you won't be alone. And we won't be too, too long, so just hang tight here for a while, and then we'll come grab you, and we'll head back home. Okay?"

This time, I hesitate. "Okay," my tiny voice replies.

"Not too, too long, I promise," Cyra says.

"Mm-kay," I mumble reluctantly.

"Hey, Snuggle Bear," Andy says, dropping into frame next to Cyra. "I think something's missing from that lunch." He reaches into his tuxedo pocket and pulls out three Reese's peanut butter cups, placing them on the floor next to the apple. "Beats an apple any day, am I right?"

Pause. "Yeah," I mumble.

"And what do you say?" Cyra prompts with uncharacteristic condescension.

"Thank you," I say flatly.

"Thank you, *who* . . . ?" Andy squawks with playful indignation.

"Thank you, Andy Reese's."

"You are welcome!" he says. "Oh, man," he marvels, looking at me. "Look at that face. Pure as the driven snow."

"What is it?" Lou asks. "What's wrong?"

I back my chair away from the console. "No," I say, shaking my head. "No, I don't need to see this."

"Why not?"

My body is all sweat and chills. "Because I know what happens."

I can feel her slipping away from me. Yesterday, she didn't exist, and now she's the most vibrant, living thing I've ever seen, and somewhere in the next hour of this tape, she's going to disappear again. A birth and a life and a death all in a hundred and twenty minutes. No, I don't need to see this. I don't need to lose her twice.

I suddenly hate everything about video recording. I despise it with all my heart, because you could lose someone over and over and over. Now all I want is to forget her again. I want to un-know everything I know and un-see everything I've seen. I want to make my mind a blank slate—just cross her out and start from scratch. Just like my mother had done.

But then, what is the point? Why have I put myself through all this? And that is exactly what I've done. I have put *myself* through all of this. Because I need to know. There is something I've been desperately trying to tell myself and I need to know what it is. I need to know what really happened—not just bits and pieces, but everything. Because I'm not my mother. I don't want to live my life playing make-believe.

SpongeBob dances across the TV screen as Theo-Cam sits perfectly still.

FAST-FORWARD . . .

SpongeBob at four-times-speed. Commercials, SpongeBob, commercials, SpongeBob. Then the camera suddenly tilts over, and my tiny hand reaches out of frame. It returns with the remote control and flips off the TV.

A sound echoes from somewhere down the hall. My sister is giggling.

The camera rises from the floor and begins to move down the hallway, past Room Seven, Room Eight, and then it stops. The plexiglass window is too high to see through, but there's light flickering through the glass, and I can hear her voice.

"I can't believe you did this," Cyra coos. "This is *so* beautiful. You didn't have to do this. I already know it will be worth the wait. You're worth the wait, Andy."

Faint, almost inaudible sounds. Kissing.

My tiny hand rises up and inches the door open the slightest crack. (Five years old and already too curious. Already needing to know the whole story.) It's only a crack in the door, but it's enough. Andy's overstuffed backpack is on the floor, empty of all its contents now. There's a fireplace lighter and two rows of white tea candles flickering all around the bed. A bed layered with blankets and colored chenille throws.

Cyra has stripped down to her white bra, panties, and pearls. Andy still has his pants on, but the jacket, tie, and shirt are gone, leaving only his white V-neck T-shirt. They kiss, and they grab, and they roll around on the bed, but Cyra suddenly sits up and pushes him back an inch. He waits, looking unsure if she wants to stop, but it's just the opposite. She reaches down and quickly unbuckles his belt, reaching for the button of his pants.

"Whoa, whoa, whoa." He laughs. "Slow down. We've still got some time."

"Oh, I think I've waited long enough." She laughs, reaching again for his pants.

"Hey." He giggles, swatting her hands away. "What's the hurry?"

"Andy, it's *okay*," she says. "I trust you. I'm ready. You don't have to worry."

The playful smile drops from his face. "Worry about what? What do you mean, you're ready? What does that mean?"

"What? No." She smiles. "I just mean I'm not scared. Come here." She slides down farther on her back and grabs his hips to pull him closer.

"Jesus," he snaps, pulling away onto his feet, shuffling the tea candles across the floor. His expression grows darker than any version of him I've ever seen. "Have you done this before? Do *not* fucking lie to me."

"What?" The first glimmer of fear appears in her eyes. "Andy, no. *God*, no, we said we'd wait. You know I've never been with anyone else. I've hardly even dated anyone else before I met—"

"That little *move* just then," he spits, "that was *not* someone who's never done this before." Within that one sentence, his rage and his volume jump from ten to sixty. "Are you *pure*?" he hollers. "Are you PURE, or are you a slut? Because if you want it like a slut, I can do that."

He collapses on top of her, crushing her flat against the blankets as his feet kick tea candles under the bed.

"Andy, no," she whimpers, trying to push him away. She digs her fingernails into the bottom of his T-shirt, ripping jagged holes in the cotton.

(I was only five years old. Could I even process what was happening? I must have been too petrified to scream.)

"Get off of me!" Cyra shouts. "Andy, get *off*." She slaps his face.

Whatever's left of Lester Andrew Wyatt drains away, and all that remains is a monster. A black-eyed vulture with a blank, unreadable gaze. He grabs her pearl necklace and twists it around her neck till she gasps for breath, till the necklace breaks apart, and the pearls go rolling across the floor.

He shoves her across the room, and I hear glass shatter on the other side of the door as he follows her out of frame. Then I hear something that sounds like a hard punch, and Cyra doesn't make another sound. But it's all out of frame now, all out of view. Seventeen years old or five, I would have done the same thing:

I finally push through the crack in the door and step around to the other side. Andy is straddled over Cyra's limp body as black smoke begins to pour into frame. She is covered in shattered mirror glass. A piece juts from her stomach. I finally scream.

Andy looks up to camera with those soulless eyes and jumps to his feet, rushing toward the lens. But there's a *whoosh* from behind me, and he freezes in place, suddenly lit up in a bright red-orange glow.

I scream again as the camera pivots and backs away from the wall of flames that has broken out on the bed. The camera pivots again, and Andy's face fills the frame. He looks lost and confused as smoke begins to billow all around us. I can see his eyes trying to process, trying to make quick decisions. And then the sound. That blaring siren sound, distorting in the microphone as a red light flashes on the ceiling.

A smoke alarm. It's the sound from the smoke alarm. And somehow that's enough to make up Andy's mind. He leans down over Cyra's body, lifts her limp left hand, and pulls the wedding ring from her finger, stuffing it in his pocket. Then he pushes me aside, and I hear the door to Room Nine open and shut.

He has abandoned me in the smoke-filled room with Cyra's body. I crouch down to a close-up of her face, and there's just enough visibility to see the deep red gash running down her left jaw. The smoke alarm drowns out every other sound, and then it's only smoke. Nothing but a pitch-black screen.

For how long? How long did he leave me there?

FAST-FORWARD . . .

Something finally moves.

PLAY . . .

The smoke thins out just enough, and Andy's face comes through from an angle beneath his chin. The camera rocks from side to side. He is carrying me toward the lobby of K.O.P. The sounds of shouting men fill the halls. Firefighters. *Those* were the shouting men Andy remembered (*I* remembered) in the halls. Not a bachelor party; a brigade of NYC firefighters.

Andy leans so close to the camera that he becomes a fleshy blur. "You will never tell anyone what you saw in there." He shakes me so hard on the word *never* that I'm surprised my neck doesn't snap. "Never," he repeats. This time he shakes me so hard you can hear the microphone rattle inside the camera. Then he pushes through the front door of K.O.P. as daylight floods the lens.

"I've got her!" he shouts to a squad of firefighters.

And there, at last, is our "Heroic Teen."

The sky cuts through the center of the frame as I'm passed from a view of Andy's chin to the chin of an NYC firefighter.

"I got her out, thank God," Andy pants. "I think she's okay. But there's another girl inside." His voice breaks into forced tears. "My girlfriend . . . I couldn't get to her in time. I couldn't save her."

His lies fade to silence as I'm carried toward an ambulance and handed into one last man's arms.

My father's handsome, stubbly face leans into frame. It seems at first like he's trembling, but I realize it's the camera that's trembling. Theo-Cam is trembling. My father sets me down and throws a blanket over my shoulders. Dusty ash flies across the screen like flakes of gray snow. "Don't be afraid, darlin'," he says. "Don't you ever, ever be afraid."

He wraps the blanket so tightly around me that it covers the lens and kills the sound.

Blackout.

I have no way of knowing what happened next because I can't remember. Maybe I was taken to the hospital, maybe not. Maybe my father or a cop took me home. All I know is that I kept my promise to Cyra. Somehow or other, I got back home, and I hid that cassette in the Magic Story Box, where it sat dormant for the next twelve years.

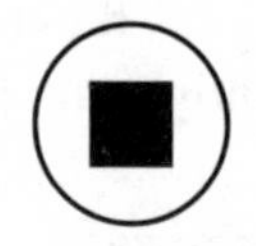

Chapter Twenty-Two

I knew what Max and Lou expected next. They expected me to sit at that editing bay in a state of shock. They expected me to go totally catatonic, maybe conjure up some more imaginary friends to play with, anything to escape the awful truth we'd seen on the screen. But it was just the opposite. I couldn't move fast enough.

"Jesus, what time is it?" I demanded, kicking my chair out as I rose to my feet.

"It's almost one," Max said. "Why?"

"No, that's too late. We need to move. We need to move *fast.*"

"Thee, what's wrong?" Lou tried to console me, but she didn't understand. Neither of them had put it together yet. There was something I'd been trying to tell myself, something I'd been trying to do. A purpose. A reason for it all. And I finally knew what it was. I ejected the tape and tossed it to Lou as I moved for the door. "Lou, how fast can you can upload this to my cloud drive?"

"All of it?" she asked.

"Just the last two minutes." I urgently searched my pockets for my iPhone.

"I'd need to convert it first," she said. "Then I can upload it to—"

"Do it," I interrupted. "Do it now. Send it to my drive, post it, Tweet it, send it everywhere. I have to get a cab."

"A cab to where?" Max shouted as he tried to follow me.

"To the Ritz-Carlton," I shouted back. I don't know if he heard me. I was too far ahead of him, and it didn't matter. I didn't need Max just now; I only needed speed. There was no more time to waste. *Please be dancing with him, Emma. Be dancing, drinking, toasting each other on that windy terrace, stuffing each other's faces with cake, laughing with each other's families. Anything but the suite. You can't go back to that honeymoon suite.*

FLASHBACKS RIDDLED MY HEAD like machine-gun fire as I barreled into the Ritz-Carlton lobby: *"We went to the courthouse this morning, and we did the deed."* That's what Emma had told me in the hospital. *"I mean, not* the *deed,"* she'd added. *"We haven't done* that *yet."*

She still hadn't slept with him. She'd been saving herself for this night, and she had no idea. She had no idea what was in store for her if I couldn't find her in time. If I wasn't already too late.

I raced to the elevator and poked like mad at the button for fourteen, trying to will my way up to the Rise Bar and Terrace. Even at one fifteen in the morning, people were hopping on and off like a goddamned merry-go-round. My stomach twisted into tighter knots each time the doors slid open and closed.

"We're just going to have a little makeup wedding night with the family at the hotel," she'd said.

Oh, please, Emma, let that still be true. Please, please be dancing.

It had all started with her picture, with her wedding announcement in the *Times*. Yes, I'd been searching for "Sarah," embroiled in my crazed psychodrama with Andy, but where had that search really led me every single time? It had led me to Emma's engagement party. To Emma's rehearsal dinner. To Emma's wedding. And I'd ruined them all.

I remembered what "Andy" kept saying in my ear at the wedding (what *I* kept saying to myself): *"We can't let it happen to another girl, Theo. Do you understand? Tell me you understand."*

I didn't then. I did now. I understood it completely.

All this time I'd thought destroying Emma's wedding was just a tragic side effect of my mission. But it wasn't a side effect at all.

It *was* the mission.

The doors finally slid open on the fourteenth floor. I shot out of the elevator and searched for signs of her thousand-dollar highlights or his ski-slope nose. What I found instead was Charles and Sally Renaux, sipping on mint juleps at the bar.

"Where is she?" I asked, butting my way between them. There was no time for etiquette or explanations. "Where's Emma?"

It took them a moment to recognize me, and once they did, they scowled. "They've retired for the night," Mr. Renaux answered gruffly.

"No," I moaned. "No, she *can't.* She can't do that."

Mr. Renaux put his drink down. "My dear," he said, oozing with condescension. "What exactly is it we can do for you now?"

"Just tell me where the suite is," I demanded.

Sally Renaux smiled. "Well, honey, I really don't think they want to be disturbed just now."

"Tell me where it is!" I barked. "She's in trouble!"

I must have spooked her because she blurted it out. "Fourteen-twelve." Maybe she was just drunk. Or maybe some part of her, too, knew that Lester Andrew Wyatt was not a saint. "Why? What's wrong, honey? Why are you so—?"

I was already running. *1412, 1412, where is 1412? Take your time, Emma. For God's sake, just take your time* . . . But I already heard the screaming. I heard it from down the hall. Screaming so familiar it froze me like a child again.

"Are you pure?" his unmistakable voice echoed down the hall. "Are you PURE?"

I raced the final feet, shouting her name. I pounded on the door with both fists. I pummeled it, kicked it, hurled my side against it. "Emma, it's Theo! Emma?"

But I was drowned out by the sound of glass shattering. And then the loudest scream of all. And then silence.

All the doors on the fourteenth floor began to open as my head fell against the door. "Somebody call 911," I said, but I'd lost faith already. "Call 911," I repeated, but I knew. I knew that deathly silence. It was the same sound I'd heard in that hallway all those years ago. The sound that came after he'd thrown her against the mirror, after he'd ended her life with one jagged piece of glass. It was the sound of a person who'd suddenly ceased to be.

I was too late. I'd failed my mission. It had all been for nothing.

I heard another faint whimper through the door. Was he crying over her now? Crying over what he'd done to yet another woman he supposedly loved?

No. It was a woman. I knew the sound of Emma's cries.

"Emma?" I spoke through the door. "Emma, is that you?"

"Theo . . . ?" It was her voice. Thin and hoarse, but her voice.

"Yes, it's me!" I shouted through the door, heart racing again. "It's Theo. I'm here, Emma, I'm right here. Open the door!"

"Theo?" her voice whimpered from the other side.

"Emma, let me in! Andy!" I hollered. "Andy, the cops are on their way right now. They're already coming for you, so you better get the hell away from her!"

"No," Emma cried through the door. "No, Theo, no police. I can't—you can't let the police in here."

"Emma, please," I begged. "Please just let me in."

There was an endless silence, but the door finally cracked open just enough for her to see my face.

"Theo," she said. There were tears in her eyes, but her voice was numb. I think she was in shock. And then I saw the blood. Blood on her chest, blood on her bare stomach. She was only wearing panties and a camisole.

"Jesus, what did he do?" I cried. "What he did to you?"

"No," she said, dazed. But I pushed my way through and slammed the door behind me.

"Andy!" I growled. "What did you—?"

Andy was sprawled out on the blue-and-gold carpet. But I shouldn't say "Andy," because Andy was gone. It was only Andy's body, flat on the floor, surrounded in a pool of blood. His blood this time. Not Emma's. A gold-framed floor-length mirror had left tiny shards of shattered glass all over his pants and his blood-soaked V-neck T-shirt.

I finally turned around and saw the weapon in Emma's trembling hand: a shard of mirrored glass, stained with blood. She was definitely in shock, still clutching the glass so tightly that it cut into her palm and forefingers.

"I had to," she breathed. "He just . . . he snapped. He turned into another—"

"I know," I said. "Emma, I know." I reached for her hand and cautiously pried the glass from her rigid fingers, letting it drop to the floor. Then I grabbed a room service napkin from the bed and wrapped it tightly around her palm.

"It was self-defense," she said. "I didn't have . . . I had to, Theo. He would have—"

"I know," I said, locking my eyes with hers. "I know exactly what he would have done."

"But the police," she said. "The police will never believe—"

"They will." I pulled out my iPhone. Lou must have finished uploading the video to my cloud drive by now. "When they see this, they'll believe you. Everyone will believe you."

I turned back to Lester Wyatt, splayed out on the floor in a bed of his own blood—the bed he'd made for himself. I couldn't grieve for him. He didn't deserve it.

Chapter Twenty-Three

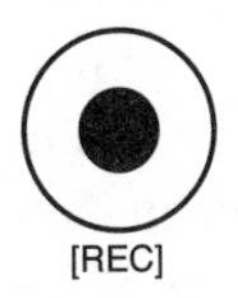

My camera fades to life in a shade of pale indigo. It's the spring sky in New York City, just after Magic Hour (as some mildly annoying filmmakers call it).

Date stamp: March 15, 2016. Time stamp: 7:21 P.M.

I am shooting a new documentary project, a movie about all the people who have come out tonight to see my movie. We've all gathered together for an outdoor screening on the roof of a women's shelter called Keeping Our Promise—a place I now hold very near and dear to my heart. A place where I made some of the best friends I will ever have: Helena Reyes, the star of my last two short films; Emma Renaux, my surrogate older sister; LeAnne Stemson, who brought me a string of pearls as a gift for the premiere. (Fake pearls, of course, but just as meaningful to me.)

They've all come for the premiere of a film I've been cobbling together over six months. It was not easy, given the abundance of source material: over a hundred hours of digital video from a very old box that had been hidden under a little girl's bed for many years.

It's a film about two sisters: Cyrano and Theodore Lane. They had apparently captured tons of video in their much-too-brief time together—none of it very extravagant, nothing big budget; just mundane little snippets of real life. Trips to the candy store, brainstorming a groundbreaking new mac and cheese recipe, acting out Goldilocks but with lightsabers.

Each clip alone might have seemed boring to anyone other than Cyrano, Theo, and their mother Margaret. But when you put all the clips together, they formed a story. A story of two girls who understood the preciousness of all the moments they were bound to forget. The times we loved each other with ease, without thinking, without doubting, without caring what the future might hold. Maybe we were just eating string cheese on a Thursday afternoon after school. But the sight of that cheese getting momentarily sucked into my sister's nose—that was precious.

I know: mac and cheese, string cheese. We very much enjoyed cheese.

As the movie begins to play, I grab the seat farthest in the back. My mother and Todd sit to my left. Mom squeezes my hand for luck, and I squeeze back. We have totally mastered mutual hand squeezing. It will still take us a while to work our way back to awkward hugs. Baby steps . . .

I hold out my iPhone camera and pan across the backs of my audience's heads until I land on the profiles of Max and Lou, sitting to my right.

I tug on the sleeve of Max's black suit. (Yes, he wore a suit for my premiere—though he stuck with Pumas and white socks.) "You want to take a walk?" I whisper.

"Now?" he whispers back, surprised. "Your movie just started."

"Yeah, I've seen it about a hundred times," I say. "Let's walk."

We begin to stand, but Lou stands up with us. "Where are you guys going?"

It's an awkward moment. One we'd been working on for the last few months. I see the look in Lou's eyes, and I think of Emma Renaux in her bridesmaid's dress at age eighteen. There's a hint of that in Lou's eyes. The look of a girl who has lost the love of her life to her best friend. We could never be the same threesome we were again. Not really. But we did our best to approximate it.

"We're taking a quick walk," Max whispers.

Lou forces a smile. "Cool," she mumbles.

"We'll bring you back some popcorn," Max adds.

"Right on," Lou deadpans. "You're a prince among men, Max." She sniffs and turns away. "I swear, I'll get better at this. There will be, like, a hundred dudes way better than Max at Oberlin."

Max laughs. "Thanks, Lou."

"Shhhh." Todd stops snacking from his bag of dried pumpkin seeds and gives us a stern look. He has a point. It is, after all, my movie.

"Go, go, go," Lou whispers. "I promise I'll have this down by the time you guys get married."

"Whoa!" Max coughs nervously. "Who said anything about—?"

"*Lou,* will you *stop* with that?" I whisper.

"I'm *joking,*" she whispers. "Go *walk* already."

"Still bringing you back some popcorn," Max says as we climb over the backs of our folding chairs.

"Hell, yeah, you are," Lou says.

I TWIRL SLOWLY IN place, shooting a panoramic view of Parker Street, then the West Side Highway, and then Max. He smiles for the camera.

"Okay, I lied," I say. "I didn't really want to take a walk. I just wanted to come down and see it again. It makes me happy."

"Like I didn't know that's why we came down," Max says.

"Would you?" I hand him the camera.

"I'd be honored," he says.

He takes the camera from me as I lead him to the corner of the K.O.P. building, where a small blue placard with white writing has been nailed high on the wall. It looks identical to the blue street placards in Paris. Max kneels down so he can get a good angle of me pointing up to the sign with a joyous smile on my face.

CYRANO LANE, the sign reads.

The small alley that runs adjacent to Parker Street now has a name. A permanent name. Now Cyrano Lane is a name *and* an address. And no one will ever forget her again.

"Come on," I say, grabbing the camera back from Max, beckoning him to join me for one last picture.

Max puts his arm around me and leans in for a selfie. "Wait," he says.

"What?"

"Your hair's in your face." He grabs the strands of my long hair and tucks them back behind my left ear. "There," he says. "Beautiful."

"Thanks," I say as I snap a few shots. But Max starts to crack up for the last few. "What? What's so funny?"

"No, nothing," Max says. "Just Lou with her whole 'married' thing. She's freakin' hilarious."

"I know." I roll my eyes. "Like that will ever happen."

The New York Times,
"Weddings and Celebrations" section, page ST22

June 3, 2022

Theodore Lane, 24, daughter of Ryan and Margaret Lane of Brooklyn, N.Y., and stepdaughter of Todd Simpson of Norwalk, Conn., will marry Maximus Fenton, 24, son of Bernard and Mona Fenton of New York, N.Y., on Saturday. The reception will be held at lower Manhattan's Battery Gardens.

The couple first met as eighth-graders at New York's Sherman Preparatory School when Ms. Lane was reluctantly enlisted as Mr. Fenton's algebra tutor. They stayed the best of friends for many years before Mr. Fenton finally proposed.

He popped the question during one of their Sunday morning walks, kneeling suddenly on the corner of Parker Street and Cyrano Lane, her favorite spot in all of New York. He presented a uniquely shaped ring that held deep significance for Ms. Lane, which he had secretly procured from a close friend of hers, and he offered what he termed his "very wordy" proposal:

He asked Ms. Lane if there was any possible way she'd consider marrying him, even though it would absolutely evoke all the clichés of guys asking girls to marry them, and would be blatantly romantically suggestive in every way, and would, in fact, become even more romantically suggestive fifty years from now when they would be very old but still very much in love.

Ms. Lane needed a moment to thoroughly consider the question. Ultimately, she concluded that, yes, she could in fact do that.

Acknowledgments

I am deeply indebted to Daniel Ehrenhaft, Bronwen Hruska, and the entire team at Soho Press for making this book possible.

For their wealth of knowledge, support, and professional acumen, my sincerest thanks to Edward Necarsulmer IV, Robert Scharf, Jennifer Grossman, and Robert S. Perlstein, Esq.

Special thanks to Lawrence Alexander, Jane Huyck, and Carole Demas. You turned my humble quest for reprint permission into the most unexpected gift. Thank you, too, to Alton Alexander and George Kayatta. Apparently, the creators and custodians of *The Magic Garden* were and are just as soulful and welcoming as the garden itself.

For keeping me sane in the darkest hours, thanks to Arthur Miller, Barbara Miller, Jed Miller, Heidi Miller, Holly Hemingway, Martha Plimpton, and the founding members of Tiger Beat: Libba Bray, Natalie Standiford, and Daniel "Knuckles" Ehrenhaft. There are few wounds that "Whole Lotta What'cha Want" cannot heal.

Bobby Weissman and Theo Cohen, I thank you for the inspiration. You will never be forgotten.

Thank you twice, Ms. Libba Bray, for being Ms. Libba Bray.

Dan Ehrenhaft, you are a scholar, a saint, a brilliant editor, and quite possibly the hardest working man in the YA business. Thank you thrice, Mr. Worthy, for all of the above.

And thank you, John Starks, for "The Dunk."